Weapons of the Gods

(Matt Drake #18)

By

David Leadbeater

Thriller, adventure, action, mystery, suspense, archaeological,
military, historical

Other Books by David Leadbeater:

The Matt Drake Series
A constantly evolving, action-packed romp based in the escapist action-adventure genre:

The Bones of Odin (Matt Drake #1)
The Blood King Conspiracy (Matt Drake #2)
The Gates of Hell (Matt Drake 3)
The Tomb of the Gods (Matt Drake #4)
Brothers in Arms (Matt Drake #5)
The Swords of Babylon (Matt Drake #6)
Blood Vengeance (Matt Drake #7)
Last Man Standing (Matt Drake #8)
The Plagues of Pandora (Matt Drake #9)
The Lost Kingdom (Matt Drake #10)
The Ghost Ships of Arizona (Matt Drake #11)
The Last Bazaar (Matt Drake #12)
The Edge of Armageddon (Matt Drake #13)
The Treasures of Saint Germain (Matt Drake #14)
Inca Kings (Matt Drake #15)
The Four Corners of the Earth (Matt Drake #16)
The Seven Seals of Egypt (Matt Drake #17)

The Alicia Myles Series
Aztec Gold (Alicia Myles #1)
Crusader's Gold (Alicia Myles #2)
Caribbean Gold (Alicia Myles #3)

The Torsten Dahl Thriller Series
Stand Your Ground (Dahl Thriller #1)

All genuine comments are very welcome at:

davidleadbeater2011@hotmail.co.uk

Twitter: @dleadbeater2011

Visit David's website for the latest news and information:
davidleadbeater.com

Weapons of the Gods

CHAPTER ONE

"We are the core elements of Tempest," General George Gleeson told CIA high-flyer, Mark Digby. "But our goals are too widespread to reach on our own." He waved at a bank of monitors positioned on the desk in front of them. "Switch them on."

Digby activated all five monitors with the push of a button. Gleeson waited for the newcomers to realize they were on-air, settling back in his padded leather chair and basking in the ambiance that surrounded him: four walls of solid oak paneling, low light bleeding from underneath gold colored lampshades, a whole wall full of old hardbacks that he'd never even looked at, and a vast, imposing desk—the centerpiece and workstation of his private house.

Digby coughed. The new attendees looked up.

"Are we ready?" Gleeson asked.

Digby jumped straight in. "The events in Egypt didn't pan out quite as we hoped," he said. "And the Sword of Mars eluded us before that. Other players got in the way," he conceded. "SPEAR. FrameHub. Luther. Even the goddamn CIA." He chuckled at the joke made at his own expense. "It was too dangerous, too much risk. Tempest were exposed and some people out there are now aware that we exist."

Five faces returned his gaze with unhappy glares of their own, among them a judge, a police commissioner, a Wall Street wiz and a presidential aide. The latter spoke up first.

"Where does that leave us?"

"Well, Mr. Troy, it leaves us with a challenge to overcome. Tempest was created to gather together the greatest weapons known to man—the weapons of the gods—and to discover if there's a way to use them together, concertedly. To date, just a single one of those known weapons has surfaced. The Sword of Mars, which now resides in London . . ."

Gleeson leaned forward before Digby could continue. "From

here on in, gentlemen, we're at critical mass. Or, to put it another way you'll understand—we gotta throw everything at it, tirelessly, dispassionately, even unethically. If you want to win—it's no holds barred from here on in."

Troy nodded. "Do we have the new, up-to-date list of weapons?"

"It's in your inbox. All twenty of them."

"And Luther? Did we lose Luther?"

"At this stage of the game," Digby sighed, "we must assume that we did."

The banker and the police commissioner shook their heads in anger. Gleeson reminded them of the contingency plan.

"The Syrian camps are well underway. They're already radicalizing hundreds and our mercs are training them. Soon, we'll have an army to distract not only the masses but every police force of the First World. Then we can barnstorm our way to the weapons."

"Are we strategically ready for all those lines of attack?" the police commissioner asked.

"Truthfully . . . no. Not yet. But it won't be long."

"And all the disavowed, alienated and disordered Special Forces teams out there? How long can we keep a lid on it?"

Gleeson deferred to the presidential aide, Troy, to answer that.

"I'm working tirelessly at it but even I—with the General's help—won't be able to alleviate suspicions forever. A few weeks maybe."

"Another reason why speed has become imperative," Gleeson said. "We can't use CIA assets anymore. We're fortunate we prepared some of our own. The camps are viable. Let's start using them."

The general took in the mood of his comrades as best he could. He preferred face-to-face at the place he'd dubbed The Chamber. The military was all about physical confrontation, but he was also forced to admit modern communications were far faster when matters were pressing. This wasn't a case of deciding which one of them was in deep and who dangled their toes in the pool. No, they were all up to their necks in it. This had become more of a test of courage.

His mind also considered the possibility that one of them might betray him.

"Questions?" he barked.

There were none. Gleeson didn't like it. These people should be spouting, chattering all sorts of rhetoric back at him. Their silence betrayed their doubts and the fact that they weren't fully invested.

Well, that would change.

He glanced over at Digby, the one man he could trust. "I think we should convene a meeting."

"I agree."

"That's gonna be extremely hard for me," the presidential aide said negatively. "I'm juggling a hundred balls over here."

"The Chamber," Gleeson said, ignoring Troy and then snapping out a time and date. "No excuses, gentlemen. It will be good to catch up."

He tried not to let any malice seep into the tone of his voice.

Once they agreed to it, Gleeson signed off. He took a moment to confer with Digby and then rechecked the status of their Syrian terrorist camp with his commanders on the ground. All was progressing well, and at speed. The weapons of the gods were almost within reach. Gleeson knew they could be tracked due to an incredibly rare element in their makeup, but the tracking device had to be close in order to work. That still left them with the problem of getting close.

Not so much the Sword of Mars.

He allowed a smile to grace his heavy features, patting his fresh stubble of hair down as he did so. The mole he'd planted in the British government six years ago would finally prove worthwhile.

Maybe tonight. Damn, how he would like to get that first weapon under his belt. Figuratively speaking, of course.

Gleeson laughed at his own small joke, ignored Digby's stare, and left the room. Once in the hallway, he fished out a cellphone and called a private number.

"Hello? I need a whore."

The woman he knew as Madam Masuda sighed in her worldly way. "Another so soon? Okay, I have Nightshade here and ready to go. She is . . . exotic."

3

"I bet," Gleeson laughed and then thought: *Nightshade?* But his desire got the better of him. "Send her right over."

"Good. Please give her one hour."

Madam Masuda never took her eyes away from the tall, dark-haired woman sat before her. "I cannot say how dangerous this is. He might recognize you."

Lauren Fox inclined her head as a sign of agreement. "This is the opportunity I've been waiting for," she said with a sassy accent. "Bring it on and let Nightshade live one last time."

"I can make you up."

"Good. But make it heavy. We don't want him to recognize me now, do we?" She laughed, feeling good. At last here was a way to help her friends, get close to Gleeson and maybe even find out who the presidential aide was—the man or woman that had been blocking all her attempts to reach President Coburn. When Secretary of Defense Kimberly Crowe came to their side, Lauren had been hopeful that her knowledge and experience with Gleeson would pay off.

Gleeson may or may not have seen her photo when he decided to target SPEAR after Peru and then during their Egypt jaunt.

But he'd never seen Nightshade.

It was time to start destroying the evil pyramid that rose against them, their reputations and the entire civilized world. She would start at the very top.

CHAPTER TWO

Ignoring the clamor of internal warning bells, Lauren Fox slipped into her Nightshade persona. It had been a while, but Lauren and Nightshade had been alter-egos for many years and the traits soon came rushing back. Of course, her "costume" was back in New York these days, but Madam Masuda was able to lay her hands on almost anything.

"Leather," Lauren had confirmed. "Boots mostly. The outfit can be lacy, I guess, but not too revealing. I'll need whips and gloves. Good gloves. If I have to touch this creep I don't wanna feel it."

Madam Masuda held up a black object. "Strap on?"

"No! I don't even wanna get close to this guy."

Traveling in the car on her way to see Gleeson, Lauren recalled the time, not so long ago in Peru, when she walked away from the team, returned to DC and started unearthing the truth. It had been a frustrating period—striking one closed door after another—but now she sensed a better opportunity. She imagined the conversation she would need to engineer to extract all the right answers.

The car stopped, the big, burly driver half-turning in his seat to look at her. "You okay, miss?"

He saw only Nightshade wrapped in a knee-length beige coat. "Yeah, thanks. The hardest part is meeting them."

"I'll be right here," his voice rumbled deeply. "You need me, you hit the button."

Lauren nodded and climbed out of the car. Gleeson had invited her to a hotel about half a mile from the Capitol building, set back from a busy street and popular with tourists. The old perv probably had a bellboy on retainer, one that could loan him an empty room for an hour or so. Lauren had seen it many times before. Money corrupted in every imaginable way, and people like Gleeson in their powerful roles used it to get exactly what they wanted.

Through the hotel doors Nightshade stalked, heading down a

level to the elevators and then punching the button for the third floor. She swept along a quiet, echoing corridor, then stopped and knocked at a door. Within seconds, it was pulled open.

"Come in," he said. "I have less time than I thought. The wife wants to meet me for dinner."

Nightshade stepped inside and closed the door, thumb hovering over the button that would summon her driver. Gleeson appeared to be at ease but hurried. She saw nothing dangerous in his body language but that might change. She slipped off the long coat and waited until he turned around.

"Answer me this first," she said. "If a girl told you she had a whip, would you want her to use it on you, or would you want to use it on her?"

Gleeson struggled with a reply, but he was also distracted by her lithe body clad in stockings, suspenders and skimpy underwear. Finally, he said: "Both?" in a husky, questioning voice that told her she already controlled the room.

"Right," she said. "Let's start by removing those trousers."

Nightshade fell into her role, taking over, giving orders that Gleeson certainly appeared to appreciate. The darker persona took over, propelling her easily through the first half hour. The action was pretty much routine until Gleeson asked to switch roles.

You're fucking kidding me? No way in this world would she let this pompous, corrupt wedge of debased beliefs have any power over her. But this was where the Nightshade personality helped. The game expanded, the stakes went higher, and she took him to a higher realm of dominance.

She was conscious of the opulent room, the tightly closed crimson drapes; the widescreen television on low volume and tuned to a sports betting channel. She wondered if Gleeson would be signed in. She noted a carryall perched upon a small, round table and a change of clothes neatly pressed. Of course, the objects she preferred were a cellphone and a laptop.

And time.

The essential trick was getting away with it, and she had to act whilst Gleeson was still excited about being immobile. Luckily, this was Nightshade's last outing. Lauren would never use the identity again. In truth, Nightshade had retired some time ago— this final collision with her questionable past was only to help her friends survive the trouble they were in.

With a flourish, she stuffed Gleeson's own jockey shorts into his mouth, smiling at the faint confusion that came across his face. She pulled duct tape from her coat pocket and fastened it first across his mouth and then around his wrists and ankles. She made sure all coverings were off the bed because she wanted this ass to feel maximum embarrassment when they found him— assuming he could feel anything beyond superior. Time was short, so she made a point of searching for his wallet, his jewelry and any other valuables. She then took his phone and laptop.

Gleeson's eyes bulged and he writhed around on the bed. Lauren shook her head at him. "You're going nowhere, bud. Keep struggling and you'll break that baby-white skin. I'd wait for maid service tomorrow, if I were you."

Gleeson looked like he was reverse-humping the mattress he struggled so hard.

Lauren cast a sad glance between his legs. "And, I'd seriously think about retiring that wrinkled insect between your legs, bud. It ain't up to much."

Quickly then, she hefted her burden and blew him a kiss. The last indignity was to unhook the do-not-disturb sign from the door and indicate she would hang it outside.

"Enjoy your evening."

Gleeson grunted and shouted at her, every syllable muffled by the gag. Lauren gave him a last pout and some quick words to embellish her cover.

"Hey, calm down. You'll get most of this shit back anyway once I've sold it on. Business is business and I'm pretty sure I need the cash more than you."

The door clicked loudly behind her. She made sure she hung the sign around the door handle then headed for the stairs.

Next stop, Shake Shack. Kimberley Crowe's contact would meet her there—a man, she had assured Lauren, that could hack into anything with a circuit board.

CHAPTER THREE

Deep underneath London, in dank and wet subterranean caverns, a surprising amount of work gets done and not even half of it by known criminals. Drake was surprised when Captain Cambridge of the SAS asked to meet the SPEAR team there, but couldn't think of a better man to help them in their current situation. Cambridge had led the SAS team that had taken the Sword of Mars and, presumably, organized its journey to England. Kimberley Crowe had initially arranged the London meet to introduce SPEAR to a new influential figure inside the British government and gain support for their search for the weapons.

The entire team stood waiting at a crossroads of arched tunnels, each one leading to an unknown destination. Noises echoed out of the dark and the incessant drip of water soon began to scratch at their nerves. The walls were black and slimy, dripping with damp. Smyth and Yorgi stood at the back, covering the tunnel they'd used whilst the others spread out around the small, circular space.

"Talk about British hospitality." Alicia sniffed. "It's not quite Kensington Gardens."

"It is the SAS," Drake reminded her. "Remember?"

"Puts me in mind of real spy stuff," Kinimaka said happily, not even bothered about his wet shoes. "Y'know, authentic, real-deal occurrences."

"We are spies, dude," Hayden told him. "The real deal."

"I wouldn't go that far, Hay."

Luther was a very large presence in the enclosed space. "How long we waiting around here, boys? I've never been comfortable underground."

"I can see why." Alicia turned and admired the muscles bulging out of the tight T-shirt. "A man with assets like those should always be seen in the full light of day." She paused. "Or by bedside lighting."

Luther glared. "You're not feeling them again, girl, so don't even ask."

Alicia pouted. "You gotta know that just makes me more determined."

Drake nudged her. "Really? You felt his arms?"

"I felt more than his arms, Drakey." Alicia laughed loudly. "But don't worry, you're still my man."

"Oh, thanks." Drake knew it would do no good questioning her. Alicia was quite simply Alicia and she would never change. God help the man that tried to tame her.

Luther leaned in close to his ear and whispered, "If it helps, when she touched me, I only got half wood."

Drake pushed him away, laughing. "Are you kidding me? I don't need to know that. Crap, now I'm wishing we'd beaten you down and left you in the desert."

"You beat me down?" Luther looked surprised, the enormous head rearing back. "I seem to remember saving and capturing you in that desert, boy."

They heard footsteps rattling along a tunnel, saving Drake the indignity of replying. He focused on the opening and the team spread out to make ready for surprises.

None came. Instead, Captain Cambridge and another man exited, both standing there and looking a little bemused.

"Wow," Cambridge said in a deep baritone. "I didn't realize there were so many of you."

"We're a big crew," Drake admitted. "It's good to see you again, Cambridge. Thanks for your help with the nukes back in the Ukraine. We were close to wiping out there for a while."

"Not again," Luther barked. "Sounds like you guys need child minders."

Cambridge held out a calloused hand. "My pleasure. And may I introduce you to Major Bennett, Secretary Crowe's contact over here."

Drake shook and then Hayden stepped forward, perhaps feeling a little left out. "And what do you have for us, Major?"

"Just Bennett," the man said. "I'm no Major down here. And I don't feel like a Major up there at present." His blue eyes shot up toward the ceiling. "Having to tread lightly. We don't know who's involved with this Tempest group and who isn't, I'm afraid. It's all very . . . underhand. It's so clandestine . . ." He glanced at Hayden and Drake. "If Kimberley hadn't put her full weight and reputation behind this I'd say you were wasting our time."

"Well thank God for the Americans," Alicia breathed. "At least they have sense."

Bennett blinked at her. "I doubt there's any British in the higher echelons of Tempest," he said. "But there may well be a few lackeys over here. We're still rooting around. Now, Kimberley tells me a wild story about seven weapons?"

Drake nodded. "Seven that we know of. I doubt there's any particular order to them but the first—the Sword of Mars—is in your possession."

"I'm only privy to so much," Bennett admitted. "I run the DSF out of Whitehall which, as I'm sure you know, is the entity that oversees all British Special Forces operations. Yes, I have contacts, but I still have to take great care."

"Understood. Where is the sword?"

"We'll get to that in a minute. I understand you can track these weapons?"

"That we can," Dahl spoke up, nodding his blonde head. "We recalibrated a GPS device to search for the still unnamed material that is part of their structure. It worked."

Drake looked across at him. "That's Dumb Swede for 'yes.'"

Dahl gave him the sly finger.

"Well, good," Bennett said. "Then you can track all seven down."

Drake thought he'd misheard. "All . . . seven?"

Cambridge jumped in. "The Sword of Mars is missing, I'm afraid."

"For how long?" Hayden asked.

"A couple of hours," Bennett said defensively. "We're all over it."

"All over it?" Drake repeated. "That sword was our biggest hope. We don't know what they'll do if they find all seven."

"We have to recover it," Dahl said. "Tempest already proved they care nothing about military and civilian life. They have to be stopped."

"Swords must never fall into the wrong hands," Kenzie said from across the other side of the chamber where she stood apart, leaning against the damp wall. "They should be in mine."

Bennett nodded hesitantly at the Israeli and then addressed everyone. "The op is ongoing. London city and airports have the heaviest surveillance in the world. We will find the perpetrator by backtracking from the moment of the theft of the sword. Then, we'll have facial match." He glanced at his phone. "It's already been narrowed down. It's nothing more than a matter of time."

Drake found it hard to accept the major's word in light of recent information. Still, the British hadn't known the significance of the weapon until this very moment. "It's partly our fault," he said. "We should have contacted you sooner."

"Thank you, but I will take it on the chin," Bennett said. "Kimberley only just broke away from Tempest and is living with a sense of not knowing what they'll do to her next. To anyone. There's a lot going on here, gents and ladies."

Alicia made a point of glaring. "You realize you've just excluded poor old Yorgi, right?"

Bennett opened his mouth to question her but then his phone started to ring. Cambridge watched him closely as he checked the screen before answering. Drake watched them both.

"What do you think?" he mouthed at Hayden.

"It all feels laborious," she said. "We need to shift it up a gear. Tempest clearly has an agenda and Luther here was not their only attack dog."

"Dog?" Luther frowned.

"Yeah," Alicia nodded at him. "Rhino would be more precise."

"Thank you."

"Oh, any time."

Drake interrupted their flirting which, he knew, stemmed from Alicia's suspicion that Mai was attracted to him. Surprisingly, the Japanese warrior had remained silent and calm this entire time.

"Fact is," he said. "We can't touch Tempest yet. They're too well insulated which, I hope, Major Bennett here and Secretary of Defense Crowe will soon change. We're at the sharp end, as usual, but this time we have everything to fight for."

Hayden nodded. "Couldn't be bigger."

"Yeah," Dahl agreed. "Our freedom. Our todays and tomorrows. Tempest must be destroyed."

"We're fighting for men and women that don't even know they've been disconnected," Drake said. "For soldiers out there, risking everything, thinking there's a real support system at their backs where, instead, there's a kill order." He paused. "And that's another thing. Somehow, some way, we have to pull these teams together. United, we will be stronger."

"Agreed," Hayden said, looking around. "Karin would have been perfect for that. I still don't agree with her decision . . . but she is her own tour de force now, I guess."

"FrameHub do need taking down." Drake shrugged. "And I guess she's being hunted too, by the US Military. Send a geek to catch a geek. That's what I say."

Luther shifted his feet. "Molokai has some experience with military communications. Nothing fantastic," he acknowledged, "but I think he could try."

Drake looked to the side of the chamber where the mysterious man lurked, face covered to the nose by a desert scarf, body bulked out by innumerable layers of clothes, protected by the flak jacket he never removed, and a big coat.

"We need a base," Hayden told Bennett, but by then the man was answering a call. When he finished he stared expectantly at the SPEAR team.

"How about that?" he said. "We've found the wankers that stole the sword. Are you ready?"

"Lead on, Major," Drake said. "This isn't business anymore. It's fucking personal."

CHAPTER FOUR

The old, abandoned hospital sat amid several overgrown acres near Muswell Hill. It was a timeworn Victorian villa that had once been used as a home for disturbed psychiatric patients and people with a high drug dependency. Today it sat in decay, similar to many old buildings in London, with no clear signs as to the owner and nobody paid to maintain it.

Alicia viewed it from the street, a military scope in her hand. "I don't like it," she said. "Looks creepy."

"The team's resident scaredy cat," Mai told Luther and Molokai in the back of the transit van. "I once saw her jump into a pit to escape a spider."

"In my defense," Alicia said, still observing, "it had legs the size of my arms."

Hayden's voice crackled over the comms system, coming from the van parked in front of theirs. "You guys see anything?"

"Rundown asylum," Alicia said. "Abandoned. You say the power's back on?"

"According to Bennett, yes. Nothing official, it's not like they applied to the electric company. But there's a power surge coming from that house and all utilities are working. It's a big ass house."

"Correct. A dozen people could get lost in there."

"Are we sure this is the right place?" Dahl asked from the seat beside Drake.

"You heard Bennett. CCTV cameras reverse-imaged two of these guys, from the moment they killed the soldiers guarding the sword, through London, to here. Arrived ninety minutes ago. Haven't a clue what they've been doing since."

"Playing chess?" Kinimaka suggested.

"I doubt it dude. They're mercs."

"Good point. I Spy, then?"

Alicia chose that moment to comment. "Well, I spy a whopper in the front window. Could be ex-military."

Luther leaned forward. "A whopper?"

Mai grunted. "With Alicia? That could mean a number of things."

"A goon," Alicia confirmed. "I guess that's enough corroboration." She threw the scope on the dashboard in front of her. "Can we go in and talk to them now?"

"I thought you said it was creepy," Dahl said.

"Don't worry. I'll keep my eyes closed."

Drake cracked open the door. "Dahl, she's with you. The rest—let's go."

Silently, the team exited their vans under a leaden gray sky, smelling rain on the mid-afternoon air. Bennett had provided weapons and other military trappings, so Drake found himself outfitted with an HK MP5 sub machine gun, a 9mm Sig Sauer, stun grenades and tear gas canisters. They wore assault suits, fireproof knee and elbow pads and a bullet-proof armored waistcoat designed not only to stop a bullet but also to absorb its kinetic energy.

Kinimaka and Smyth carried the breaching gear. A sledgehammer and battering ram, pneumatic tools and explosives. Others carried ladders and ropes.

They were all out, ready to strike the old asylum like a bolt of thunder. Drake leapt the short wall, landed in overgrowth and ran with his head low, gun aimed carefully ahead. The team were with him, their boots swishing through shrubbery the only sound. Trees were positioned here and there, providing brief shelter, and then they resumed, running for the wall of the house.

Drake arrived in seconds, putting his back to the brick. Half the team would go around back; half around the side. Drake gave it a minute and then crept under the nearest window, heading for the side of the large house. Another window loomed and then they grouped, preparing to breach. Drake waited for the "go" from the other team before giving the signal. Instantly, Mai and Dahl raced around him, taking point. He went third and knew Alicia was at his back.

A dozen targets stood between them and the sword.

A narrow path ran down the side of the house, covered by a triangular, tiled roof. It ended at the side door. Drake signaled

Smyth to come around, who then breached the entrance with a battering ram. Dahl jumped in first, backed by Mai as the thick door swung back against its hinges. They were going in loud and hard, hoping to surprise their enemy into mistakes. Drake found himself inside a narrow kitchen, consisting mostly of shelves, cupboards and sinks, and then turned left along another narrow passage and through a much larger kitchen. To the left a staircase with a red threadbare carpet led to the first floor. To the right more rotting archways ran deeper into the house.

"Split," Dahl called.

Alicia chose the house, followed by Kenzie, Yorgi and Molokai, the last man looking beastly, clad not only in his own clothes but in the SAS get-up too. Alicia couldn't think of a time when she'd run with anyone more imposing. They cleared one room and then another, each a small sitting room still furnished with old sofas and spiderweb-coated bookcases that reached up to the ceiling. Old paintings, covered in dust, hung on the walls.

"It's as though someone fled very quickly," Kenzie breathed. "Spooky."

"If this were a horror movie the original patients would still be here," Molokai intoned. "Not that I watch horror movies much."

Yorgi couldn't take his eyes off the many potential treasures, though none of them sparkled any more. The Russian thief appeared to be cataloguing an inventory for later.

Gunfire sounded somewhere in the house. Alicia didn't waver, just swept as fast as caution allowed around the eastern wall. They were nearing the back of the old hospital now; she could see overgrown garden through the windows ahead. Alert as she'd ever been, she saw a patch of shadow spreading across the floor from the doorway in front and fired instantly through the wooden paneling that protected it. There was a grunt, followed by a thump as a body fell into her path, chest pouring blood. She hurdled the dead mass, came down and saw another figure sheltering behind an overturned refrigerator to the right.

No fucking about today, asshole.

She hurled a grenade, then ran in the opposite direction, now following a corridor that ran parallel to the back of the house. The grenade exploded behind her, shrapnel flying everywhere, flames licking at the ceiling. A window smashed to their right, a frame buckled, but the refrigerator itself had stopped most of the blast— well, the refrigerator and the merc, to be fair.

Alicia sped along, stopping to clear rooms along the way, working in concert with Molokai and Kenzie as Yorgi searched for signs of the sword. By necessity, this was a rapid shock attack, but it would help to take at least a couple of the mercs alive.

Up ahead, there stood another closed door. Alicia saw vapor seeping through the gap along the bottom and pulled up sharply.

"Fire?"

"Doesn't smell like fire." Kenzie sniffed the air. "And it looks more like steam."

Alicia readied herself, feeling a little bemused, then grabbed the brass doorknob. It turned easily, allowing her to crack it open a little. The spectacle beyond caused the corners of her mouth to curl up.

"Interesting," she murmured. "It's the men's shower room."

Kenzie shifted from foot to foot. "Is it occupied?"

"I'll say."

Alicia opened the door wider, an inch at a time. The noise of the three running showers and the banging rock music from someone's phone boomed out, masking any noise they might have made. Alicia slipped in first, then Kenzie, Molokai and Yorgi. Before them lay a makeshift, open shower area—just six shower heads in a row and a sloped wet floor that led to a drain. Three naked, muscular mercs were soaping and rinsing, completely engrossed. Alicia paused for a moment at the edge of the wet area.

"Yogi, cover your eyes. You're too young to see this."

"I believe we should attack right away," Molokai said, still giving Alicia the creeps in his voluminous robe-like clothes. "Whilst they are preoccupied."

Alicia nodded. "I agree."

"Then why are we waiting?"

"Welllll . . . I'm feeling quite relaxed right now."

Yorgi approached the edge of the dry floor. "Do you see any weapons?"

Alicia glanced at him and choked. "Are you kidding me?"

Kenzie crouched. "Best show I've seen in a while."

"I'm still worried about weapons," Yorgi said, casting his eyes all around the room.

"Believe me," Alicia still hadn't taken her eyes away from the showers, "there's nothing here that should worry you."

Molokai leveled his gun. "Less talk," he said. "More death."

"Whoa," Alicia reached out a hand and grabbed his cloth-covered wrist, noting the puff of dust that rose. "You can't just shoot 'em. They're naked."

"You think they wouldn't shoot us, given the same circumstances? They're mercs—led only by money and power. They have no morals. You know this."

"I guess." Alicia nodded. "But don't join them, Molokai. Rise above and be better."

Kenzie rose now. "I'm all for killing the fuckers to be honest."

Alicia regarded her. "And I thought you'd changed."

"That was yesterday," she said. "Today . . . I really don't care."

Alicia knew she was smarting badly from Dahl's rejection. "He has a wife and children. You can't ask him to give that up."

"I won't," Kenzie said. "Soon, I won't even be around."

Alicia didn't push it. She'd never liked the Israeli but grudgingly admitted she was a powerful asset to their team. Molokai moved again and Alicia strengthened her grip on his arm.

"Wait," she said. "The guy on the right just dropped his soap."

Seconds passed. Alicia peered harder, but then the taller of the three men wiped soap from his eyes and spotted them.

"Hey!"

Alicia set off without thinking, blocking Molokai's aim. She couldn't watch the bloody destruction of three unarmed men, despite their choice of occupation. An annoyed grunt sounded behind and then she was totally committed, dashing quickly toward the three naked mercs and feeling somewhat surreal.

The things I do for my job.

Kenzie was alongside, clearly wanting in on the action. The mercs lost their expressions of shock and discomfort, and took defensive positions. Alicia knew there was simply no point in bouncing off a musclebound body, so she dropped and slid in, using the water to smooth her approach. A kick upward as she neared the tallest merc, and a foot hooked behind his knee, caused him to buckle and fall forward and then she was up, at his back. She slammed an elbow down on his neck, felt him stagger.

He turned as she struck again, taking a hit to the ribs. His soaking wet body helped divert some of the power of her blow. It also helped him slip closer. She punched again, a double strike to the sternum. He staggered backward this time, head forced forward. Alicia front-kicked his stomach. The man slipped to one knee. She attacked but he grabbed her around the waist, pulling her close.

"Shit, dude, this ain't how I roll."

"I won't let go." He squeezed harder, trying to crush her ribs.

"Didn't realize you cared."

She used his own slippery body to squeeze down through his hands, and then they were both rolling on the floor, soaked through.

Kenzie certainly didn't stand on ceremony, using her opponent's nakedness to help herself. The blows she struck were telling, and well placed. In his desperation though, the merc grabbed her knees and forced her to the floor, so that she also was grappling through the sloshing waters. The third merc ducked behind the wrestlers too as Molokai lined him up in his sights.

"Typical mercenary," Molokai intoned. "Yorgi, my friend, go get him."

The Russian thief stared. "Why can't you?"

"I don't want to get my feet wet."

"Oh, sorry, is that a leper thing?"

"No, it's a sanity thing. Just lift his head up a little and I'll do the rest."

"I remember now. You feel the cold quite badly, yes? Well, so do I. And I don't want to feel anything else, thank you. Those guys are naked."

"It doesn't seem to bother the women!"

Yorgi shook his head at the huge man. "You have a lot to learn about Alicia Myles."

The showers still surged and the banging sound of guitars screamed from the cellphone. Alicia lifted her man by the ankles, knowing she didn't have to do too much to set him down hard on his spine. It worked, but she fell onto his midriff, getting a bit closer than she'd bargained for. It was impossible to lay down the power and the telling blows amid such slick mayhem. Her clothing was soaked, her boots filled with water. Maybe this idea hadn't been such a good one after all.

She used the slick surface to crawl up his top half, grabbed hold of his head and forced it beneath the shower's pounding flow. He gurgled and struggled; Alicia using her knee to force the breath from his body. To her right Kenzie struggled with her merc and now Alicia saw the third crouching behind her and looking scared.

Molokai?

The man should come with a fucking leash, never mind the enigmatic robes. Alicia held her opponent in place and then heard the sloshing of boots as another attacker came from her right. It was Yorgi, and he launched himself at the third merc with what looked like a broken piece of tile in his hand. Despite all the incredible, witty one-liners this opportunity offered Alicia she couldn't help but feel a shiver of fear for the Russian.

He was no fighter, and clearly wanted to knock the third merc into unconsciousness rather than kill him. Alicia was forced to wait extra seconds as she saw Yorgi smash the merc across the temple, draw blood, and then slip heavily onto his own tailbone. The air rushed out of him; his face turned white. The merc rebounded and kicked him in the face. The tile went skimming away.

Alicia hammered her merc hard until he moved no more, then pulled him so that his face was clear of the water. She saw Kenzie employing an interesting handhold with her opponent, one arm passing under his groin and half way up his back whilst the other choked him into unconsciousness. Clearly, the girl had a few cool tricks in her arsenal. Alicia met the third merc boot-first, making sure it contacted heavily with his right cheek. Then she rose cautiously and moved in as he fell away. By the time he looked up she was standing over him.

Yorgi scrambled up to her. "Hurry."

"You sure you don't want get it on with this mammoth?"

"No. I was just saving his life."

"You hear that?" Alicia bent down and smashed the merc in the face. "He . . . was . . . just—" each word signaled a punch "—saving . . . your . . . life."

The man bellowed loudly and rose up, shedding water. He came at Alicia. She grabbed his shoulders and spun him away, but he somehow arrested the slide with a solidly planted back foot and then came again. Alicia smashed an elbow into his nose, stunning him, then proceeded to lash out half a dozen more times. The merc fell back every time, bleeding profusely from the nose and forehead.

He put his head down and attacked once more, a bull in a shower stall. She stepped smartly aside as he reached her, caught hold of his head, and added some momentum of her own. Unable to stop, he smashed skull first into the concrete wall where the showers were set, then groaned as he leaned there, trying not to slip to the floor. Alicia allowed him no dignity, planting her foot against his ass and pushing until he lost balance, falling among the flowing waters.

She whipped her head around. Kenzie had choked her opponent out and now rose, dripping water and soaked to the bone. Alicia stared at her, feeling the liquid sluicing off her own body in waves.

"Still think that was a good idea?" Kenzie asked.

"It wasn't my best," Alicia admitted. "I guess the sight of man-sausage just confuses my brain."

Molokai met them as they exited the shower area, trying to shake the worst of the water away. Alicia squeezed her hair and Kenzie smoothed her clothes. Yorgi emptied his boots. They turned for a last glance back at the showers.

"Surreal," Alicia commented.

"Waste of time," Molokai said. "Five seconds and I'd have ended them."

"Sometimes," Alicia said, "you just have to try harder."

"And now we leave live, capable enemies at our backs."

Alicia hadn't failed to notice. She'd taken their cellphones, clothes and discarded weapons. "I doubt that, my friend."

Molokai ignored her and headed for the exit door, taking a moment to peer up and down the corridor. The coast was clear, and gunfire raged from a distant corner of the house.

"We have to go."

"Lead the way."

Leaving the mercs and that area of the extensive asylum behind, the foursome raced for the side where the other teams were engaged in battle.

CHAPTER FIVE

Drake smashed through weak, wooden paneling, leaving it in splinters in his wake, and then rolled twice until a spray of bullets had temporarily ceased. He was pinned down, but fortunately it was all a distraction. Drake was the bait and Luther was the hook. The single merc that targeted Drake didn't see the enormous, bald-headed behemoth charging in from his left, and paid a hefty price. Luther struck, bones smashed, and the merc entered unconsciousness before he even knew what had happened.

Luther looked for Drake. "You okay?"

The Englishman was already up, shaking his head in disappointment. "Bloody hell, man. C'mon, let's find the others."

Two minutes later and they were stealing up behind Mai, Hayden and Kinimaka. It was the Japanese woman that turned.

"Did you find out where the sword is?"

"Nah. Luther the Hulk decided to show up instead. Knocked our merc out cold."

Mai widened her eyes at the big man. "Oh, Luther. Really?"

Drake was incredulous to see Luther lower his head. "Yeah, sorry Mai."

"For fuck's sake," he muttered. "You two sound like a pair of pansies."

Hayden waved for their full attention. "There's another merc bedded down just ahead. Pretty soon he's gonna realize that this corridor is constructed of wooden paneling, but he's hired help so I think we have a few minutes. I'm thinking . . . percussion?"

Drake nodded along with everyone else. At that moment Alicia and her small team arrived and made them whole again.

"How many?" Kinimaka asked.

"We took out five in total."

"Okay, so that leaves our friend here and three more. They must have the sword. Anything from the perimeter?"

Hayden checked her comms. "No movement out there. Cops have the place ringed and sealed."

Drake was staring at Alicia and her team. "Why the hell are you all wet?"

Alicia shook droplets over him. "Stopped for a shower."

"So why isn't Molokai wet? And why is Yorgi blushing?"

Alicia stroked the Russian's cheek. "What happens in the asylum stays in the asylum, right Yogi?"

Drake sized Alicia, Kenzie and Yorgi up, all three soaked through and sporting fresh bruises. "Had to be a hell of a threesome, guys. You ready for more?"

Hayden threw the grenade and jammed her ears with her fingers. When the blast erupted, they moved quickly, firing hard on the hidden man but ensuring they fired high. When Drake slipped around the side of a sturdy overturned bookcase he found the merc on his back, blood leaking from his ears.

"Shit. Doesn't look good, people."

Hayden righted the merc as Kinimaka swept his weapons away with stroke of a hand. Carefully, she planted his back against the bookcase and let his eyes swim back into focus.

"Can you hear me?"

The merc blinked.

"I think percussion grenades were a bad idea," Kinimaka commented.

"Ya think?" Hayden patted the man's cheek gently. "Speak up sooner next time, Mano. This dude's less use than a carrot."

The man's eyes cleared suddenly and he blinked up at Hayden. "What?"

"You can hear me now? Oh, good."

She dropped to her knees and framed his face tightly with her hands, not too hard but still making sure he could feel her. "Where is the weapon you guys stole from the Brits? The Sword of Mars."

The merc stared and then tried to look around. Hayden let him see Kinimaka, Drake and Luther, all standing menacingly close, and then asked the same question again.

"Last chance, dickhead," Drake added.

The merc kicked his legs but they were jelly, pushed his arms against the floor but found he had no strength. Finally, he slumped. "All right," he moaned. "The pizza just arrived."

Hayden bit her lip. "I think the blast must have confused him."

"No, no. The pizza guy delivered so the boss took the boxes to the comms room. To eat. He has the sword."

"Where's the comms room?"

He relayed the information, then Smyth and Dahl rendered him immobile with plastic zip ties. "Don't worry, the cops'll be along soon." The Swede grinned.

As a team, they slipped toward the comms room, wary of traps and wondering when the last three remaining mercs would make their appearance. The asylum brooded heavily all around them, its scarred, cold walls bearing the weight of oppressive secrets; its half-closed, creaking doors having endured with a stoic silence all the arduous years it housed the criminally insane. In the air, Drake imagined, there still might linger ghosts of former terrors, watching over the new trespassers, gathering in the gloom.

He shook it off, treading the old boards as cautiously as he could, for more than one reason.

Hayden stopped as a new smell infused the air. "We're close."

Drake smelled it too. The mouth-watering aroma of several pepperoni pizzas. Up ahead, a shadow darted. Shouts went up among the SPEAR team, most hitting the deck and others falling into nearby rooms. The shadow appeared again, this time holding a machine gun, becoming solid as he peered around a corner.

Shots rang out. Bullets struck wood, plaster and block work. Hayden threw another grenade and, in the aftermath, used the confusion to charge ahead, Kinimaka at her side. It became a full-on assault as Dahl, Luther and Molokai joined in, jostling for position along the hallway. Drake was up and chasing them with Alicia and Mai alongside.

"New boys are keen," Drake muttered.

"Mai's got her Luther all wound up," Alicia baited.

"Don't be a fool, Taz. You know Drake's the only one for me."

"I'll give him back when he's all worn out, bitch."

"Hey!" Drake shouted. "Quit it."

The leaders burst through a door frame, quite literally. Dahl and Luther were shoulder to shoulder and neither gave ground.

The wooden frame splintered, smashed apart. Dahl went through a step ahead, gun raised, and Drake was barely a step behind Luther.

The room was small, almost fully occupied by a central table. A computer desk and monitor sat in one corner, practically inaccessible because of the table, a live Skype screen in use. The monitor was blank, but the "live" light still blinked.

On the table sat six enormous pizzas in distinctively colored boxes.

Resting atop the highest box of pizzas was the Sword of Mars.

Now that's surreal. Drake entertained the fleeting thought as men attacked from both sides. The onslaught was weak at best, both men affected by the grenade. Drake didn't blame them. He'd been some way from the explosion and could still hear the ringing in his ears.

Luther and Dahl put the two men down with ease. Drake relaxed, looking around at the beaten enemy and the weapon they had come to reclaim. "Well, I'm starting to feel a bit superfluous."

"Finally," Dahl nodded, "the Yorkshire bell end sees the glaring truth."

"Says the man from the land of blonde porn." Drake pushed the Swede aside. "Are we done here?"

Hayden reached over the pizza boxes and grabbed the sword. "Looks like it hasn't been damaged." She turned it over in her hands. "Not that we saw it too well last time."

"We were fighting a shitload of enemies and Kenzie was riding her nuclear weapon," Alicia pointed out.

"Ah, yes." Kenzie smiled, remembering fondly. "And I haven't ridden anything like it since." She glared at Dahl's back.

"We good?" Kinimaka asked. "I secured these guys, but there are some still unaccounted for. And hell, I can barely turn full circle in here."

Luther backed through the shattered door frame. "Follow me, big guy. There ain't room for all of us in there."

Kinimaka held up a hand. "Wait. We can't let this pizza go to waste." He scooped up all of the boxes.

With a steady prudence they exited the comms room. Hayden

stayed behind for a few seconds, trying to trace the live communication, but it had been disabled already and she couldn't find anything. "We'll ask the Brits to deep-dive this," she said. "See if they can come up with something."

Drake took control of the sword, keeping it away from Kenzie, whose eyes glazed at the sight of it. Drake let the pizza-carrying Hawaiian go first, noting that Hayden quickly followed. It was good to see the pair trying again. *Where would we all be without affection and passion? And more importantly, where would we all be without family?*

He studied the team that left the house; the newcomers adding their own peculiar personalities to the mix; the usual crew that had fought for civilians and the innocent from the beginning, and still fought—despite the ambiguous severing of their friendship with the US government.

A temporary thing.

Maybe. But if it was that easy to disavow a team, possibly alienate several teams, why would they continue to aid this government? This administration? It should be as hard to estrange a Special Forces team as it was to get close to the President.

But sadly, the opposite was true.

Drake noticed the rain had started to fall as he left the asylum and wondered if the sky was weeping tears for the damned.

Or was it for all the soldiers?

CHAPTER SIX

The following day, the morning was bright and crisp, the blue skies an unbroken dome above. Hyde Park was teeming with dog walkers, cyclists and joggers. Luckily, it was a considerably large place and the SPEAR team kicked their way across the glistening grass with morning dew on their boots, meeting Major Bennett and Captain Cambridge on the path that ran past the statue of Achilles.

Hayden held the Sword of Mars, wrapped in two supermarket carrier bags. Bennett couldn't hide the smile when he saw it. "Really?"

Hayden shrugged. "Best we could do on short notice and all the sword-wrapping shops were closed last night."

"Interesting place to meet." Dahl eyed Achilles. "Topical."

"We aim to please," Bennett said. "It's also tourist free at this time of a morning. Now, we do have much to talk about . . ." He paused and picked up two cardboard trays full of steaming hot drinks. Cambridge picked up another and offered them around.

"Civilized." Luther nodded his thanks.

"Don't get used to it. First things first—Tempest are totally hell-bent on gathering all the weapons of the gods. There appears to be no order to them, no clues on how to find them. We're relying on getting close and then using this rare element to pinpoint the location. The point of that recap is to highlight the words 'getting close', which is the problematic part. So, what do we know about these weapons?"

Cambridge held up a thick folder. "Most of the gen's in here." He flapped it backward and forward. "Pages full of information on the Sword of Mars and the others. Read it." He slapped it down on a bench right in front of Hayden.

She stared at the generous file with fear. "Jeez, dude, I haven't read that much since high school."

"Mars was, or is, the Roman god of war," Bennett said. "Identified with the Greek god, Ares. These classical deities are now thought to once have been real men, or perhaps real gods that walked the earth. Some are even identified with the Atlantis myth and, it is said, were the kings of Atlantis, later worshipped by lesser races such as the Greeks and the Phoenicians, and thus their legends turned them into the gods we know today."

"You're telling me Atlantis is real now too?" Smyth grumbled.

"Well, no, my friend, but rumors are starting to surface, some new evidence has come to light. Who knows? Perhaps another team will chase that, but we must concentrate on finding the weapons, defeating Tempest and proving all your innocence."

Hayden liked this man and the way he set his goals out quite clearly. She sipped strong black coffee and stood in the sunshine, letting its warming rays soothe her soul. It was good to take a moment to feel the sun on your face.

"Mars was the son of Jupiter. He was virile, a thriving life force. The spear of Mars is most associated with him, but the sword is a good second."

"This raises a question," Hayden butted in whilst Bennett took a breath and a sip of his drink. "If we're scouring the planet for these weapons, presumably under fire, we need a safe place to send them when we find them. A secure network of contacts, so that we can ship them to you, Major, allowing you to store them with the Crown Jewels, or something. We can't be lugging them around the world with us."

Bennett nodded. "Yes, we came up with the same idea. We will provide for you a state-of-the-art communications system and have already tasked a special unit to shadow you at all times. Between all of you, and them, we should be able to extract the weapons without risk."

"Sounds great," Alicia spoke up and Hayden glanced at her. "Any ideas what's up next?"

Her question raised most of the crew's eyebrows, Hayden noticed, including Mano's. She found her attention briefly fixated on her old flame. The big Hawaiian was as solid a home as she was ever going to get and, incredibly, was still interested in her. Hayden didn't want to blow it this time, so she was taking everything slow, creating no expectations and offering no promises. The hope was that it would all just fall into place.

Wouldn't that require a period of stability?

Sure, and that wasn't even on the horizon. A network of criminals had to be taken down first, a network that had entwined its way through the power-halls of Washington DC. Its contacts would be formidable, its reach all-embracing. Even here . . .

"Let's get on with it," she said, snatching up the folder. "We'll get savvy with this and be prepared for the next few weapons. Maybe a little knowledge of the gods will help us find them."

"Well," Bennett held out a hand as she prepared to wrap the meeting up, "we do have an idea as to the whereabouts of the next weapon."

She stopped. "You do? Why didn't you say so?"

"It seemed best to surprise you." Bennett shrugged. "With no path to follow it's like putting a pin in a map and going after the closest. We chose the Key of Hades first simply because it was originally found in the tomb you all discovered."

"Which one?" Dahl asked.

"There was more than one? Ah, well, I suppose you have your secrets. The Odin tomb. The place where you found the bones of Odin."

Hayden thought back momentarily to a time when she first met Drake and his friendly associate, Ben Blake, gone but never forgotten. At that time Alicia had worked for the other side and Dahl was a fixture of the Swedish government. Kinimaka had been involved in some other mission centering on the Blood King. So was Mai, for that matter. Karin had been involved also, kidnapped by a madman, and Kennedy Moore too—yet another lost soul.

"Feels an age distant," Dahl said reflectively.

"Yeah." Hayden hid her emotions and addressed Bennett. "Please go on."

"The Key of Hades was discovered along with a whole host of other items inside your Icelandic tomb. Many of these items were removed before the tomb collapsed or exploded or whatever happened to it—"

"The Swords of Babylon," Kinimaka rumbled. "That's what happened to it."

"Right, well, the Key of Hades is a small object about the size of a big man's hand. Obviously, we don't know its purpose for being or why it was inside Hades' tomb, but we do know it's on Tempest's list. Now, after the key left the tomb under guard it was sent to a museum in Stockholm for study, and from there it was very quickly stolen."

Drake glared at Dahl. "Typical."

The Swede closed his eyes in a long-suffering way. "I remember an awful lot of archaeologists coming and going in those days. I guess not all of them were real."

"It was a busy, frenzied few months. It's always the same. Nobody knows who's really in charge or who their actual superior is, and then the carrion swoops in to take a piece of it. Money talks, and in this case it talked the Key of Hades right out of that museum and into the hands of a thief known worldwide as Aladdin."

Alicia gawped. "Fuck, don't tell me he's real too."

"No, no, just a moniker given to him by some agency somewhere. Aladdin is known to steal without trace, a true ghost, but also never to properly tidy up the breadcrumbs that could lead to his benefactor. He leaves that to them. Some, of course, don't realize or think they're too important, and here we have one such individual."

"You know who has the key?" Yorgi asked.

"We do, son. He's a shipping magnate that owns the Gad Shipping Line and, specifically, the *Enlargo* yacht."

"One of the biggest ever produced," Cambridge added.

"Quite." Bennett nodded. "This man—Gordon Demba—has lived aboard the *Enlargo* for a decade, sailing from port to port. He's not especially troublesome, stays off all the main radars, and I'm guessing he has no idea that we know about the key."

"Did you send the heavies in?" Smyth asked.

"Of course not. The key has to be taken covertly. We must leave Tempest guessing. And Demba will have his own security detail."

Hayden had guessed they would be chasing the shipping magnate down. Smyth, of course, was hoping for a swift return to Washington. Lauren hadn't been in touch for a while. She finished her coffee and threw the cup into a trash can.

"Where we headed, Bennett?"

"The Pacific Ocean," the major said. "We'll sort out the coordinates later. Are you ready to go?"

"Sure," Hayden said. "But there is an issue. Is it wise to seek just one weapon? Won't that let Tempest grab at least a few?"

"We don't have the backup yet," Bennett admitted and Cambridge nodded along. "We don't know who to trust. Why do you think we're meeting here instead of MI5 or 6, or somewhere closer? I want you people and a select team or two, soldiers I can rely on."

"Honestly," Hayden said. "We feel the same, and we can always split the team. But let's stay together for now. This is what . . . a two-day op?"

"At the very most," Bennett agreed. "And it's relatively simple. In . . . out . . . Demba is no soldier and employs no mercenaries."

"We need a thief," Drake indicated Yorgi, "and a bodyguard. Take your pick. I guess it's a go."

"The Key of Hades is on that boat," Bennett said. "And the jet is equipped with the retro-fitted GPR device you requested. It has been recalibrated and will seek out the one specific element we need. If it doesn't beep, I've sent you on a wild goose chase."

"It'll beep," Hayden said. "Have faith."

"Oh, I have faith," Bennett sighed. "But, right now, only in the people I see around me."

CHAPTER SEVEN

Flying at full speed toward the middle of nowhere, Drake was reminded of the vast size of the Pacific Ocean. It was no surprise that there still existed officially uncharted waters and even islands out here. The scale was staggering.

They sat in the back of a big Chinook cargo chopper, forsaking the preferred military alternative because of the size of their group. Alicia was complaining about the bumpy ride and Mai was reminding her that she usually enjoyed that sort of thing. Kinimaka and Hayden were chatting; Smyth was looking distant and holding a phone to his ear; Kenzie and Dahl were sitting apart, trying desperately not to stare at each other; Yorgi was passing the time with Luther and Molokai, the latter wrapping his heavy robes tighter as cold penetrated the chopper's fuselage—so it was business as usual really, with Drake watching over them all.

Still no word from Lauren, or even Kimberly Crowe, so they were flying blind with no fresh updates on Tempest. Drake wondered how Karin was getting on. He didn't expect to hear from her or her team so soon—infiltrating FrameHub would be extremely perilous even for her. The odd bunch of supergeeks that had targeted Egypt with a missile a short while ago were clearly unhinged.

But now she has training, and so do her new friends. And what the hell did she mean by saying: I'll interrupt my agenda for this?

What was her agenda?

The pilot communicated that two of them should go up to the cockpit. Drake and Hayden rose first, so they trudged steadily along the steel fuselage, listening to their own reverberating footsteps and the quiet murmurings of their team.

Drake glanced sidelong at Hayden. "You good?"

"Feels like we've been on this damn road a decade, Matt," she said. "Always another crisis. I do believe the world would continue to turn without us."

"I'm not so sure," he joked, but then grew serious. "We do make a difference. Sure, there are other teams, other agencies, all good men and women, but work at it like we already won it, Hay. We do good."

"And who works for us?" Hayden said as they reached the cockpit.

The pilot turned to them so Drake could say no more, but he knew what she meant. The situation with DC and lack of understanding from President Coburn's allies and even the man himself was challenging. Of course, with all the missions they had been through during the last few weeks, the time period seemed far longer than it was.

They had been safe in Transylvania only a few short weeks ago. Peru and the Incas just before that, each op leading straight into the next.

A drifter with a gun, in the full-time employment of the government that wants to kill me, he thought. *That's what I am, what we all are. Helluva job description.*

"Thanks, guys," the pilot was saying in what Drake recognized as a Yorkshire accent. "We're twenty minutes out so you might wanna prep. Gonna belay you whilst we hover. Shouldn't take too long to reach deck; we have four lines."

Drake grinned. "Ey up, mate, are you from God's own country?"

"Ey up." The pilot turned with a genuine smile. "Don't be shoutin' down me lug 'oils, pal. Where y' from?"

"Ponte," Drake said, pronouncing it "pontey." "You?"

"Cas."

"Hey, Dahl!" Drake called back into the hull. "We got a bona fide Yorkshireman right here!"

"Oh, fuck," came the long-suffering reply. "If only we had a half-intelligent translator."

The pilot looked over his shoulder, through the door of the cabin. "You wanna understand Yorkshire, mate, go watch *The Full Monty.*"

Hayden disrupted the mutual northern solidarity. "Are you staying close?"

"I'll hang around," the pilot guffawed, all jovial now. "Judging by the fuel level you will have about . . ." He made several clucking noises. "Forty minutes."

"That'll give us time to steal the key, tidy up after ourselves and probably even re-paint the boat," Drake said.

"Maybe even a spot of shark fishing." Dahl poked his head through and stared at the Yorkshire pilot as if inspecting a new species. "Is this the inbred layabout?"

"Y'see any other pilots on board, ya blonde wazzock?"

Drake choked back laughter. The pilot held up a hand in apology. "Seriously, people, we're ten minutes out."

By the time the pilot called out again the team were lining up by the doors, rappel lines in hand. Drake and Hayden were staring out of the windows, trying not to let the rolling blue waves hypnotize them. They tested comms and checked weapons. Soon, Drake saw the shipping magnate's boat on the seas.

"It's bigger than I thought," he admitted. "Better work fast, team, and sweep in pairs. Plenty of places aboard for guards to hide themselves."

The *Enlargo* was a mixture of silver and black panels, the front end as sleek as a speedboat and the stern a sweeping fusion of elegant lines. Three decks above water were visible, but there would be at least two more below.

"Nobody in sight," Hayden said. "Good start."

"Time to go," the pilot shouted.

Luther opened a door and then Drake, on the other side, did the same. Lines were dropped, spooling down to the clear, clean deck. The first two descended, guns ready, covered by those still up top. Soon, the next batch went and then the last, Drake and Hayden among them. Luther touched deck first, with Molokai and Smyth a second behind. The soldiers dropped low and checked their surroundings. Drake landed softly and heard no noise other than the lap of waves against the hull and the chopper overhead.

Weird.

Somebody should have heard the chopper's hover pattern, if not the approach. Quickly, the team divided and moved aft and forward. Drake saw highly polished brass rails, gleaming windows and one cold, but half-drunk ceramic mug of coffee. He saw an open door, a misplaced throw heaped in a corner, a yellow bottle of sun cream with the top still open.

A small pile of coins as if someone was in the middle of counting their change.

But no signs of people.

Alicia voiced his feelings before he could. "Well, this is fucking creepy."

The boat rocked gently, soundless except for the newcomers. Drake wondered if they were all hiding below, or all passed out, or . . .

Don't think. Search.

"The key may still be here," Hayden said in his earpiece. "Move your asses."

He climbed a set of stairs quickly to the top deck, but it was nothing more than a pool surrounded by sun loungers. The second deck was an outside viewing area and recreational room, bordered by smoked glass windows and a pair of sliding doors. He went through drawers and a cupboard with minimal hope of finding anything and wasn't surprised.

"Heading down to main deck," he spoke over the comms. Alicia, his partner, tapped him on the shoulder.

"Are you thinking what I'm thinking?"

He wasn't in the mood for a witty comeback. All his senses were on red alert. "Probably, love."

"Good. Because I'm a few minutes away from abandoning ship."

The comms blared into life. "Thought you should all know—that thing is drifting," the pilot said. "Not much, but it's a very calm day. See if you can drop the anchor, folks."

Drake continued walking, trying to ignore the tiny shiver that traveled the length of his spine. Drifting? He'd been around boats enough to know where the electric anchor winch control would be situated and found it easily. The sound of the anchor deploying was raucously loud in the quiet day, causing both Alicia and him to check their perimeter uneasily.

Another transmission: "Scrubbing to the side of the boat. Looks like something came alongside."

Drake moved within and helped Dahl and Mai search furniture and nooks and crannies for any sign of the Key of Hades.

Cambridge had provided them with a photograph of the original artifact found near Odin's tomb. Again, he found it surreal that they were weaving through another tale connected to their first mission and the old gods. The Key of Hades was a mediocre item as far as artifacts went, but its title and more likely its size was what made it appealing to thieves and collectors. Big money, small risk. They checked under sofas and behind the television, opened every paperback and a thick photo album, but came up with nothing.

"Below decks," Mai said. "What do you see down there?"

Kinimaka responded. "Rumpled beds. A toothbrush with toothpaste still attached. Full coffee cups. The staff quarters are clean and empty, the kitchen too. I believe we have a ghost ship on our hands here."

Alicia breathed out sharply. "Don't say that."

"Yeah," Luther spoke up, surprisingly for Drake given the man's level-headed and candid attitude. "I remember being lost back in a desert somewhere in some Taliban-infested shithole, and this young soldier with a busted helmet came walking down the road and told me where all the buried IEDs were. I lived, thanks to him, but it turned out he didn't . . . I looked him up later, and the kid died three months previous."

Drake felt Alicia shiver at his side. "Is that true?"

"Of course it's fucking true. You don't mess with shit you don't know nothin' about, boy. And that includes you, Hawaii Five-o."

Kinimaka grumbled. Smyth, Yorgi and Molokai were searching the lowest deck and announced similar findings. No key, no signs of life. Hayden told them they had five minutes to double-check everything and then meet up on deck. Drake wandered over to a window to scan all the rolling horizons.

"Ghost ship," he whispered aloud. "Where'd you all go?"

"If it were a Kraken there'd be more damage," Alicia said with conviction. "So don't worry."

"Thanks, love."

Of course, these days, there were several clear reasons why a ship might end up deserted, and none of them good. Pirates. Terrorists. A criminal undertaking. Ransom. But he was concerned at the lack of evidence, the sense that a full crew had been interrupted, surprised. The waters were empty to all the compass points; just blue, undulating ocean.

And it left them with one enormous problem.

They reassembled quickly, taking themselves out onto the main deck and up toward the prow where there was room for everyone. The chopper hovered above, its rappel lines snaking softly in the gentle breeze.

"It's a new one on me," Drake said first.

"Do we abandon the key?" Kinimaka asked, then added: "And the boat?"

"The Dagger of Nemesis comes next on the list," Yorgi informed them.

"Bollocks, I hate losing," Dahl said. "Somebody mentioned this thing was drifting, right? Pilot—can you track a path along which it may have drifted?"

"Aye, mate, that I can. But you gotta tell me first—why did the GPR device point us to the boat if it's not there?"

Dahl waved it around, checked the batteries and then tried again. "A residual signal?" he ventured. "Or maybe it was here when Bennett ordered the check. Maybe . . . it's only recently moved."

The pilot offered a grudging, "Maybe."

While the team waited for him to finish charting the drift of the *Enlargo*, they stood, trapped in the unnerving ambience that lay over the empty boat like a heavy shroud. Minutes later, the Yorkshireman came back on the comms.

"Must have drifted between five and seven miles assuming you're right and whatever happened, happened this morning. They wouldn't be drinking coffee at night, right?"

"The beds are slept in and unmade," Mai pointed out.

"Aye, so let's get you all winched back up and take a short trip."

They left the *Enlargo* where it was, abandoned and lonely, and watched out of the windows as the chopper retraced the boat's itinerant path. Empty blue seas greeted them and what had, at first, been a splendid vista was now humdrum and a little alarming.

"No rafts, no lifeboats, no . . . nothing," Hayden said.

"Big storm could'a took 'em?" Kinimaka wondered.

"Nothing on today's forecast," the pilot said.

"I'm thinking something more physical," Alicia said. "And with teeth."

"Stop thinking." Mai sighed. "It doesn't work well for you."

"Says the frisky Sprite."

Drake ignored their bickering, watching Luther and Molokai. The two new members of the team rarely spoke to each other, but often communicated in shared looks and gestures. Clearly, they knew each other inside out. Drake got the impression that Luther could fit easily into any team and any situation, whereas Molokai would always be detached and uneasy. The story of their pasts would be a bloody interesting one.

He returned his attention to the window as the pilot told them they'd arrived at an approximate spot. Two minutes later he called out for people to come forward.

Drake crowded into the cockpit. Through the wide glass window, he saw a surprising mass. Surprising because the map on the instrument panel didn't acknowledge it.

"Is that an island?"

"Aye, mate, it is, an uncharted one."

"Shit." Drake shared a glance with Mai, remembering another uncharted island they'd visited and what had happened there.

"Pull up," Hayden said. "We need to see the size of it and check for others."

"A few miles in circumference," the pilot said. "Nothing you couldn't walk around in a couple of hours, and I see no other land masses to any horizon. We're pretty much on our own here."

"Strangely," Kinimaka said. "That doesn't help."

Even Molokai pulled his outer robe more tightly around him.

Dahl pointed the adapted GPR at the island, lowering the chopper's window as they drifted nearer, now able to make out a small mountain chain, probably volcanic, and several stands of dense, green trees. A valley lay beyond the beach, bristling with shrubbery. Dahl switched the device on and there was no mistaking the sudden red pulse that started blinking in the center of the screen.

"The key," he breathed softly. "It's there."

"Then put us down," Hayden said. "Right there on the beach."

Nobody spoke. They all remembered the *Enlargo* only too well and, with their imaginations fired up, they couldn't help but wonder exactly what unknown hell they might be about to walk into.

CHAPTER EIGHT

The beach was pale in color, almost white, and belied any sense of wrongdoing. Drake waited, standing in the thick sand, staring at the treeline ahead and wondering what manner of escapade awaited them.

Dahl broke out his GPR and studied the signal. "North." He aimed his hand in the direction of travel. "Dead north."

Alicia was studying the treeline. "Got a machete?"

"Oh, hang on." Kenzie rummaged around her jacket's various pockets. "Ah, no, must have misplaced it."

Alicia groaned, but Molokai withdrew his arm from under his thick coat, brandishing a three-foot-long gleaming blade. "Will this do?"

Kenzie practically ran over to hug him. "Oh, wow, what else do you have under those robes, man?"

Alicia tried not to stare at him, but waved at the trees. "Lead the way."

The day was hot, but Molokai revealed not an ounce of sweat or discomfort as he walked up the beach toward the greenery. The team spread out, careful to watch for any movement and to keep an eye on the sea too. The pilot left his helicopter as securely as he was able and joined the team.

The going was tough at first as Molokai forged a way. It didn't take long to find the gaps between the trees though, the machete was put away and they were able to walk easily between thick tree trunks, wading through a bed of vegetation. The air was heavy beneath the boughs and the sunlight intermittent. A wave of heat fell over them. They ranged left and right, always alert, but came across nothing untoward and no tracks.

"Could be as uninhabited as it looks," Kinimaka said, trying to disentangle his bulk from a bush. "Maybe we're—"

"Barking up the wrong tree?" Drake asked. "Yeah, maybe. But Dahl's gizmo says not."

The red pulse beat consistently a few miles ahead of their

position, judging by the scale of the island.

"This Key of Hades," Luther asked as they walked. "What is it, exactly?"

"It's the key to the underworld," Hayden said, tying back her hair as the heat grew. "It opens the locked doors that lead to hell."

"Shit." Luther shook his head. "Like we need that in our lives."

"I don't think it means anything to Tempest," Drake told them his thoughts. "They're simply gathering together a list of known weapons."

"It seems that way," Hayden agreed. "But I'm reserving judgment for now."

Gradually, the density of the trees lessened and the ground began to slope. They emerged onto a short field where the earth fell away in a regular gradient, turning into a mile long, mile wide, incredibly green valley. The sides sloped sharply—the far side was almost a cliff face—and there wasn't a visible structure in sight.

"So," Hayden mused. "Into the valley? Or around?"

"Bad place." Molokai stared ahead. "No cover, and raised hills all around. I don't like it."

"Gotta agree," Luther said. "Sitting ducks and all that."

"No structures of any kind," Dahl said. "But that doesn't mean nothing's there. And the GPR says the key is . . ." He pointed a hand again, dead north. "Right at the head of the valley."

"You sure?" Smyth asked. "Or is it at the top of the cliff above the valley? 'Cause, dude, that's a world of difference when we're walking."

Drake saw Smyth made a good point. The cliff could only be accessed by walking around the valley top and negotiating a range of ragged boulders, whereas the end of the valley could be reached simply by continuing along their path.

"Let's split," he said. "Any preferences?"

Opinions were voiced but the team soon separated. Drake and Dahl took their time, scanning the whole area for movement, but saw nothing out of place. Soon, they started to descend into the valley.

Alicia gave all their thoughts a voice. "I don't like it," she said. "Maybe it's the drifting boat giving me the creeps but then this uninhabited island? And I can't help but think . . ."

"We're being watched?" Drake finished. "Yeah, I get that too."

"If that's the case," Dahl said. "They're very good. We have a world of experience here among us."

With the Swede's words rattling ominously in their wake, the team continued, watching their step as they approached the valley floor, feeling the soft loam underneath their boots. Drake was the first to see the raw earth ahead and then the great, fresh delve in the ground. He slowed, sensing something horrific.

"Oh, God," Mai breathed and then stopped in her tracks.

A mass grave lay before them, dug deep and filled with dead bodies. Drake saw roughly a dozen, most shot but at least two with grenade wounds. The sight was as grisly as he'd seen and made him stare rigidly toward the end of the valley. The smell was ripe, almost overpowering, making even the seasoned soldiers breath only through their mouths.

Dahl jumped on the comms, relaying their find to the rest of the team. Hayden asked if it was the ship's crew.

"I think so." Dahl walked around the perimeter of the grave. "I see several white uniforms on males and females. Also, a man wearing a suit and an older female. Best guess? These are our missing people and one of these bodies is Gordon Demba."

"Understood," Hayden said and signed off.

The team raised weapons, moving past the gravesite with its accompaniment of flies and insects. Nobody spoke. They stayed low, more aware now of the lack of cover and the utter lack of movement anywhere inside their vision.

"Signal is still good," Dahl said. "Same place."

"Did you see the bodies?" Mai said. "Stripped of everything except their clothes. No jewelry. No watches or rings. Whoever did this also robbed them."

Drake saw the tripwire three feet in front of his boots and held up a hand. It was a thin strand of cord, flexing in the slight breeze and blending in with the floor. What gave it away was its uniform straightness when all the earth around it was arbitrary. Crouching, he studied the style of it and found the trap.

A claymore, old as the hills and covered with grass.

"Soldier?" Dahl ventured.

"This gets weirder and weirder," Drake said.

"Could be any inbred criminal enterprise," Hayden said over the comms when they warned her. "We're taking it steady."

Drake moved to the slopes, where cover was easier to find. Dahl dropped to his knees and used field glasses to study the end of the valley, now only half a mile distant. After a minute, he grunted.

"Now we know what we're looking for," he said. "Easy."

Drake took the glasses and focused in. He saw a soldier's hide, a camouflaged den where a sniper might lie in wait for a target, sometimes for days.

"He's well dug in," the Yorkshireman said. "Seriously, I can't even see him."

"Could be a decoy—" Hayden began over the comms but then stopped suddenly as the high-pitched whine of a bullet echoed across the valley.

Instinctively, Drake dropped, checking himself for holes even though he knew the bullet would already have struck. Alive then, for now. The entire team called out their status. All was well.

"Any idea where that came from?" Dahl asked.

"Not a clue," Drake said. "But we gotta split up right now."

They parted and crawled from cover to cover, taking it slow. Two more bullets were fired, one kicking up dirt close to Alicia's elbow and the other sent toward the valley's perimeter where it tore hunks from a fallen bough.

"Big caliber," Kinimaka said, hiding behind the bough.

"No movement at all," Dahl said. "We have to watch our backs too. Consider some kind of remote mount."

Kenzie whistled. "Good call. He could be calling these shots in over his damn phone."

Drake studied the terrain once more, aware that too much scrutiny was little better than none at all. If you stared at a patch of grass long enough it would move eventually. Equally, it would also start to blend with its surroundings. Above, Hayden's team were pushing away from the edge and homing in on the cliff face. Below, they started up the slope that led to the hide and the place Dahl's retro GPR device pointed them.

Drake breathed shallowly, wiping sweat from his brow. Mai and Luther watched their rear. Finally, Drake spied a camouflaged rifle inside the hide that appeared to be mounted on a swivel. He relayed the news quickly and then spotted a second hide.

"We should halt," he said. "There's a reason this guy isn't shooting us to bits."

"The key is right there," Dahl said. "Inside that first hide." He breathed deeply. "Who's with me?"

"No," Hayden said quickly. "We don't know what the hell's going on."

"We don't need to," Dahl said. "Anyone up for a brisk jog?"

Drake saw the Mad Swede come to life and knew there would be no stopping him. Better to tag along than to watch disaster unfold without being able to influence it. Alicia was there and then Mai and Luther, ready to charge in.

Dahl didn't wait a moment longer. He rushed up the last stretch of the valley, straight at the hide, and then flung himself down as the barrel of the gun swiveled toward him. Bullets shot out, ear-splittingly loud this close, but Dahl was underneath its trajectory and the others were alongside. The Swede crawled up fast, coming under the gun and ripping it from its moorings. Drake saw the remote box and disabled it. Luther took the gun, checking its ammo. Dahl was already searching the hide.

"Duffel bags," he said. "Army issue. Full of the crew's belongings. Looks like he stripped them of their wealth and then executed them, stashing the goods up here. Bastard could have a dozen of them all around, I guess."

Drake had eyes on the second hide, but Alicia and Luther were already there, deactivating the rifle. Alicia held up another duffel, brimming with items.

"I don't know what this is exactly," Drake relayed it through the comms. "But it's not good."

"We've been scanning the valley and the slopes," Hayden said. "No more hides, but nothing human either. Did you find the key?"

Dahl sat looking uncomfortable, still with the duffel in his hands. "He murdered all these people."

"He?" Hayden said. "What makes you think it's just one 'he'?"

"Sniper stuff," Dahl said. "They usually work alone. The fact that we haven't been attacked points to a low-number adversary. I'm guessing one, or two."

"But how would one person force all those people off the ship?"

"Easy," Drake answered. "If he's a trained soldier. Brute force and aggression would go a long way and maybe he took someone hostage. Someone important—the old woman maybe. He brought them here and then killed them."

"But why?"

Dahl's face was set in a miserable frown as he sorted through the contents of the duffel bag. Bracelets and rings came out, and a brace of watches, but finally at the bottom of the bag he found the object they were searching for.

"Is that it?" Alicia asked. "I expected more."

Dahl waved the GPR over the key and watched it light up. The key was black in color, inlaid with golden bands and serrations at various intervals. The shoulder was high and twice-spiked, the cuts complex and notched out all along its length. Even the tip was fancy, tapering to a point where a cloven hoof swept back toward the bow. Dahl handled it carefully, not wanting to get cut.

"Ah, listen up," Hayden spoke over the comms. "We've found something up here."

Drake's heart fell in anticipation of more bodies. "What?"

"A cave, well hidden. The guys are exploring it now but it's a pretty safe bet that it belongs to our sniper. There's a huge stash of armaments up here. Army fatigues, combat vest. Camo jacket. Rucksacks, rifle cases. You name it."

"So it's pretty safe to say this man was a soldier," Mai said.

"Yeah," Kinimaka said. "There's even medals in here. Two ACMs, that's Afghanistan Campaign Medals, at least. We could have a war hero."

Mai's tone turned severe. "Whatever he was, he's a murderer now. And we will treat him as such. Do we have a position yet?"

Smyth's responded instantly. "I've been tracking the last few shots. He's dug in somewhere along the other valley rim. Can't pinpoint it, but he has the high ground and the scenic view, all the advantages. It's gonna be a cluster fuck, whichever way you look at it."

"Maybe not," Dahl said. "I have a plan."

Drake winced and glanced over at Alicia and Mai. "Is there any way we can talk you out of it, mate?"

"You haven't heard it yet."

"I know, but when you said you had a plan, I knew we were in deep shit."

CHAPTER NINE

"Am I the only one wondering why this guy's here?" Drake asked.

"Deserters end up all over the world," Alicia responded. "And so do war heroes that can't cope."

"Two opposite ends of the spectrum right there," Drake said.

"Don't judge anyone, Drake," Mai said. "You should know that, my friend. Smile and accept how people are, even if you don't like it, because there could be a pain lying behind their eyes that you could never imagine."

Drake inclined his head, acknowledging the small reprimand. In truth, this situation was different, but many people kept their own demons barely leashed and there were far worse things than being shot at.

"Not happy," he said grumpily.

"Well, that's because Dahl chose you to be the decoy."

"Yeah, and why's that? I think he's been secretly scoffing down on the sausage sarnies."

Alicia glared. "Don't be mean. If Dahl's comfort eating it's because of that Kenzie bitch."

"You two still not getting along?" Mai asked sweetly. "Funny that you see every other female as a challenge, Taz."

"Not you, Little Sprite. You're less of a challenge, more of an experiment."

Mai stiffened, fists clenching. Drake got between them. "Stop it," he said. "Get used to our situation being awkward, and move on. And besides, I'm more worried about being in the middle of you two than I am being a decoy."

"Good to hear that," Dahl said over the comms. "Because it's time to go."

Drake stared at the women, then shook his head. "Bloody comms."

Alicia looked like she didn't care, and Mai was already getting down to business. The trio waited inside the hide, waiting for the moment to leave. It came quick, with Dahl and Luther peppering the valley rim with bullets. Drake raced out and to the right, head down and keeping his center of gravity low. The sniper only had time to squeeze one wild shot off, the bullet flashing past Drake's left, before Molokai and Kinimaka opened fire from elsewhere, using the cache they had found in the hidden cave.

Bullets snarled up the hillside near where the sniper lay, huge gouts of grass and clods of dirt erupting several feet into the air. Drake gained the far slope and raced upward, leaping from mound to mound. Molokai and Luther kept firing and then Hayden's voice barked loudly in their ears.

"Out of the cave! Out of the hide! Get away now."

It was expected. They couldn't be sure that the sniper hadn't booby-trapped his belongings, so they played it safe and got clear. They hauled ass around the valley rim, heading for Drake. The Yorkshireman gained the top of the slope, finding level ground— the sniper could be anywhere from thirty steps ahead of him to a hundred. So far, he had seen nothing.

Tricky.

Alicia and Mai jumped out of the hide and made their way to the valley floor, one spotting and the other firing. They were Drake's best hope of staying alive.

He continued at speed, handgun drawn in case he needed to adjust quickly. From left to right, the terrain looked the same. It was a surprise then when the flat earth itself shifted ten meters in front of him, and he understood what he had to do.

Dug himself a hide, and then a small tunnel to the edge of the valley from where he sees all. Ingenious.

It would be the man's downfall. And this was no capture mission. They didn't have the time; other weapons were out there and the murdered souls of the *Enlargo* sure as hell wouldn't mind. Drake plucked two grenades from his webbing and launched them into the air.

"Heads up," he told the team and rolled to the ground.

Two explosions and a large displacement of earth followed. Drake saw a figure caught in the wave of soil that spilled down the slope. He was on his feet before the upwelling had even reached its zenith, racing toward the valley rim, showered by falling dirt. Others stood at the edge and in the lee of the valley. Alicia and Mai dashed toward the explosion.

Drake scrambled down. Upturned earth lay everywhere, in piles and in pouring rivulets. A figure was struggling amongst it, a figure covered in earth and wearing camo fatigues. Drake grabbed him, spied his weapon, and threw it aside before hauling the man upright.

A fist connected with his nose, staggering him. He hadn't expected a man who'd just been blown up and fallen over five meters to be quite so spry. He brandished his handgun but the man ignored it, too far gone to care. Drake saw only the whites of his eyes as he leapt, but heard the report of Alicia's gun. The bullet struck the man in the ribs, sending him to the ground. Drake took aim between the eyes.

"Stay down, pal. You have any friends out there?"

A heavy wheeze was all he got in return. Everything pointed to this man being a loner, though—from the single size and style of clothes, the utensils and old photographs they had found in the cave to the solitary weapon that had been firing at them. Alicia and Mai arrived and stared down at him.

"What's your name?" the Englishwoman asked.

Mai bent down and held her hand over the bullet wound, trying to staunch the flow. Her face betrayed the knowledge in her brain. When Hayden and the others ran up she shook her head.

"I . . . I am . . ." The sniper seemed to be trying to make an effort to sit up.

"What is it?" Mai supported him with her body.

"George . . . Mclean . . ." he said, in pain. "SBS. I'm glad you came."

Drake felt surprise. "How the hell did you end up here?"

But Mclean was fading. Mai held him as life drained from his body but he did manage a few more words. "The things I saw . . . I had to get away. It . . . changed me. No help. Sailed here . . . and stayed."

The body slumped; Mai let him fall to the floor. The team stared at him and away from him, thinking of all the crimes of war and the sins of the war makers. It was hard to feel sorry for a killer, but maybe they could feel sorry for the man he'd been before being ordered to a distant battlefield.

"Let's go," Hayden said. "Back to the chopper."

"What about the bodies?" Mai asked, meaning the *Enlargo* crew.

"We'll call it in, of course," Hayden said. "But right now, we have to get the key back to Cambridge."

The network they had set up involved a hand-picked SAS team and several contacts placed around the world. SPEAR would hand off the artifact to the SAS who would then dispatch one man to place it in the hands of a facilitator, someone with the resources to get it sent back to the UK, where Cambridge would store it at a secret location. The network were very hands on—and known to each other, friends from way back. As Cambridge said—a small net of trusted individuals, some relationships stretching back to school years, was the most appropriate and beneficial thing he could offer them.

The pilot fired up the helicopter as the team climbed aboard. Drake saw the stress carved into everyone's face. Yes, they had taken the prize today but were left with conflicting emotions around what they had seen and heard. As the chopper took flight and the island began to recede, Luther walked over to his pack and pulled out a bottle of rum.

"I think we all need this."

As they headed for the rendezvous with the SAS team, Hayden sought to distract her colleagues with talk of the weapons of the gods, and what, if any, significance they might have. She pulled out the Key of Hades and turned it around and around in her hands.

"You know what gets me?" Alicia said briefly. "Clearly, that thing is a key and fashioned to fit into something. I mean, what could it be?"

"Something Hades wanted to keep private," Kenzie said. "Unlike you and your feelings."

Yorgi jumped in before Alicia could react. "An incredibly complex key. I doubt even I could pick the lock it fits."

"I could," Molokai said, holding up a grenade. "My ugly friend here never fails."

Luther's mysterious brother rose then and slipped off his great coat. Drake couldn't help but stare, not having seen the man so relaxed before. The coat rattled, presumably with weapons, and emitted constant puffs of dust. Molokai threw it into a corner. Underneath he wore a flak jacket over a camo jacket, the webbing stuffed with armaments and survival gear of all kinds. When he unwrapped the scarves that covered his face, Drake let his eyes drift away.

"Leprosy is treatable," Molokai said to the whole team. "A multi-drug therapy is used. I'm lucky because the disease was spotted early and treated quickly. But I still have some lesions, sores."

Drake understood the man's words would probably be a one-time offer to the team. Just something to assuage the naturally curious. The right side of Molokai's face was a mass of small bumps that gave the skin a scaly appearance, stretching from his jawline to the ridge of his eyebrow. There was no terrible disfiguration, no misshapen mass. Molokai folded the scarf carefully and patted it as he put it down. Another pall of dust billowed into the air.

"We really need to put you through a washer dryer," Alicia commented. "All of you."

"I am just a man," Molokai said quietly. "In case you were wondering."

Drake guessed he was referring to the air of mysteriousness he kept active around him and, truthfully, he did wonder about the man's story. Perhaps another day.

Hayden was holding the key aloft. "Our second weapon," she said. "But we can't simply expect to find more. Tragedy aside, this job was easy and took way too long. There are five more weapons left."

"Do we know what and where?" Dahl asked as he meticulously checked his weapons.

"There's the Dagger of Nemesis and the Chain of Aphrodite. The Waters of Neptune and the Flail of Anubis. And the Forge of

Vulcan. Whitehall—the place in London where the DSF is housed and from where they run all the Special Forces teams—are using worldwide contacts to track the weapons twenty four hours a day, seven days a week. Our advantage here is pretty good—as we know all the weapons were stolen at some point, and that's how they survived the destruction of the tombs."

"And a shame none of the gods were stolen," Luther said. "I'd have enjoyed comparing bone structure." He flexed trunk-like arm muscles.

"Actually." Dahl raised a finger. "One of the gods was stolen. The skeleton of Kali. Remember? Kali was the goddess of death. A man named Russell Cayman became obsessed with her. He stole her skeleton and has never been heard from since."

"That's messed up," Molokai said. "Truly. You couldn't write this stuff."

"No, that's interesting," Luther admitted. "I'd track that lunatic down."

"Yeah, me too." Molokai nodded. "Just for the pre-battle chitchat."

Drake listened as Molokai rattled off more words than he'd spoken since they met. It didn't last long, both of them lapsing into brooding silence as quickly as they'd spoken up. Hayden continued with her description of Whitehall's search for the weapons.

"Nothing they're doing is transparent," she said. "It has to be subterfuge under subterfuge, which is why it's taking so long. Tempest have moles everywhere, and definitely some in the British government, maybe in MI5 or even the DSF. Only Cambridge and Bennett know the real objectives."

Hayden received a text then, looked surprised and spent a few minutes digesting it. Drake guessed it was something acute by the narrowed eyes and the depth of severity on her face. It was into an expectant silence that she spoke.

"I just received a message from Kimberly Crowe who finally heard from Lauren. It seems . . . ah, it seems Nightshade was instrumental in engineering the theft of General Gleeson's personal computer. Lauren is fine, and the computer yielded at least one thing. We have the location of Tempest's secret chamber meeting place. Lauren will now try to get close to President Coburn with the information."

"Nightshade?" Luther asked.

"Never mind," Smyth said.

"That really ups the ante," Drake said. "It's also another clear shout to get moving."

"My thoughts too," Hayden said.

"What did you have in mind?" Luther asked.

"Split the team," Hayden said. "Who's with me and who's with Drake?"

Long moments of banter passed in which Alicia waited for Mai to decide and Kenzie waited for Dahl to choose. Smyth asked about Lauren, but Hayden could literally give him nothing.

"She's okay," the ex-CIA agent repeated. "Just hang on to that."

It was several moments later that Drake voiced the obvious. "All this seems a bit premature, don't we have two objects to find?"

"It does," Hayden said. "And we do. Whitehall identified two weapons at the same time by tracking the chain of criminality. One in the States and the other in Greece. Say your goodbyes, people, 'cause we're gonna be hitting the ground running."

"And fighting," Mai said.

"Yeah, and that," Hayden said. "Tempest will be all over this too."

CHAPTER TEN

Quietly, Hayden's team stole back into the United States.

The dialogue with Whitehall grew more intense by the minute. Every hour was precious and it had taken several to fly from the uncharted island to America's coastline.

"Tempest are growing bolder," Cambridge told her.

"Do they have mercenaries in America?" Hayden asked apprehensively.

"Not mercenaries," Cambridge said with even deeper worry. "I'm afraid our sources are coming up with the word 'terrorist.'"

Hayden was shocked to her core. "In what way?"

"Not sure yet. Tempest could be hiring them, using them, or even creating them. Don't forget, they've been planning this for a year and, when ultra-clandestine methods failed, they changed everything. This is their end game, and perhaps they feel cornered, but they will stop at nothing to gain an advantage."

"Do you have friends in America that can help us?"

"We have friends everywhere that can help you. We also have enemies. So far, it appears Tempest's plan is to cloud events where weapons are stolen by using terrorist cells. This information comes from a trusted source in their outlying organization, somebody implanted in Syria, where the cells are being trained."

"And now we've crossed into America," Hayden said. "It's a big place, buddy."

"Yes, yes, I understand what you're saying. Do you have a laptop handy?"

Hayden pointed to a zippered bag and waited for Kinimaka to bring it over to her. With a nod of thanks she booted it up. "Ready."

Cambridge gave her a link to click and then several passwords, working in tandem. Soon, a clear image flashed up, showing a standard interrogation room with white walls and plastic table. A man was sat on either side of the table, but only one wore the uniform of a prisoner.

"Tell us everything and you might stay out of medium security," a man was saying. "I'm sure you'd prefer minimum?"

"I am a simple archaeologist," the man whined, his balding head bobbing up and down, tears welling up in his scared eyes. "I did not mean for this to happen."

"Right." The interviewer coughed. "But you did profit from theft, right?"

"Yes, but—"

"Don't give me any bullshit," the interviewer barked. "This is a one-time offer, Theodore. Spill and you get two years tops at a minimum security. Choke and you get the full weight of our office coming down on you," he paused. "Might even get maximum . . ."

"All right, all right." Theodore couldn't bear it any longer. "Men already asked me yesterday. That is why I was getting the hell out of there. They were more persuasive than you, threatening to cut parts off and mail them back to me over the next few months."

"Describe them," the interviewer said. "Figures, faces. Any names. Everything."

Theodore did as he was told and then returned to the main subject. "The Dagger of Nemesis," he said. "It came from the enormous German tomb, the one I worked on. It's about, oh, six inches long." He showed the measurement by using the tips of his fingers. "And perfectly obsidian in color. There are no reflections. And still, even now, it's sharp as a woodcutter's axe. I don't know which ancient civilization made weapons like this, but they sure knew what they were doing."

"You don't buy into the 'gods were once real' theory?"

"I can see its merit," Theodore said. "Real, living, powerful people worshipped for generation after generation, after which less-developed, lazier races just adopted the old stories, turning the main figures into gods. It makes perfect sense, to be honest. But I can't go that step further and believe these gods had powers. Of any kind."

"Okay, understood. Please go on."

"The dagger is unique, certainly priceless. One of the most irreplaceable objects the world has ever discovered, but—"

The interviewer couldn't help but interrupt, to Hayden's

annoyance. "Then why did you steal it and sell it to a member of the public?"

"Money." Theodore shrugged. "I had gambling debts. Two children. A wife that outstripped both our means. I guess it was the easy way forward." He hung his head.

"Who did you sell it to?"

"Joseph Berry," Theodore said. "The oil man from Dallas."

Kinimaka was peering over her shoulder. "I heard of that guy."

The interviewer confirmed the name and soon Cambridge came back onto the secure line. "This man, Joseph Berry, lives less than three hours west of Dallas by chopper. We have all his addresses and liaisons, more coming as we speak. I suggest you head that way right now."

"Tempest have a day's start on us," Hayden said.

"So it seems. I'm activating all Texan contacts now. Stand by, Miss Jaye, and I'll soon have more information for you."

Hayden relayed their destination, guessing they were about two hours from Dallas itself. The rest depended on where Joseph Berry had his home and where he was right now. She studied her companions—Mano, Yorgi, Molokai, Dahl and Smyth. More than enough muscle to take down Berry and take on Tempest. Of course, she had no idea how the new terrorist angle would present itself, but speed, valor and vast experience would see them through, she was sure of it.

Theodore Brakski, the archaeologist inside the interrogation room, had been captured in Stockholm by a small cell connected to the British SAS. It was sad to see they had been a day late, otherwise they may have whisked him away. Hayden thought that might be a good idea even now, but then Cambridge was back on the comms, ruining her thought process.

"Obviously, Mr. Berry is wealthy. He's a troubleshooter for a very large oil company and often stays in Dallas for weeks on end. We're using credit card information and CCTV to track him right now, but online presence shows him at home in Arizona just a few hours ago. He bought a last-minute economy class train ticket to Dallas and right now, I'm looking at him boarding a train, carrying a backpack about an hour ago. As we speak, he's on that train."

Hayden thought it through. "So this wealthy guy buys a cheap ticket to Dallas and boards with a single backpack. Is he running?"

"Could be he got wind of Theodore's arrest. Maybe he knows about Tempest and is running to Dallas to collect his more influential belongings before scarpering for good."

"Well, let's ask the guy nicely," Hayden said. "Let's get to that train."

"How are we with the second GPR device?" Cambridge asked.

Yorgi held up a black box. "Technically it's not GPR," he said. "But Dahl left detailed instructions. It's more of a cross between a GPS and a long-range metal detector. But we're not searching for the world's most precious metals here—not rhodium, extremely rare and valuable, or platinum, gold or iridium. We're looking for the unknown element and we can only calibrate it by taking readings from an object that contains the same. Hence, these shavings I took from the Key of Hades."

Smyth shifted uncomfortably. "Was that a wise move?"

Yorgi shrugged. "We shall see."

Hayden gazed at Yorgi. The young Russian had become more distant over the last few weeks, ever since he revealed to them the tale of his past and why he killed his parents in cold blood. Something was brewing there, Hayden knew. Something that retelling the tale had resurrected. Yorgi still needed closure, and Hayden could think of only one way he might achieve it.

"Set us on the path of that train," she told the pilot. "We're ready back here."

Cambridge's voice suddenly snapped into life. "Damn, we have a big problem. Local authorities are reporting that terrorists have taken over the train and hostages taken . . ."

Hayden closed her eyes. Were they already too late?

CHAPTER ELEVEN

"What exactly are we looking at?" Hayden asked Cambridge.

"It's bad. The terrorists are threatening to drive the train into Dallas Union Station and explode it. They have hundreds of hostages on board, who they'll kill if the authorities try to stop them. Double-edged sword. If you didn't know it by now this is what we call deep shit, people."

"Details?" Kinimaka asked, always the inquisitive agent.

"Eight hostages, all with bombs. Possible suicide vests. Our man, Joseph Berry, should be in the third car from the front. There are eight cars, so I'm guessing one terrorist per car. But that's a guess." He let out a ragged sigh. "I hate to think this is all Tempest's doing."

"It sounds like it could be," Hayden said. "They have had a full day to prepare this terrorist cell, for starters. Enough time to make plans. They steal the dagger and let the train burn. Cover up a theft with an atrocity. It won't be the first time."

"Why not nab Berry at home?" Smyth asked.

"I don't know," Hayden admitted. "Time? Surprise? Other issues. Maybe they failed and the train is their penance. Cambridge, are they diverting the train?"

"They won't. There's hundreds of hostages on board and they don't wanna risk it."

"So they're letting it ride straight into Dallas?"

"They're working on it."

"Change tracks?" Molokai suggested.

"Trains can be tracked by any cellphone," Hayden said. "The terrorists would know."

"Dead man's switch?"

"Not feasible without killing the driver."

"Kill switch?"

"Again, stopping the train would alert the terrorists. The hostages are the risk element. Cambridge, tell me, have the terrorists made any demands?"

"Just that they will in due course."

"They're searching for the dagger," Hayden said. "They have to be. Pilot, how close are we to that damn train?"

"Just arriving now."

The chopper swooped over the railway tracks, and then veered back around, trying to follow the sweeping line of rusting rails. Still flying high, but with the nose angled downward, it approached the rear of the racing train.

Gunfire came from below. Two bullets clanged off the chopper's metalwork, making the pilot veer away. He backed off to a safer distance, but Hayden and the others could still see everything that they needed to.

"We can't wait," Molokai said in a soft growl.

"Oh my God." Kinimaka gripped a portion of the bulkhead so tightly it buckled.

Hayden saw a passenger shot and pushed out of a window, then another shoved alive through a door. Others were being herded to the roof. This was not a hostage situation. It was a terrifying killing field.

"Dagger or not, we have to act," she said. "Get us down there now and don't fuck about. We need to get on that train."

CHAPTER TWELVE

The Chain of Aphrodite was causing them trouble.

Drake spun his head as Alicia dropped face-first at his side. "You okay?"

"No, I'm fucking dead."

"Is that all? Stop whining then, and get on with it."

Alicia raised her head, blood smeared within the lines that crisscrossed her forehead. "What the hell happened?"

"I think we took a hit."

"Ya do? Wow, Drakey, you got some major extra-sensory perception going on there."

"Extra-bollocks what?"

"Lookout!"

Drake ducked as rubble exploded all around them. "Where are we?"

"Greece."

"Funny."

"Glyfada. It's a beach resort."

"Yeah, I know that, love, but where the hell are we?"

Alicia sighed. "Shit, man, I have no bloody idea."

"Tempest hit us."

"There was that report . . ."

"Yeah, yeah, Tempest are in the area, I know. But Hayden said they were training terrorists, not using mercs."

"Maybe they're doing both."

"Maybe."

At that moment Kenzie and Mai crawled up. "Street's too narrow," the Japanese woman said. "We can't move without being targeted."

"Well, if we stay right here we're sitting ducks," Alicia said.

"Where's Luther?" Drake asked.

"Behind the overturned Bentley. See?"

"Oh, yeah, I see him. Is he okay?"

"I hope so," Mai said quickly, then changed her tone. "Can't see any blood."

"Ooh, good save." Kenzie laughed. "Not."

"Where are they?" Drake asked.

"This would be easier if the comms hadn't gotten knocked out," Mai said. "I spotted one with a semi-auto there." She pointed. "Third story of that building, and another with a handgun there, first floor. He's pinning Luther down."

"High buildings to both sides, narrow road in the middle," Drake said. "Doesn't bode well. Are there others?"

"Reckon so," Alicia said. "I heard four different guns firing."

"Me too," Kenzie said with a nod of respect. "Good call."

Another burst of gunfire shattered the silence that had fallen over the street, a precursor to a hail of rubble that spattered their shoulders and backs and the screams of fleeing pedestrians. Windows fractured. Car alarms started their incessant whine.

"We still have our weapons," Mai pointed out.

"They got us pinned down pretty good," Drake said. "Where does that bloody archaeologist live?"

"One block over," Mai reminded him.

"Are we sure it's him?" Kenzie asked. "I'd hate to wade through this battle and then find we got the wrong man."

"Whitehall struggled with this one," Drake admitted. "They couldn't discern where the archaeologist in question made the hand-off. No money trail either. Turns out, he kept it. Right here in Greece. Adrian Doukas keeps the Chain of Aphrodite in his home."

"Crazy, right?" Kenzie muttered.

"Takes one to know one," Alicia said, shifting position.

"I guess all relic hunters have a little crazy in them."

"All relic hunters?" Drake asked. "You know others?"

"I know all the best ones. It was my business."

Bullets rattled the Bentley sheltering Luther, but the big man shifted to his right a little, now hunkering down beneath the engine block, barely moving. His eyes moved across to them.

Drake waved. "Good job with the car, mate. I've never seen anyone overturn a Bentley before."

"Ideas?" The bellow scared at least one remaining civilian into fleeing their hiding place.

"Retreat," Mai said. "We don't have to fight every battle. That's life. Let's go."

"Every second we wait, our archaeologist friend may decide it's time to run," Kenzie said.

"No way he knows we're coming for him," Drake said. "But I guess Tempest could beat us to it. Mai's right. The job comes first. Is everybody ready?"

Whilst they complied he signaled their intentions to Luther. Alicia watched with some amusement.

"If that were me behind that car, I'd be thinking you were asking me which pizza I wanted to order."

"Then we're lucky it's a real soldier," Mai said. "He's ready."

"Wanna blow him a cute kiss first, Sprite?" Alicia teased.

The answer was silence.

Drake stretched the muscles that had been stuck in the same position for so long. "Okay, good to go."

And then, actions spoke louder than words.

Drake broke cover first, firing up at the third-floor shooter. Mai rolled along the ground. Aiming her gun at the first floor, she fired to keep her gunman occupied. Kenzie sprinted back down the street, taking cover behind another vehicle. Luther dashed from behind the cover of the Bentley past them all to join her. In seconds he had another car, a small Seat Ibiza, on its side.

"He's very quick to flip his vehicles onto their sides," Alicia commented. "Wonder if he's like that with his women."

Mai rolled back into cover and Drake ducked. Together they endured another round of aggressive gunfire, reloading as they waited. One look passed between them and then Alicia rolled out, Drake rose, firing, and Mai ran to Luther. Kenzie was already sprinting away toward the next cover, a deep alcove that formed the doorway of a shop.

In the next moment, the three runners stepped out and laid down covering fire so that Drake and Alicia could join them. By now, they had pinpointed all four shooters and were peppering their hiding places with heavy fire. Kenzie left the alcove and found another vehicle, and then the end of the street, the others following her in turn. Their guns were never inactive, bullets constantly flying at their enemies.

When Kenzie reached the corner, she laid down hails of gunfire and soon they were all around it, safe for now, pocketing weapons and sprinting headlong for the next, parallel, street. The archaeologist at the very least was in danger. It took just a minute to reach his street and much less time to spot his address. Steps led up to his front door. Drake hit them at a run and kicked at the white paneling, splintering it. Luther arrived a moment later and smashed it off its hinges.

"Nice," Drake said. "Good job I weakened it for you or you'd have taken a leg off."

"Yeah, thanks man."

Luther pounded on, going for the narrow staircase, heading for Doukas' first floor flat. They knew the man lived alone. They knew he was a freelance archaeologist. They knew he was currently working part-time for a small, local museum and that he was sixty two years of age.

Less than two hours ago a local contact had seen him entering his apartment with a coffee-and-bagel breakfast take-out.

Drake reached the first-floor corridor, saw another staircase at the far end, and thought: *crap, there could be two exits. No time for that now.* He backed up Luther as he smashed through Doukas' door without offering any kind of warning. The door resisted a little so the big soldier just tore it from its hinges and threw it several feet up the corridor.

"That works." Alicia watched the door bounce gradually to a stop.

"It fought back," Luther growled. "And like everything else—it lost."

Drake pushed him into the apartment, the team fanning out as they entered. A quick search revealed it was empty and that the Chain of Aphrodite was not present.

"Shit." Drake halted. "All this for bloody nothing."

"We'd best move," Alicia said. "Or prepare a warm welcome for the Tempest boys."

"Maybe they've already been," Kenzie said.

"Nah, they'd have smashed this place to pieces."

"Agreed," Drake said. "And see there? The remains of Doukas' breakfast. I think he left this place of his own free will."

"Hey." Luther walked over to the phone and switched the answering system on, replaying the last message. It was a brief request that Doukas help out for an extra few hours at the museum that afternoon.

Drake shook his head. "It's never easy, is it?"

"Could be just what we need," Mai said. "Kill the answering machine and then let's head over to the museum. Hopefully, we'll get this man to ourselves."

Drake glared at her. "You had to say it, didn't you? Now we're gonna have a fight on our hands."

Luther grinned as he deleted all the messages, outsize digits threatening to smash the plastic every time they pressed down. "Music to my ears."

CHAPTER THIRTEEN

Hayden held on, every muscle tensed, as the helicopter swung from side to side, trying to evade errant gunfire. The train raced along the track below them, a fearsome, destructive metal titan already frighteningly close to being out of control. Bullets resounded off the chopper's exterior despite the pilot's dexterity, and one window was smashed. In truth, the chopper's presence had distracted the terrorists from their bloody deeds, but Hayden knew it wouldn't last.

"They ain't blowing up that train," she said, "until they find the dagger. Get us down there."

The pilot dived. Terrorists screamed up at them, brandishing weapons and hurling captives from one man to the other. When a captive objected or fought back they threw them off the top of the speeding train, laughing whilst they did it.

"Let me lie down," Molokai snarled murderously. "You don't know it but my main job used to be sniper, just like the man on the island. It's another reason I wear all this crap; I'm used to it." All the time he was shifting and rolling, getting comfortable, lining up his shot.

The terrorists yelled and waved the chopper away. Hayden could only see their eyes over brightly colored scarves, their faces were obscured and they wore bulging jackets. It was hard to tell their gender, let alone identify faces. When one terrorist dropped to a knee and lined a Beretta up with their cockpit, Luther opened fire. His shot took the terrorist high in the forehead, avoiding the vest, and released a gout of blood. The man toppled backward instantly, his gun flying away, the body then flopping off the top of the train. His companion looked aghast, then turned and ran, throwing his gun up into the air and leaving a captive behind.

Hayden listened to the chatter.

"This train is thundering toward Dallas!" a sensationalist reporter eagerly told his loyal followers.

"Authorities are gathering," another said. "Trying to work out a

65

plan to stop this train in its tracks as the minutes tick down."

"Passengers tell of terrorists with bomb vests, handguns and knives," someone else stated. "Photographs from inside the train are flooding social media. The terrorists don't appear to care. The challenge has been issued and now America must watch helplessly to see what happens to the train, its passengers and crew, and the city of Dallas."

On quieter channels, Cambridge reported without emotion: "The ideas being floated range from ludicrous to extreme. Someone is trying to talk them into blowing the train off the tracks."

Hayden shook her head sadly. "Have they mentioned us?"

"You're barely on their radar right now, but somebody did order that the damn idiot reporters should be cleared from the airspace. You don't have long."

"We're ready to go. Can you help us?"

"Whitehall has as many feeds as possible up and running. Train CCTV, piggybacking from the helicopter's Wi-Fi, television broadcasts, social media photograph and video uploads, and more. You just have to go in fast before the suits cock it all up."

Hayden again instructed the pilot to dive for the top of the speeding train, and watched as the helicopter's skids came closer and closer. The team prepared themselves in the standard manner and then hooked their arms around anything sturdy to get ready for the coming impact.

"Can you land this thing on top of a moving train?" Molokai asked.

"Dunno, bud, but I'm willing to give it a go."

"That's inspiring."

Hayden closed her eyes briefly as the chopper nosedived toward the train and then struck its ungiving surface.

CHAPTER FOURTEEN

They found the archaeologist, Adrian Doukas, without too much trouble, but offered up no challenge. First, they wanted to scout the area. The civilian jackets they'd thrown over their military gear, whilst helping them blend in, shouldn't have passed careful scrutiny, but the meagre security on the door was bordering on absurd. Five-strong, they spent twenty minutes scouring the corridors, exits and various floors before putting Luther on exterior guard duty and Mai on Doukas-watch.

A large part of their attentiveness and prudence was due to the ongoing terrorist situation in Texas. Hayden was a big part of it, and Drake didn't want something on the same scale occurring here. Athens National History Museum had recently been the target of a bad attack and Greece didn't need another.

Luther took seven minutes to report in.

"All clear out here. I've checked the perimeter twice. It's gonna be hard even for me to keep an eye on all three entry points though. I could do with help."

Drake wondered if he was hoping for Mai, and sent Kenzie out. Both he and Alicia then headed down a bright corridor to where Doukas worked. Mai was seated on a bench outside the room, reading a brochure. She stood up when they walked past.

"He speaks English," she said. "I heard him relating a story to a tourist."

They had expected as such. Such well-traveled archaeologists usually spoke at least passable English.

"We're American agents," Drake told Doukas for simplicity, his brain focused on a dozen relevant concerns at that moment.

"You are?" Doukas peered at them. "You don't look it, nor sound it."

Drake acknowledged Alicia and Mai. "Aye, ya got that right. Bad start. Listen, let me get straight to the point. You're in danger. We're here to help. Problem is—we need the Chain of Aphrodite to make that happen."

Doukas stared fixedly, trying not to let an ounce of emotion leak into his face. "I have no idea what you mean."

"The tomb of the gods," Drake said quickly. "It was destroyed, but not before several archaeologists like yourself removed some smaller, more collectable items. Well, somebody found out. And that somebody wants them. All of them. They'll happily kill you and a hundred others to get just one of them."

Doukas looked scared, but still didn't cooperate. "If that were in any way true I would go to jail."

"Look, pal, we're not here to arrest you. Just tell us where the chain is, and then disappear. As I said, people are coming to kill you."

Alicia unzipped her jacket then, sweeping the folds aside to show Doukas her weaponry. Mai followed suit. The archaeologist swallowed heavily.

"I heard . . . I heard this from another man, third-hand really . . ." He paused.

"I can accept that," Drake said magnanimously. "Please hurry."

"I heard that the manacles they display inside the old weapons cabinet are not manacles at all. It's a chain. A few have questioned it but nothing stuck. And they are there whenever an old man wants to view or clean them." He smiled. "I don't know how it got there."

Drake gave the man a sidelong glance. It was a defense, he guessed, but hardly one that would hold up against the evidence. Still, that wasn't for him to decide.

"Where is the cabinet please?" Mai asked, ever polite.

"The very next room, my dear. Just to the left."

They didn't need him anymore, but Drake delayed. "You should come with us," he said. "Or run and hide."

"This is an old museum," the man said. "I know a place."

"Fantastic. Go there now."

Drake followed Mai and Alicia into the room next door, immediately spotting the large glass cabinet mounted on the far wall. In addition to brass surrounds and fittings it had two wide, ornate, golden straps across the center and was supported by a dark-oak bookcase, full of hardbacks with obscure titles.

Drake stared at the glass case. "Do you see it?"

"Are you blind as well as American?" The old man's voice came from his shoulder. "It's right in front of you."

Drake made a face. "So, you decided to stay, did you?"

"I helped start all this," the old man said. "I want to help finish it too. I have a key to that strapping."

Whilst he worked, Drake decided to make use of him. "Maybe you can help, mate. What can you tell us about this weapon?"

Doukas inserted the key and twisted. "Weapon? That Aphrodite, she was all about the love, the beauty and the pleasure of procreation. Facts which are tainted somewhat by the knowledge that we know she was created from sea foam produced by Uranus's genitals. There's a fact that, had I been Aphrodite, I might have ordered redacted. Oddly, despite her beauty, her grace, her thirst for sex, and intelligence, most of the other gods feared her. Do you know why?"

Drake watched as the man spoke and pulled the heavy gold straps to the side. Alicia held up a hand as if answering a teacher's question.

"Did she have a dungeon?"

"Not that I am aware of, and I've been studying Aphrodite since my early twenties. They feared her because her beauty could lead to conflict and war, since many came forward as rivals for her favors. Gods and men, it seems. Aphrodite had many lovers."

Mai tapped Alicia on the shoulder. "She remind you of anyone?"

Alicia looked thoughtful. "Kenzie? No, your sister?"

Drake found more and more that he was the acting intermediary. "Let's listen to the nice man," he said. "We may learn something."

"Born near Paphos, Cyprus, she was sometimes said to be warlike, often married, adulterous, and vain. She is a major figure in the Trojan War legend."

"And where does this chain fit in?" Alicia enquired.

Doukas gave her a wise smile. "After everything I just said do you really have to ask?"

Alicia blinked in surprise under his gaze. "You're kidding? You believe this is Aphrodite's sex chain, or something?"

69

"Sex is the oldest form of pleasure." Doukas opened the cabinet wide, clipping the doors back before reaching in between a short sword and a shield. "Here, feel it. The links are very light but surprisingly hard to break out of."

Drake stepped back as Alicia eyed the object Doukas removed from the cabinet with suspicion. "That sounds like you're speaking from experience."

"Ah, now that would be telling."

Alicia stared across at Mai who stared back, careful not to reveal any emotion. Neither of them reached for the chain. Drake eyeballed the dozens of links of hard black obsidian, enough to span a man's body at least four times, but nothing out of the ordinary as chains went. In fact, the only special thing about it was that it had been found inside the tomb of a god.

"Easy to see how they escaped notice," Drake said, taking the chain. "Now, let's vamoose before those trigger-happy baboons get here."

"It's not a weapon," Alicia murmured. "It's just a chain."

"Hey, the GPR confirms it. They contain the rare element. This is what we're looking for."

Exiting the room, they glanced out of a window, hoping to see either Kenzie or Luther. Drake was amazed to see Luther, standing on top of a car, firing left and right with a gun in each hand, blasting his enemies away.

"That guy is so old school he's Butch bloody Cassidy."

Mai headed for the door. "He needs help."

Drake looped the chain around his neck since there was nowhere to put them and drew a handgun. Together, they pushed out of the museum and into its grounds—two dirt paths twisting around a central fountain and statue. The car park at the far end was where Luther was doing his work, and out here they could hear it too.

Drake saw the scene unfolding as he ran closer. Luther had blocked the entrance to the museum with a car of his own and was pinning the few remaining mercs down with constant gunfire. Not the best plan by any means, but then this was Luther.

"We're here!" Drake cried out to save being shot. "Where are they?"

"And get your stupid ass down from there!" Alicia yelled.

Luther slithered down the side of the car, still firing. "I got two to the right, two to the left," he shouted out car makes and models, but Drake could see clearly the vehicles that had been sprayed with bullets.

"Kenzie?"

"Pinned behind the fountain. Didn't you see her?"

"No, no, where—"

It was then that Kenzie scaled a wall and jumped down into the car park behind two mercs. She was upon them in seconds, holding one by the throat and trying to fend the other off. Alicia and Mai knelt down and sighted their weapons but couldn't fire for fear of hitting the Israeli.

Kenzie choked the first man unconscious but couldn't stop the second from attacking her. Bruising her ribs with a boot, he then launched a knee right at the side of her head. With nowhere to go she took the blow on her ear, smashing her face against the side of the car.

She fell backward, flat out, groaning.

The merc sighted down on her. Kenzie kicked out with her legs, struck his shins. Still neither Alicia nor Mai could get a proper shot; the vehicle was an SUV, and the figures were largely hidden. Kenzie struggled, but the blow to the head had dazed her, making the constant kicks to the merc's shins too weak to bother him.

Looking down at her, he pulled the trigger.

An instant before the gun boomed the merc jerked backward, head blown backward by the bullet Alicia fired into his skull. Risking everything, she had dashed toward the car, in the line of fire, and rolled around the side, coming up with the gun in her hands.

The merc fell. Kenzie nodded in relief.

That left Drake and Luther to cover Alicia's run and try to take out the other two mercs. Several shots were fired, but then Luther got bored and climbed into the car he'd been standing on.

"Don't have time for this," he growled.

Drake set the chain straight around his neck and leapt out of the way as Luther gunned the vehicle's engine, making it scream, then set off with tires squealing and created a head-on collision with the other car. The mercs staggered back, away from cover. Drake picked them off with two bullets.

"About time." Luther slammed the car door, then surveyed the car park. "We ready?"

"Yeah, we have the chain."

"Well, I didn't think that was a lei around your neck, dude."

Quickly, they escaped the area, conscious that Hayden's team were under fire and several more weapons were still out there. This was only the beginning.

CHAPTER FIFTEEN

"Speed is our ally," Hayden said. "The terrorists won't pull the trigger until they find the Dagger of Nemesis. Maybe even until Dallas, where there'll be more people, more cover. Oh, and give these fuckers the same mercy they're offering all the people on that train."

She leapt out of the helicopter, boots coming down on the roof of the moving train. She wobbled at first, then gained purchase, suddenly aware of the rushing air and fast-moving countryside to left and right.

"Are you okay?" she yelled, approaching the single captive who'd been left behind. The man was shivering, sat with his back to her, the weight of the trauma he'd experienced already haunting his eyes. Hayden passed him back to Dahl, Smyth and Molokai, down the line, past Yorgi, and back to the chopper. It was the safest place for him right now. In the end, he didn't dare climb onto the moving chopper so Kinimaka simply reached down and hauled him up.

Hayden was moving across the top of the train. The steel was slippery, but her boots held. A stanchion of lights whipped by to the left, a row of houses to the right. Her eyes had already dried out from the rushing wind. She approached the edge of the carriage, seeing adjacent rusted railway tracks flashing past to the side like an endless, undulating snake and hearing nothing but the roar of the train.

Reaching down, crouching, she balanced herself on the tips of her fingers and peered over the edge. A face loomed. The terrorist she'd seen running away had been lying in wait. In addition to the bomb-vest, he held a knife which he thrust up at her face. Hayden felt the metal slice her jacket at the shoulder and instinctively rolled, catching herself at the last moment before falling off the train.

She grabbed the forward edge of the top of the carriage, fingertips exposed to the knifeman but with no other option of hanging on.

Dahl shouted, standing over her and peering down. He engaged the man's attention, allowing Hayden precious extra moments. The knife flashed up once, twice, Dahl dodging both attacks. On the third lunge the Swede reached down past the wrist, grabbed it, and simply hauled the attacker up. He came screaming and kicking. Dahl flung him back along the train, right to Molokai's feet.

Hayden felt one hand come loose, and screamed.

Dahl lunged across her, his weight pinning her to the top of the train.

Molokai followed Hayden's earlier advice and kicked the terrorist hard until he rolled, screaming, off the top of the train, falling, tumbling with limbs akimbo before hitting the side of a passing meter box. Cambridge would already be sending his final resting place covertly along to his contacts.

Hayden couldn't breathe, crushed by Dahl. She didn't care, since that was all that was keeping her from taking a nose dive off the top of the train. The wind whistled by as she wondered just how long Dahl could balance his body on top of her as the train took its snaking high-speed path toward Dallas central.

Someone grabbed her ankles, and then Dahl's weight was removed. She looked back to see Molokai pulling her to safety.

There was no time for appreciations.

"Six left," Hayden said. "Let's get down there."

"Six that we know of," Kinimaka reminded everyone. "The people going for the dagger may be dressed in civilian clothing."

Hayden was first back to the edge of the train, never one to be daunted by anything. She remembered being shot in the back during the Blood King's night of vengeance, an act which only forged one more layer of iron over her already resilient will.

They climbed down into the space between carriages, feeling grateful for a sudden end to the terrible buffeting. They knew the last carriage would be clear and that there was a terrorist halfway along the coach in front of them with a Smith and Wesson, a military blade, a bomb-vest and a hand grenade, according to Cambridge's extensive Intel.

"Fast and true," Hayden said. "Who's got the best shot?"

Dahl slid past her. "I'm surprised you have to—"

"I do," Molokai said. "Sniper."

Dahl blinked, not having factored Molokai into his opinion.

Hayden pushed the Swede. "No time, just do it!"

Molokai crouched, put his hand on the handle and nodded at Dahl. One second later the Swede was ready and nodded back. Molokai swung the door open, Dahl stepped through and lined the terrorist up with a hair-trigger.

Forehead square-on, shocked features frozen for just an instant in time, the true knowledge of his terrible fate suddenly very much registered upon his face.

Dahl fired. The terrorist's head whipped back, blood spraying those nearby and the side windows. The man fell dead in the aisle, no longer moving. Heads turned toward the newcomers as the screams started.

Dahl shouted above them all. "Be quiet! Go to the back of the train. All the way and then hang on to something. Close the doors. Go! Now!"

They moved aside as passengers surged by, many nodding gratefully. Hayden knew even if she pleaded and begged or ordered them to stay off social media that there was no chance of compliance. Some people just couldn't help themselves, even if it put their lives at risk.

The carriage was now empty. Hayden moved quickly along its length, knowing that even if the terrorists could communicate they couldn't be sure of the insurgents' exact position. Of course, that depended on the smarts of the guy in the next carriage.

He was peering through the glass, looking straight at them.

Dahl didn't hesitate, just charged like a wild animal, shoulder first, at the connecting door. It didn't stand a chance, its hinges shattered; and neither did the terrorist on the other side. Both flew backward, and into the air arced a gun and a hand grenade.

Dahl collapsed face first onto the door with the terrorist pinned underneath. Hayden was barged aside by Molokai as he ignored the gun and lunged headlong to catch the grenade on its way down. She recovered quickly, seeing the gun land unluckily close to the terrorist's grasping hand.

Molokai caught the grenade. Hayden picked up the gun.

Dahl rose up with the heavy door in hand, and slammed it down twice onto the terrorist until all movement stopped.

Hayden stared up the length of the carriage.

"Wait," she told everyone. "Don't move until we say, then run to the back of the train."

No point repeating the same mistake twice.

She counted carriages off in her head as they approached the next. Number four was next, and the dagger had been identified in number two. Maybe five minutes had passed since they put boots onto the train's roof. The next terrorist fired at them, causing an outbreak of shrieks and the breaking of glass. Molokai stood firmly even as the second bullet tugged at the scarf that covered his lower face, sighting on the attacker, then calmly pulled his trigger and killed the man.

They made another rush forward. More passengers were sent scrambling, running to the back of the train. Hayden heard Cambridge in her ears, saying the city of Dallas could already be seen on the horizon.

She needed to hear nothing else.

The minutes ticked by. Hayden went for the third carriage from the front and saw a terrible struggle underway. Some passengers had risen up against their tormentor, trying to disarm the man. They were bunched all around him, struggling to lash out, struggling to defend themselves, hopefully hampering his own ability to wound and maim. Two were lying bleeding on the floor and another slumped across the back of a seat with a woman shielding his body. She too, was wounded.

"That motherfu—"

The rest of Hayden's sentence was lost in growling hatred as she stalked down the aisle, reached among the fighters, took hold of the terrorist's head by the hair and raised it up until she could look into the whites of his eyes. Then, she introduced her Glock to the spot at the bridge of his nose.

"Enjoy Hell."

She ended the brawl with a bullet. People slumped everywhere. She cleared them back. Kinimaka, Yorgi and Smyth handled them, directing them to the rear of the carriage and then kneeling to tend the injured ones. Hayden knew they now faced the coach where their target, Joseph Berry the Dallas oil man, should be situated. The broken window to her left caught her eye and she remembered how, not long ago, the terrorists had been throwing people off the speeding train.

It was true that terrorists wore a mantle of pure evil, but what of the men that created them? What of the men that recruited and trained them? She would always put the everyday civilian's welfare at the top of her list and aim to hurt the people that threatened them—whether that be a vile terrorist or a powerful and malicious figurehead.

She crouched carefully at the door to the next carriage, and peered through the grimy glass pane.

It was a scene from Hell.

CHAPTER SIXTEEN

The terrorist was standing on a seat, head and shoulders above the passengers he had forced to stand all around him. One hand held a woman by the hair, the other a gun pointed at her temple. She was sobbing, her face bloodied. Those around her were either trembling, crying or trying to look strong. He could turn the gun on them in just a few seconds.

"Do you see Berry?" Kinimaka asked. "This has to be a diversion."

"Can't see him," Hayden said. "But you're right. He's in there. They haven't had the chance to get the dagger off the train yet."

"And the dagger may no longer be with Berry," Molokai said. "I'll handle this." He pulled out a rifle from under his big coat.

"No." Dahl put a hand on the man's wrist before he brought it up into sight of the terrorist. "That asshole has half the weight of that trigger loaded already. Even a dead-center bullet could cause a reflexive reaction. It needs handling differently."

Smyth stepped forward, hands up. "Then handle it."

He approached the door, easing it open. Hayden followed suit and the rest spread out, similarly displayed. Dahl retreated to the broken window and quickly perched across the sill, his head stuck outside, staring down the buffeting gusts of wind.

Mad, he thought.

But necessary. He gripped the top rim of the window and hauled himself out, hanging by fingertips and ankles hooked over the sill. Next, he balanced his feet on the sill, flexed his powerful legs and lunged up toward the roof of the train. A blast of air shook him and the train as it raced toward its destination. Out here, Dahl could see approaching buildings: warehouses, homes and shopping malls. In the skies he could see several helicopters and a smudge in the air high above, a potential fighter jet.

Oh bollocks.

Would they?

Cambridge had to be passing valuable Intel along, but it all depended on the capabilities and disposition of the man in charge. It might even depend upon the suit at the top of the chain. He believed in President Coburn's ability to do the right thing—hell, they'd fought together during the Blood King's attack on DC—but didn't believe certain people would let Coburn have his say.

Tempest would be engineering all this, right down to the last detail.

Who held the dagger?

Dahl heaved his body over the top, rolled and halted on top of the train. He sat up, bracing his body into the wind. He walked forward the number of paces that would have taken him to a face-to-face with the terrorist. He glanced over the side of the train.

Rails and heaps of gravel rushed by; the track's banking beyond that. Cambridge was silent on the comms. Hayden whispered that it was now or never.

It became an orchestrated strike. At the heart of it all was the knowledge that the terrorist didn't really want to kill the woman he held—not yet at least. She was his greatest asset. Everything in Hayden's and Dahl's training said that he would hesitate. Dahl gripped the side of the train with one hand, the rim of the window with the other and lowered himself down carefully, not quickly.

The movement caught the terrorist's eye, made his head swivel over. That movement pointed the barrel of the gun away from the woman for a split second.

Hayden broke the window of a small box that triggered an alarm.

And nothing happened.

"Oh, no,"

The terrorist started to turn back toward them but Molokai and Smyth were already in full flight. They leapt across seatbacks and through the scared passengers, hitting the terrorist at chest height and propelling him back off the seat and onto the floor. The gun went off, a bullet passing harmlessly through the roof. Smyth took his hand grenade whilst Molokai fractured all the bones in his throat. They held his arms down as he died and then quickly disabled his bomb-jacket.

Hayden took control. "Stand apart," she shouted at the mostly bewildered passengers. "Right now!"

Kinimaka and Smyth stood on the seats, covering the passengers with their own weapons. There was no time to explain; to do so would increase the overall danger. Molokai dragged Dahl inside and then they all watched with guns at the ready.

Hayden unhooked her pack from her shoulders and pulled out the GPR device. The view outside the windows changed from fields to buildings.

We're coming into Dallas, she thought. *And there's still at least one terrorist on this train holding a bomb.*

What do we do?

CHAPTER SEVENTEEN

Drake dragged the chain from around his neck as the car sped off. The museum was safe, the old man was in hiding, and the mercs had been dispatched. Not a bad few hours' work if he did say so himself.

"Wait," Alicia said. "What's that?"

"What's what?" He was never sure if she was about to crack a joke at his expense.

"Your hands, Drakey. Look at your hands."

"They're bloody black bright," he drawled. "My mum would kill me."

"That's not dirt."

She was right. If anything, it was like coal dust, a covering of inferior black paint perhaps. The incoming thought made his heart leap. "Shit, this isn't the fucking Chain of Aphrodite."

"No," Mai said, staring at his hands and then the chain links that were starting to flake and reveal the silver beneath. "That old man—Doukas—deceived us."

"Bastard," Drake swore. "But then, why should we expect anything else from a thief? Kenzie, get us back there."

"We'll never find him," Mai said.

"Oh, I think we might," Kenzie said, staring ahead through the windshield.

Drake focused. Doukas, even now, was running across the car park area in the direction of the furthest row. His face was panicked, his gait made awkward by a slight limp, and age. When he reached the front of an old gray Nissan, Kenzie swerved her car to within an inch of his knees.

Drake opened his door and stepped out. "Get in."

His tone brooked no objections. Doukas was practically dragged into the back seat and wedged between Alicia and Drake. Kenzie backed up and then swung the wheel toward the exit.

Three mercs stood in their way, remnants of the earlier force.

"Where did these guys come from?" Luther asked.

"Probably searching the museum." Drake told it as he saw it, but who really knew? "Doesn't matter. Kill 'em."

Mai slammed a fist against her own door handle and allowed it to swing open. "I'm fucking sick of these assholes."

Alicia let out a noise of shock, gawping after the Japanese woman. "What happened to Little Miss Proper Pants?"

"She's fucking sick." Drake threw open his own door. "Don't you listen?"

Mai fired instantly, not waiting on any kind of ceremony or aggression from the mercs. Her aim was never in doubt, the first bullet smashing one's shoulder blade and spinning him around, the second taking out an elbow, and the third destroying a knee. The mercs fell, weapons clattering to the ground. Mai's step didn't falter as she stalked toward them, closing the gap, lining up the kill shots. One merc groped for his weapon, claimed it, and fell dead over it. Another crawled away, aiming for a spot between parked cars, but died a few seconds later as Mai opened fire.

The last held both hands in the air.

Mai finished him before he could even try to betray her trust.

Drake let out a long breath, balanced by the side of the car with his handgun sighted. Mai turned away from the dead and headed back inside. Drake followed. Luther, in the passenger seat, coughed politely.

"Nice work."

Mai ignored the American and turned to Doukas. "That is what we do to our enemies, scumbag. Do you want to be our enemy?"

Doukas shook his head, trembling. "No. No. I—"

"Save it," Mai growled, now eye to eye. "What the fuck are you up to, old man?"

Kenzie took the opportunity to get them moving, driving around the bodies and heading out of the exit. The traffic in this relatively small Greek town was sparse, and the sidewalks quiet. Sirens were screaming in response to the earlier gunfire, but nobody had converged on the museum yet. They had to assume the police would have been led to Doukas' apartment.

Kenzie threaded a discreet path away from the noise.

Mai ground the barrel of her gun under Doukas' chin. "Talk, old man. You put us all in extra danger. That's already unforgivable, but if you spill everything now I might even let you live."

Doukas couldn't stop shaking as, finally, he came clean.

CHAPTER EIGHTEEN

The GPR device squealed, signaling that the dagger was close by. Hayden wondered if it was sophisticated enough to indicate an exact position. The little red dot blinked faster as central Dallas came closer. Cambridge's voice filled her ears, informing them that they had twenty minutes left to pull this off. The only reason they hadn't been overridden so far was because they'd now annulled seven out of the eight bombs with no loss of life. Nobody outside the train would risk their career betting against odds like that by sending in a strike team.

We can't risk the train.

"Molokai, Smyth, finish that last terrorist."

She watched them approach the end of their carriage and then turned her attention to the nervous passengers. One by one, she sent them past her position, holding the GPR in one hand and a Glock in the other. Kinimaka stood next to her, with Dahl, Yorgi and Luther opposite.

And then she knew the identity of their enemy: a woman with scraped-back brown hair, sweating at the temples, wearing a large coat and moving with her head down. She indicated the woman to Dahl and Luther and then raised her gun.

"Stop!"

Someone screamed. Heads whipped around. Hayden didn't expect the woman to attack, but neither did she expect her to fall to her knees and start wailing.

"No, no, no . . . I can't, just can't . . ."

She shrugged the coat off her shoulders, let it fall to the floor. Hayden half-expected to see a bomb-vest, but the woman wore only a simple white blouse. The Dagger of Nemesis fell to the floor and Hayden got her first real look at it.

Around fourteen inches long, with a wickedly serrated and notched blade, the dagger emitted no radiance despite the bright strip lights shining down on it from above. The dense, black surface absorbed everything. The handle grip was man-size and ribbed along its entire length and, when Hayden placed the GPR upon it, it made the device go crazy.

Good to know.

The fallen woman was sobbing into the floor. Hayden lifted her head. "What is it?"

"They have my husband. Forced me to board the train. I was supposed to jump when it slowed, then make my way to a phone box on Ross Avenue." She nodded at the dagger. "With that."

Hayden hung her head for a moment. The evil of men . . . and women . . . could never be underestimated.

"Sit tight," she said, then opened the comms. "Cambridge? Sit rep?"

"More telling info from Crowe and Lauren, gleaned from the general's computer, but we'll discuss that later. This is your last chance, Hayden. They're literally lining up guns on anyone all along the final route. They're on the ground, crammed in second and third story windows. They're on rooftops. You have . . . four minutes."

Hayden screamed for Yorgi to race right down to the back of the train, to make the passengers lie down. She raced with Dahl and Luther toward the front carriage to see what the hell was happening with Molokai and Smyth.

The last terrorist stared, eyes huge, the terrifying gleam of utter fanaticism glowing from his face. He'd tied one man to the headrest of a seat and was making him hold tight to a grenade.

A grenade from which the pin had already been pulled.

The terrorist knelt on the seat behind him, a gun aimed at the rest of the passengers that were lined up at the front, some kneeling, some standing. Smyth and Molokai were halfway down the aisle.

With no options.

Hayden stole inside the carriage without being acknowledged, knowing she had to be there. The others followed. The terrorist saw them immediately, but knew he had the upper hand.

"I will kill everyone," he said.

"Oh, I know you will," Hayden replied. *Because you're a mad little fucker.* She addressed the captive holding the live grenade:

"What's your name, bud?"

"Mark. Mark Starzynski."

"You have kids, Mark?"

"Yes, I do. Two."

"Well, Mark, you hold onto that lump of iron like it's gold, the winning lottery ticket, and your kids' futures all rolled in to one. Got that?"

"Yeah, right, I got it."

Good. Now, fuckhead?"

The terrorist narrowed his eyes at her, gun wavering.

"Yeah, you, fuckhead. You look at me, not at those poor people. Just me. You wanna know why?"

"You are a crazy bitch."

"Well, that's something you got right today. It's was me that killed all your deranged pals. I gave the orders. I pulled the trigger. How'd you like that?"

"Two minutes," Cambridge said inside her head.

Kinimaka's voice replied with real fear. "There are loads of passengers being forced to stand," he hissed. "At the front. And the team too. Pass it on."

"Ah, shit, I'll try but they've gone dark now."

The ominous phrase that nobody liked to hear. Hayden glared at the terrorist standing in front of her.

"I sent all their worthless lives to a shitty hell, and spat on their filthy corpses. What do you think of that, asshole?"

"Back away!" the terrorist yelled. "You back away now or I will kill everyone!"

"You said that already." Hayden came to within arm's length. "How about you stop being such a fucking coward and point that gun at me?"

"I blow your head off! You stay!"

Cambridge whispered: "Thirty seconds!"

Hayden leaned forward and hissed: "Boo."

The terrorist shrieked and whipped his gun toward her. Before he'd even pulled it halfway round both Dahl and Molokai had put bullets into his chest, above the bomb-vest. Hayden wasn't watching. She saw Mark Starzynski shaking badly through her peripheral vision, and reached out to steady the hand that gripped the grenade.

"You're safe now."

To Cambridge she said, "All clear."

The train thundered on, minutes from Dallas Union Station. Hayden ordered everyone on the entire train to lie down and hoped to everything she held dear that Cambridge managed to get the message through.

Dahl pulled the emergency brake and the train began to squeal, wheels shrieking as it came to a fast stop. Hayden slid forward. Dahl hung on and smashed through the nearest window.

"We're not waiting," he said as the train finally came to a halt. "The bureaucracy would end this entire mission."

He was right. Hayden pulled her body upright and related all she knew about the woman with the captive husband to Cambridge.

"Try to help them."

"Will do."

Not knowing where the shooters were, but knowing they had no choice, they put their trust in Cambridge's contacts and exited the train.

Already dashing headlong toward the next mission.

CHAPTER NINETEEN

They never stopped running.

It was in their blood, in their heart and soul. The mission, the world, and those they fought against demanded it, and they always rose to the challenge.

In the darkness of a luxury minivan, in the rear of an empty, unlit parking area, they came to a stop after many hours of traveling. Finally, they were able to rest, but the updates kept on coming, never ceasing, keeping the mission running at top speed.

Cambridge described the aftermath of Dallas. "Incredible outcome," he told them. "Only the rambunctious twats that missed out on theoretical glory are even questioning it. And those we can handle. You still have the dagger?"

"Are your people close?"

"Yep. I have men on the way so we can feed it back through the network. Back to England and the Key of Hades. This will be the third of the weapons in our possession, including the Sword of Mars."

"Didn't the others get the Chain of Aphrodite?"

"Ah, they're still working on it to be honest."

Smyth grunted at that. "Not cool."

"Yeah, they hit several snags over in Greece. But nobody got hurt, so we're good."

"Earlier you mentioned receiving some important information from Crowe and Lauren," Hayden reminded him.

"Of course. Whoever they're using to delve through General Gleeson's laptop has uncovered something significant. It seems the list of weapons that Secretary Crowe acquired was by no means the definitive one. There's another . . ."

Hayden sensed the bad news wasn't quite finished. "And?"

"It's quite a bit longer. We're counting at least seventeen weapons so far, with the potential for more. But this does explain why we're encountering Tempest at every weapon site, and why some of their team are mercs and some terrorists. It also explains why they initiated the terrorist training camps."

"They're stretched very thin," Smyth said. "We get it."

"Like Marmite on toast," Cambridge said. "This also helps explain why they're not unduly disturbed about losing all the weapons that we obtain."

"Working from a bigger list," Dahl said. "No doubt they're still getting the majority."

"Exactly. I'm seeing items ranging as far back through the gods' roster as the very oldest—the Spines of Erebus and the Rivers of Styx. The biggest—the Gates of Ishtar—is referenced as being 'practically unobtainable' and 'infinitely desirable.' But there are many more."

"Some of those," Dahl said. "Don't sound as though they came from any tomb."

"Well, that's the last thing we know, for now," Cambridge said. "Not only weapons were found at the tombs. Maps were found too."

Hayden sat back in her seat, taking stock. "You're saying we're beat? Even before we start?"

"Of course not," Cambridge snorted. "We're taking them apart, and we're close to exposing Tempest. We'll work on that end, you work on the weapons."

"Nemesis," Dahl said then. "What's the significance of her dagger?"

"She was the god of retribution, consort of Zeus himself. She gave birth to Helen of Troy, apparently. Her father was Erebus. A winged goddess bearing a dagger, she is ruthless divine justice, a true avenger of crime. Using her scales or tally stick she decided the fate of mortals and gods alike, and rides in a chariot drawn by griffins. It is she that is credited with bringing Narcissus the greatest sorrow of his life, by bringing him to a pool where he saw his own reflection in the water and fell in love with it. In the end, it was what killed him since he couldn't bear to turn away from the beauty of his reflection."

"Y'know," Dahl said, "I have the same problem. Anything else?"

"That's about it," Cambridge said. "For now."

"Good, then what's—"

"Oh, apart from one thing."

Hayden sensed it might not be good. "Cambridge?"

"Sorry, the info just came in. Several US powers know you're in the country now. I kept your identities hidden on the train, of course. But they will yield to pressure from the powerful members of Tempest and launch a manhunt for you."

"Do we need to leave the country immediately?"

"I'm afraid that you do."

Hayden started the car. "We're heading out now," she said. "Whilst darkness lasts. Just point us in the direction of a friendly landing strip."

CHAPTER TWENTY

Drake wouldn't listen to the old man until they'd reached a quiet destination, parked the car, and were seated on concrete benches at the edge of a small park. Swings moved to and fro in the distance and the happy sounds of children playing drifted like delicate blessings on warm streams of air. Mai, cooler now, and Luther, having volunteered to watch the perimeter, split up, and wandered off. Drake watched them both go with a substantial question in his heart.

How do I feel?

The place he was at now, with Alicia, had not been of his making. Mostly, it had been of Mai's. And perhaps here was a chance for her to make a fresh start. Luther too.

Alicia interrupted his thoughts, deciding to play team sweet-talker. "Let's hear the pitiful confession, Doukas, every scrap. Remember, me believing you is how you get to survive."

The old man placed a hand on each temple and studied the ground between his feet. "I acquired the chain like you said, from the old tomb. I escaped without detection, by the skin of my teeth. Felt lucky. Took the chain to my home and then began to wonder what the hell to do with it."

"You didn't steal for gain?" Drake asked.

"Didn't even enter my mind."

"Weird," Kenzie whispered. "It's in mine all the time."

"I kept it and kept it and, like all first-time thieves I guess, grew so paranoid that I had to do something about it. I thought—what would be the best place to hide it? That question overlapped a memory of an old enemy of mine, bringing the perfect place to mind."

"An old enemy?" Kenzie asked.

"Yes, yes. Lars German. He is the police commissioner around here."

Drake did a double-take. "Come again?"

"You heard correctly, sir. He is the police commissioner and a childhood antagonist of mine. The man was a bully."

Drake didn't like the sound of where this was going. "Doukas—how the hell does your enemy, the police commissioner, tie in to the whereabouts of the Chain of Aphrodite?"

"That is where it gets tricky," Doukas admitted. "I figured out long ago that the chain didn't set metal detectors off. Just like half the scientists working inside those tombs. I swathed them in bubble-wrap and tape, then came up with a plan to get inside the station. I walked them right in. I pretended to meet with German to bury the hatchet and, after a cup of coffee, excused myself to go to the toilet. I left it hidden right there, with my enemy, because what better place can you think of to hide it?"

Drake had to admit that Doukas' plan was bordering on foolproof, but he was furious with the old man. Time was passing and they'd already put their lives on the line. Now they were being told the chain was hidden inside some old police station?

"Is it still activé?" Alicia asked.

"Yes, yes, I'm afraid so. Though not terribly."

"Not terribly? What does that mean?"

Alicia gazed over at Drake. The Yorkshireman stood up and kicked the overgrown grass at the base of the bench. "Does anyone else know?"

He expected a negative reply and received one.

"On the one hand it doesn't sound like a hard target," Alicia said. "But on the other, what's our response if the cops resist?"

Drake stared with sad eyes into the graying skies. "The response will be as light as can be," he said. "But we have to get that chain and it has to be tonight. Tempest could be scouring this entire town right now with a GPR like ours. We have no time."

Kenzie squinted then. "Hey, why did our GPR think the chain in the museum was real?" she asked.

Drake shook his head at Doukas. "I have an idea about that," he said. "Why don't you tell them, mate?"

"I scraped flecks from the chain," he admitted. "Added some paint scrapings, coal and water. Made a good paste. You see, I still wanted the chain. Couldn't help myself. So I kept a small portion of the links."

"Weirdo," Kenzie glowered at him.

Drake called in Mai and Luther and then told them the bad news. The team gathered to make a plan.

"A shame we don't have Yorgi," Drake said. "The kid makes a fine cat burglar."

"He was a cat burglar," Alicia said, "who got caught."

"Not through his profession," Drake said. "That was something else."

"Yes, I know. Family. He should go back there."

"I could do the job," Kenzie said. "I've carried out similar operations before. But I'd feel safer with someone like Dahl at my back."

"That's a much different operation," Alicia said bluntly. "It's called doggy-style. Let the grown-ups talk, bitch."

"I do love a cat fight." Luther looked between the two of them. "You two ever get it on?"

"Once or twice," Alicia responded. "Almost as many times as your girlfriend and I."

"My girl . . ." Luther raised a hand. "Now, whoa. I'm not part of your little life-experiment and never plan to be. I have a job, a calling, and as soon as this Tempest mess is sorted out I'll be getting right back to it."

Mai didn't look happy. Alicia saw it but decided to let it go. There were too many broken hearts already in this team. Kenzie moved next to Drake.

"Do you want me to do it?"

"Not on your own, Kenzie. You shouldn't have to take on that kind of risk. We'll all go in together, including Doukas here. Let me tell you this, mate, if you're still lying I'll put you in one of those overnight cells, straight through the goddamn bars."

"I'm telling you the truth."

"Move out and prep," he said. "We go in just after midnight."

CHAPTER TWENTY ONE

With no easy choices, they chose the most direct of several problematic ones. A disturbance on the other side of town would draw away the bulk of the night force and, before searching for the chain, they needed to obtain some Tasers. Luther was sent to devise a disturbance.

Everyone else headed for the police station.

Drake stood in the darkest shadows, silent, cold as midnight passed. *At this rate we're gonna have to storm the bloody place.*

It had already been a long delay, just waiting for an opportunity. At first they had found good fortune—a patch of greenery lay within sight of the police station's rear gates. They were able to scope out approximate numbers, coming and goings, even civilian activity. Luther's distraction was due any minute.

Alicia stretched. "I'm bored."

"But you're still luckier than us," Kenzie told her. "Because we're forced to look at you."

"Oh, you wound me." Alicia gripped her heart and doubled over.

"Not yet," Kenzie murmured, turning away.

Mai watched them and then shook her head. "Please someone, hand me a Taser."

Drake counted down the seconds, watching the silent Doukas. Luther's distraction should have happened minutes ago, but with no active comms they were ignorant for now. Luther would probably be too busy to contact them by cellphone. Drake saw a police van leaving the police station, light blazing across their patch of land as it turned into the road. The team hunkered down behind old tree trunks and a thick hedge, hidden on all sides. Darkness set in again, leaving the team to twiddle their thumbs.

"Wait," Mai said. "That sounds promising."

The Japanese woman's hearing was as acute as it could get. Drake heard the noise a few seconds later—the sound of a van approaching.

Alicia saw it first. "We're on."

They broke cover, walking briskly and as unobtrusively as possible toward the rear gates of the police station. As the white transit van approached, they slipped out of sight behind the pillars that anchored the gates on each side.

A low buzzing noise signaled the gates being opened by remote control. Drake waited for the van to drive in, bouncing down a ramp into the station, and then slipped around the slowly closing gates, following it down a slope. Alicia and Mai were right behind him, backed by Kenzie. Quickly, they dispersed into the accumulated darkness between parked vehicles and hoped the man studying the CCTV images covering this quiet, small, out-of-the-way police station had missed those last few seconds.

"Silence is golden," Mai said. "Let's go."

At that moment the van came back, followed by two police cars. The gates grated apart and both vehicles raced out. Drake nodded happily.

"That'll be Luther."

"Perfect."

Breaking cover, Drake found himself praying for luck and moved toward the rear doors of the police station. An unusual sentiment when starting a mission, but this undertaking was entirely different. Very little needed to go wrong to turn it into an absolute disaster.

The building had two rear doors—the first a single opening which Drake assumed led to a cage that held a small number of people, and a second with sliding double doors. A well-placed explosive charge shattered the doors, enabling them to crow-bar the frames apart. Mai slipped in first.

The desk sergeant crawled around the side of his wooden counter where he'd fallen, gun in hand. The man's hand trembled and his eyes were wide. Mai rolled, took cover behind the desk and then jumped silently up onto it. She watched the sergeant crawling beneath her, picked her moment and then dropped down onto his back. With a twist she disarmed him, pocketed the gun and unhooked his Taser.

"Done," she said aloud, rendering him inert before zip-tying his hands and legs.

"Masks." Drake slipped his own across his face, before any CCTV could spot them.

A second policeman came into the room, an enquiring expression on his face. The blast had been deliberately quiet, just powerful enough to crack the glass and sound like a hundred different things. By the time this man realized intruders were breaking in, Mai had spun back across the deck, pinned his upper body between her legs and flipped him onto his back. Before he even caught his breath, she'd zip-tied and gagged him.

"C'mon, Sprite," Alicia complained. "I'm feeling unnecessary back here."

Mai dragged the second policeman over to the first. "Finally. She gets it."

Kenzie walked out into the station, foregoing the luxury of a mask. Her words: "I'm already in the system, and it might help maintain the rep, you know?" didn't exactly reassure Drake, but it certainly wasn't official that she currently ran with Team SPEAR so maybe her identification would in fact help deflect suspicion.

A rough estimate told Drake there were at least three more policemen to deal with. He saw a corridor to the left and glanced along it—noticed a row of cells. A voice shouted out inquiringly but he ignored it. They found and used a keypad to move further into the building. Beyond a waiting area they found several more rooms with closed doors. Mai slammed through the first. Drake heard an exclamation of annoyance and then a muffled shout. So, that was three to Mai. Not to be outdone, Alicia and Kenzie breached the next two rooms, leaving Drake standing in the corridor.

He hurried to help, saw Kenzie bent over, already tasing her target who had been pouring coffee from his machine. Figuring she was fine he moved on to Alicia and saw her bending a man's elbow so she could get him in the right position for a gentle tasing.

Now who's feeling redundant?

"Is that all of them?" Doukas asked.

"Should be. Lead me to the men's restrooms, quickly."

Not a sentence he'd ever imagined asking a man.

The old man shoved past, then stopped at the bottom of the corridor. Drake saw no toilet signage, but Doukas was staring at a closed door to the right.

"That's his office. My bully. Do you think he might be inside and I might borrow a Taser?"

Drake viewed all bullies as cowards and held a memory of a boy from his school days; a boy that stole his lunch money and intimidated him for a year. Somehow, he doubted that boy would try it now.

Ergo: coward.

"Sure," Drake said. With a quick flick he turned the doorknob and opened the door. The police commissioner was sitting with his legs up on the desk, idly tapping away at a laptop with one hand and holding alcohol in a diamond-cut glass with the other. When Drake rushed at him, he spilt the drink, choked on liquid, and fell off his chair. Drake dragged him around the desk and handed Doukas the Taser.

"One."

The mask lifted around Doukas' lips, so happy was he. Drake supervised the tasing and then looked up as the others came into the room.

"Couldn't handle it alone?" Alicia asked, voice muffled.

"Yeah." He remembered to be cautious about what he said. "It's complicated."

"Oh, I get it," Alicia said. "I really do."

Once the police commissioner had been restrained, they made their way to the toilet area. Doukas pointed out the correct stall, upon which Drake climbed to remove the paneled roof and search for the bubble-wrap full of chain links. At first his questing fingertips found nothing, but he knew it couldn't have gone far. A change of direction and he found it—a medium-heavy package that strained his biceps as he lifted and passed it down to Alicia. Once they were done, they ignored its contents to make haste before any more police officers showed up.

Drake hastened toward the rear doors, passing the men they'd already tied and checking on their welfare. All were fine and, except for the commissioner, they apologized too. As they headed for freedom a nightmarish sound split the air.

Explosion. Drake dropped to the ground. The building shook. Glass shattered somewhere not far away and rubble fell to the floor. Loud voices could be heard as the noise of the detonation faded away.

"In here! Now!"

"I'm not happy breaking in to a cop station, bro. Just the opposite."

"Quit yer damn whining and move ahead. The tracker's squealing like a pig in heat."

"Speaking of pigs, when do I get to blast one o' dem fuckers?" A new voice.

Drake halted. There was a chance they could slip away unnoticed. "I think the enemy just arrived."

"Tracked the chain," Alicia said. "We'll have to be quick."

"What are you waiting for?" Kenzie growled. "Go!"

"I don't—" Mai began.

"We can't," Drake said. "They'll kill those policeman, or at least hurt them. They're helpless. I can't let that happen."

Alicia stopped in mid-stride. "You're right."

Kenzie regarded them as if they were insane. "The way out," she breathed, "is right there."

"Then use it." Drake hid behind a corner as footsteps rushed along the bisecting corridor. A hurried estimation put the count at five men. Drake let the first go by and then hit the second, assuming that the first would turn soon anyway. The second rebounded off the far wall and tripped all those pounding behind him. Men sprawled face first, weapons tumbling. Those wearing scarves across their faces lost them. Fingers were broken, curses vented. Drake fell among them.

Kenzie raced past Mai to tackle the first man, grabbing his gun as he sought to level it, and pushing it up toward the ceiling. It became a metal bar between them, rolling back and forth. With a free hand the merc pulled a knife from its sheath but this was exactly what Kenzie wanted.

She smiled. "Thanks, man."

In mid-thrust he blanched. Kenzie gripped the wrist and let it pass her by, twisted viciously and caught the blade as it fell toward the floor. The merc bellowed as fingers snapped. Kenzie flicked the knife up in the air by the blade, then waited for the handle to fall back into her hand.

The merc's eyes followed the weapon.

She caught it and rammed it home just under his ribs. All strength fled his body. She stepped away and watched him fall, now holding his gun.

Drake elbowed and kneed and nutted his way through the battle. Every gun he found, he threw back to Mai. Alicia was with him, crawling among the downed men, the narrow corridor giving them little room in which to work. It was more like a hellish death-struggle; a tight, claustrophobic melee with everyone crammed together.

Drake rolled off a body to find a leg wrapped around his neck, which he removed with the touch of his Taser, but he knew the charge was running low. He rolled back, rose with an elbow to a sitting man's face, then flung his body headlong atop another. Alicia was giving no quarter, tasing everyone in the most easily available parts of the body, using her boots and a knife she had pulled loose from one man's sheath.

Mai strapped two guns over her shoulders, another across her back, and held a fourth leveled at head height. At the end of the corridor, a shadow shrouded by light, she was a vision—not least because her demure, slim figure belied the fact that it could bristle with such a collection of weapons. But the shadow had bite.

A new merc came through the shattered façade of the police station, his semi-auto Mauser leading the way. Mai didn't let him fire, just opened up with her own weapons instantly and watched the figure bounce off the rear wall, turned into a lifeless rag-doll without even spotting his killer.

Another crouched down at his side, surveying the scene. Mai shot him too. Drake realized he'd disarmed most of the men, and scrambled back the way he'd come, dragging Alicia along by the elbow.

"Time to leave."

"But they won't take long to recover."

"Long enough." Drake tapped his ears. "Listen."

Sirens wailed in the distance.

They reached Mai and Kenzie; the Japanese woman distributing weapons. Drake took a last look at the bound policeman, saw all was okay and almost dashed on. But it was the look in the desk sergeant's eye that stopped him—the fear, the slight shake of the head, the deliberate widening of the eyes.

Without hesitation, he fired at the rear doors. A figure fell, groaning, followed by another mercenary, that he shot through the chest. Nodding at the policeman he lay the gun on the floor.

"Thank you," he said.

The others did the same, recognizing they had little use for the weapons now. Doukas had been carrying the chain, but now Kenzie took it off him and hurried him out through the station's rear parking area, back toward the gates. Drake used the same keypad as earlier and then they were squeezing through.

They ran left between buildings and threaded a path back toward their waiting car.

To meet up with Luther.

And get the hell out of town.

CHAPTER TWENTY TWO

Drake's heart sank when he heard Hayden and the others were on the run, trying desperately to escape America before they were caught. Even Secretary Crowe and Lauren, who were relatively close by, couldn't help them. Lauren continued to be blocked in her efforts to meet President Coburn, and Crowe had been forced into hiding. For now, they were only able to pull covert, invisible strings as they tried to make a difference.

Similarly on the run, driving down a road somewhere in Greece, Drake's team checked the Chain of Aphrodite and then dropped off Doukas. Drake made a call to Whitehall.

"We're sitting in a rented Merc C class, following a B-road through some form of flat purgatory to be honest. I have no clue where we are."

Alicia pointed at the satnav. "Tells you right there."

"It does, but I'm so pissed off I can't be bothered to look. Cambridge, can you track us?"

"Got your phone triangulated right now. We'll collect the chain. Just keep going."

"How do these bastards keep on tracking us, mate?"

Cambridge wasn't slow to answer. "It's not you, it's the law of averages converging. It's a worldwide web of facts and details stacked against you. They have instruments to track the weapons which are better than ours. Crowe found out there are many more weapons than we first thought, over twice as many. Tempest have a wide net, using terrorists and mercs. The chain gives us four weapons, and I'm betting they have double that. They're jumping all over the world from job to job. One of the bigger problems is this terrorist camp. We don't know where it is and Tempest will have a small army pretty soon."

"Understood." Drake took in the mood of the people in the car. Still taut, they lived by the minute knowing they were fugitives and that Tempest had put a kill order on their heads. Of course they were fractious. Of course they were on edge. But over a dozen other estranged Special Forces teams were out there too—living every day under threat.

"What can you tell us about the chain?" Alicia asked. "Doukas seemed to think it was Aphrodite's sex toy."

Cambridge snorted. "By all accounts she was a bit of a minx, but I doubt she needed to resort to chains. It was fashioned for and given to her by a potential suitor, something about it symbolizing the way his heart felt every time he saw her."

Alicia choked. "Yeah, Drakey says that all the time."

Cambridge went on: "It wasn't quite that easy. Aphrodite was married of course, and as her adulteries went on so her husband grew wiser. She grew bolder. The only way men could court her was to send gifts, the more heartfelt the more chance they stood of a midnight tryst."

The length of chain felt light to Drake as he handled it. Small links and slender metal made it suitable for any hands.

"Makes more sense," he said. "These wouldn't even restrain Alicia, and she's a wimp."

The Englishwoman made him groan with a punch to the shoulder, no doubt raising a new bruise. "Add that to your assortment," she said.

"Whilst we're waiting for the collection," Luther said. "We're wasting time. Where are we headed next, Dartmoor?"

Drake knew it was a nickname referencing Cambridge's SAS background and smiled.

"Well, we have that in hand too. The next weapon that we know of in your vicinity also happens to be in Greece, and you're headed right toward it."

"We are? That's great. What is it?"

"We have a problem with this one—" Cambridge waited as the chorus of groans and "again" settled down. "I'm sorry, nobody said this was going to be easy. Next up is an artifact called The Waters of Neptune. Basically, it's in Thessaloniki, a large Greek city, and we have a very good idea of where it is."

Drake scratched his stubble. "I'm guessing there's a but."

"Name me a day when there isn't. But . . . a man named Mattheus has it."

"Somehow, that doesn't bring to my mind the image of an aging archaeologist," Luther said.

"It isn't. Mattheus and Doukas don't even live in the same universe. Mattheus is a criminal that runs a nightclub in a police no-go area of the city, a particularly violent type. He's aware that the artifact is being sought and has surrounded himself with a small army. To be fair, the army is business as usual for him."

"There must be a story about how he came to own the artifact." Kenzie sounded interested.

Alicia leaned across to Drake and cracked a one-liner: "She's hoping she didn't sell it to him."

Kenzie turned, face serious. "In all honesty I've been wondering for some time if any of these artifacts might have crossed my path. Doubtful, but . . ." She shrugged.

"You didn't sell this to Mattheus," Cambridge said. "He murdered an entire line of succession until it passed down to him."

Drake wished he could be surprised at the news, but wasn't. "So, his father purchased it?"

"Father to big brother to him, yes. Black market. Possibly even purchased at the last Bazaar of Ramses. You remember that?"

"Oh, yeah. A lot of shit went down that day. Can you send us all the information you have on Mattheus and his nightclub?"

"On its way. Mattheus's father bought this at the last bazaar and then kept it hidden inside his home for some time. Mattheus saw it one day and coveted it, then brought it to his own home, which is this bloody nightclub. It's a four-story building and we believe Mattheus has apartments comprised out of the top two. And I mean, a proper, ritzy abode. None of your cheap crap. Underground parking garage, dedicated elevator, the usual stuff that criminals love. No doubt a slew of disposable bodyguards. You really do have your work cut out for you here, Drake."

The Yorkshireman rolled his eyes. "I'm wondering if Tempest are cherry-picking their jobs. Leaving the hardest until last."

"Probably," Cambridge affirmed. "They could be waiting for their terrorist camp to come fully online."

Mai sat upright in her seat. "And that's something else we can't allow to happen."

"Any luck contacting any of the other teams that have been left out in the cold?" Luther asked.

"Ongoing," Cambridge answered. "You can imagine the logistical problems involved with approaching a dug-in, hyper-wary Special Forces team in enemy territory. Let's say, we're working carefully on it."

Luther tapped the satnav screen. "We're approaching Thessaloniki, guys. Where is this nightclub?"

Cambridge reeled off the coordinates, which Luther tapped into the vehicle's navigation system. "Twenty three minutes," he said. "We should find a hotel close by."

"Not too close," Mai said. "In case you're all wrong and Tempest are here already."

"Not a problem," Alicia said. "We'll kill anyone that gets in our way."

"That's not always the answer," Mai said obstinately.

"Works for me," Alicia said. "They'd do as much or worse to us. And besides, I still have a demon in my soul that needs appeasing."

"Since birth," Mai muttered.

"Hey," Alicia said. "You have to admit I'm better than I used to be."

Mai grimaced. "In the same way a predator is better when it cuts down by one meal a day."

"Eh?"

"It's still a predator and it's still only happy when it's eating."

"You're saying I'm only happy when I'm fighting the scumbags? That's not true."

Mai gave her a long look and then turned away. Alicia looked deep in thought. Drake decided it was best to ignore them both and watched the wet city streets passing by through a raindrop spattered windscreen.

"Hotel." He pointed. "Let's get registered and make a plan."

CHAPTER TWENTY THREE

"Place looks clean," Luther said, studying the nightclub's exterior and surrounds through field glasses.

Alicia shook her head sadly. "Poor Luther's never been inside a nightclub," she said. "He thinks they're clean."

"No, I didn't mean—"

Drake watched the building from a different angle. It sat wide and squat on a piece of land between two diagonal-running streets, somewhere near the heart of Thessaloniki, in the tourist district. Four concrete steps led up to the front doors, which were black and, currently, shut tight. A-boards sat outside, advertising events and opening hours. All the windows were opaque, some on the first floor covered in sign-writing. Drake could see a clear difference between the bottom and top two floors—the latter obviously having had some lavish expense thrown at it, including ornate balconies, a roof garden and, he imagined, much more besides. The stonework was dirty and unwashed, which backed up Alicia's experienced presumption of a grungy interior.

Luther was rephrasing. "No obvious signs of enemies," he said. "Tempest, or otherwise."

"Agreed," Drake said. "When does the place open?"

"According to the website," Kenzie said. "Nine p.m. tonight."

"Why do they open at bedtime?" Dahl wondered.

"Latest Intel just arrived." Cambridge was talking on Drake's cellphone. "This is recently in from a deep-cover informant, and I'm quoting here: 'Mattheus stores this weird idol thing in a safe in the nightclub.'"

Alicia bit her lip. "By the sound of this guy that could be anything."

"I guess," Cambridge said. "But if it isn't the Waters of Neptune then it's some twisted coincidence."

"An idol, not a statue?" Mai said. "Do we have any information on the artifact?"

"Yes, they documented it briefly before it went missing. The problem with these artifacts is—the people stealing them are the ones documenting them, so they make the description as brief as they can with 'more to follow.' Neptune was, of course, the god of the sea, the Roman counterpart to Poseidon. The description depicts an obsidian block with a smooth granite feel and a representation of the god and his trident. A rough estimate of size places it no larger than, say, a microwave."

"Which would fit in a safe?" Alicia questioned.

"Yes. The informant tells me Mattheus's safe is floor to ceiling. It'd fit."

"Could be the break we need," Drake said. "We do have access to the club at least. Not like the rest of the building."

"If you call access to a room full of sweaty, heaving bodies being watched by over a dozen guards, bouncers, CCTV cameras, and a mezzanine level of offices," Cambridge said. "Then, sure, you have access."

"I call that more than access," Alicia said. "I call that party time, baby."

Cambridge made no comment, instead returning to the artifact. "Neptune was also the god of lakes and springs, hence the 'waters' reference in the title, I guess. Only a single temple existed to him in Rome, built before 200 BCE. I'm quite sure you will know the idol when you see it."

Drake was staring at Alicia. "What do you think?"

The Englishwoman read his mind. "You mean Mai and me? I'm thinking the same thing."

Luther put the field glasses down on the scarred wooden table of Drake and Alicia's hotel room with a thunk. "That worries me."

"I don't see why," Alicia said. "We're both females looking for a good Greek time. On vacation. Both young . . ." She paused. "At least I am. Mai's chomping on that chain a bit."

"It's fine." Mai nodded. "A good idea. They won't suspect us."

"They will if your photo's in their database."

"Why would it be?" Mai was already rising to her feet. "Tempest are the loudest players here. We're just background noise. C'mon, Alicia, let's get ready."

"Why? Are you gonna dress me?"

"You wish. We need to coordinate. Find a place to hide all those cameras."

"Sounds fun. Is there anywhere—"

Kenzie cut in. "Hey, I'm going too. Can't hurt, right?"

"Three's a crowd, bitch."

Drake wasn't watching but didn't need eyes to know whose response that was.

"The problem," Mai said seriously. "Is that they may have your photo. A result of your previous employment."

"I never came across these people. The only Greeks I used for business were based in Athens and various Egyptian cities."

"I'm sure we can work it out," Mai said, and then in answer to Alicia's groan: "She's right, Taz. Three is better than two on this occasion."

The woman started walking toward the door. Alicia voiced the comment that she was looking forward to a great night out.

Drake winced and glanced glumly at Luther.

"Shit," he said. "This isn't gonna end pretty."

Alicia leaned on Kenzie's shoulder as they entered the club, whispering exactly what she thought of her. Kenzie smiled and grinned at the doormen as they pranced by. Mai stayed close to the back of the pair, playing mother. Due to lack of time and ease of purchase they'd been forced to wear new jeans and tourist T-shirts, but weren't too far removed from the norm. This nightclub at least, didn't have a rigid dress code but cared more about patrons handing over money.

Mai laid a hand on each of her companion's shoulders. "Stay cool, girls. Do what we came here to do and get out."

Alicia pushed Kenzie away, playfully yet with force. The Israeli barely managed to catch herself before striking a wall.

"Oh, don't be silly," she cried as if she'd inhaled a bottle of red wine on the steps.

Alicia moved to push her again, faking a laugh, but Kenzie defied her inebriation and slipped deftly around Alicia's other side. "Miss me, bitch?"

Leaning in, she hooked an arm around Alicia's neck and squeezed. Alicia let her tongue fall out, acting the fool, but in truth finding it increasingly hard to breathe.

Mai parted them with difficulty. "Focus, kids. We're in."

A wall of noise abused their senses as they were allowed through a final door and into the heart of the nightclub. One enormous room, it was roughly circular with mini-dancing-stages all around the outside and a lengthy bar to the right. Glasses and bottles sparkled under bright lights all along its length, the glitz instantly attracting the newcomers.

Alicia stepped down onto the central dance floor, taking it all in. Couples and groups capered to and fro and screamed into each other's ears to make themselves heard. A dance beat pounded from wall to wall and through the floor, thrashing its way into Alicia's bones and dampening her senses.

She leaned back, grabbing Mai by the head and shouting into her ears. "Fuck me, I do not miss this shit!"

The Japanese woman smiled softly. "It's different when you're young."

"Yeah, damn right. I was far stupider then."

"Are you ready to do this?"

Alicia steeled herself. They knew where the guards were. They knew where the guns were. They knew where Mattheus was, and where the criminal boss that ruled this police no-go area kept his safe.

"Bring it on."

CHAPTER TWENTY FOUR

Knowing in advance that communication would be verging on impossible outside the restrooms, they had decided on a series of hand signals. Used by the military, they were quite familiar with them, but hoped no ex-army bodyguards would also recognize the gestures. The trio cut through the crowd, hands in the air, skirting a shrill hen party and then several couples and a man dancing on his own.

Alicia leaned against the bar, using the interminable wait for service to get a better feel for the place. Flashing lights shone overhead and were set into the walls. The small exterior dance floors were packed, people only managing to stay on the small squares by hanging onto the floor-to-ceiling dance poles. Two heavy, golden curtains covered a door at the end of the bar, and two more across the far side. Several nondescript doors marked *Private* were also dotted around.

"Help you?"

Alicia turned to see a friendly faced bartender staring at her. "Champagne," she said. "All round."

She hated the stuff but didn't intend to drink it.

The mission parameters centered on the safe, not Mattheus, so the women drifted over toward the door that led to the criminal's inner sanctum, glasses in hand. If the informant was correct, there would be men directly behind the door with another three or four sets positioned after that—guards for several rooms used in various nefarious operations, and then a comparatively snug, dingy office at the far end.

Of course, they weren't here to deal with the safe.

They were here for Mattheus.

Strolling past the first door, they approached the golden curtain with its thick, overlapping folds. Two men stood in front of it, guns holstered but in clear view, watching the people on the dance floors and all those milling around. Their eyes were blank, like a shark's; their faces could have been chiseled out of solid stone.

Alicia peered between them. "What's in there?"

"Private room," one grumbled. "Move on."

Kenzie widened her eyes. "Oh, and how do we get an invite?"

"You don't. Now get the fuck out of here."

"I can be very persuasive . . ."

The man on the left gave her a hard stare whilst the man on the right moved a hand down to his gun. Mai dragged the women away, laughing.

"Take it easy," she told them under the musical blast. "Just take it easy."

Alicia found a corner and turned on Kenzie. "Jesus, girl. I can be very persuasive," she mimicked. "What the fuck?"

To her credit, Kenzie hung her head. "It just came out. Total blooper."

Mai checked her watch. "We have to think of something fast. The guys are gonna be knocking at the door in a few minutes."

Alicia glance at the guards. "Plan B," she said.

"Which is?" Mai looked blank and resigned to a new plan.

"Well, if my name were Kenzie it'd be to approach them naked."

The Israeli scowled. "Do not tar me with that brush."

"Why? Would you rather I used whipped cream?"

"Stop it," Mai said. "Just get on with it."

"It's not hard to figure," Alicia said, ignoring an obvious comment from Kenzie as she continued. "We wait for the boys to knock. In the commotion we grab Mattheus, or at least the part of him that we need."

Mai took another glance down at her watch. "Four minutes," she said.

"Best get ready to fight then." Alicia couldn't keep the grin off her face.

Drake drove the slate gray transit van through the dark streets of Thessaloniki, seeking out the quietest routes. They weren't in danger, but wanted the route of the van to be as inconspicuous as possible. Getting the gear they needed hadn't been easy. The van was stolen from Mattheus's own cache of vehicles; the winch borrowed from a store downtown. The bolt gun came from a shop, bought and paid for, and as for the rest? Well, Cambridge certainly had to pull the most resourceful of strings down here and use up all the British government's favors.

"Approaching Mattheus's rear," Luther said.

Drake shook his head. The American really needed to work on his delivery. The side street was pitch black, unpopulated and dotted with piles of rubbish that showed up in the van's headlights. Even narrower, darker streets branched off to the sides as they crept along. Soon, Drake found the marker they'd placed earlier which denoted the place where Mattheus's small office should be along the outer wall, according to the informant.

He pulled the van over to the curb and turned to Luther. "You're up."

"Keep your eyes peeled."

Drake nodded, mostly listening as Luther set up their offensive. The big American muttered to himself as he worked, first checking the bolts that held the winch to the floor hadn't shifted during the journey, and then the winch's winding mechanism. Both were approved and then Luther jumped out, bald head gleaming from the lights that shone from Drake's instrument cluster. With a powerful flashlight he measured back from the edge of the building and then marked out an oblong vertical shape on the wall with tape. Working fast, he'd finished by the time Drake checked his watch two minutes later.

"Wait," Drake said.

"I haven't set the charges yet, boy."

Drake cringed at the moniker, but accepted it because he knew Luther wasn't being disparaging. This was just the warrior's personality taking over and, supposedly, part of his charm. Drake was on the fence about that one, but waited until Luther had set all of the specially shaped charges.

"Forty seconds," he said.

"All good here. Just need the detonator."

"Get around to the other side of the van."

"Yeah, yeah, Ma, give me a second."

"You don't have a second."

"It can't go off whilst I'm holding it," Luther hissed back, then added: "Said the vicar to the choirboy."

He stomped around the side. Drake squeezed his eyes shut and wondered how he'd ended up here. His watch flashed and he called a "go," but Luther was already on it, pressing the detonator button. There was a loud, but not booming explosion, and the side of the van was showered with rubble. Drake slithered over to the passenger seat as Luther came around the van, flashlight in hand, to view their handiwork.

"Not bad," Luther said. "I've seen worse."

Drake thought it was shoddy work, but didn't comment. The brick wall that formed the back of Mattheus's nightclub, and his office, now included a vertical four-foot-high hole. Bricks jutted here and there, still clinging on to the main wall, and mortar rained down. A pile of debris lay on the sidewalk. Luther cleared the excess away and then returned to the van. Drake jumped out with a fresh Smith and Wesson handgun at the ready. The van was still running, the lights switched off.

He imagined the chaos inside the nightclub. No matter the sound-deadening qualities of their explosive, the minute quantity of it or the way the charges had been shaped—an explosion was an explosion and easy to recognize.

Staying low, he scanned the street both ways and the buildings above. All lay in darkness. Nothing moved. Perhaps Luther had done a better job than he'd first thought.

"Fastening the chain." Luther breathed heavily.

Drake stayed on watch but hissed back: "You okay? Need a sit down?"

"Fuck you, man."

Luther took up the slack in the chain and carried it inside Mattheus's office. A guard was dead inside and another on his knees, staring at the floor. Luther finished him quickly and propped the only chair left intact behind the inner door, securing it for a short while. It would have to do and they didn't need long. Quickly, he looped the chain around the short safe and shackled it, then moved back to the truck and started the winch.

A grinding began that made Drake wince. The iron safe scraped across broken brick and mortar, shoving it out into the street as it came. Its edges collided with the wall, loosening even more bricks, but came through as the winch started to strain. Luther jumped out and straightened the safe, seeing it though the gap.

"I hear noises inside," he told Drake. "They'll be through the door soon."

The safe was dragged frustratingly slowly but inexorably toward the van.

Drake jumped into the hole it had just passed through and fired three shots into the heavy wooden door that led back toward the nightclub and Mattheus's other rooms. A scream attested to his accuracy or his luck—it didn't matter which at this point. The hammering sounds stilled and Drake put his back into helping the safe across the sidewalk and down onto the road.

Luther positioned flat metal ramps that ran from the lip of the van to the road. The safe scraped like a ship running aground as it bumped down onto the tarmac and then began a slow incline up the ramps.

"Still need a few minutes," Luther said.

Drake watched the door and the street, alternating between the two. This was one of those moments when he wished more than half the team weren't in America. Usually they had strength in numbers. Not so today.

"Hurry the fuck up," he hissed apprehensively at the safe. "We're about to get bludgeoned by the might of a Greek crime boss here."

When the deep rumble shook the nightclub not everybody noticed. Alicia detected it, as did Mai and Kenzie. The guards noticed. Most of the guests partied on, but some pulled away and cocked their heads with sudden worry.

Alicia saw the curtains twitch before several guards hurried out. Already, their weapons were drawn which started a panic in those that saw them. Screams broke out and panic spread quickly, but the guards couldn't care less. They headed for a door marked *Private.*

Alicia dashed back to the curtain, face distraught.

"Oh, please. What's going on? Should we leave?"

Both guards drew their guns just as Mai and Kenzie stepped around Alicia to disarm them. The process benefited from being a surprise and took far less time than ordering a drink at the bar. The guards collapsed as the two armed women stepped around Alicia and drew back the curtain.

A wide passage led to yet another door. No guards stood before it, although Alicia guessed they probably had before the explosion. A few seconds later and they were at the door, peering through the vision panel. A room lay beyond, sumptuous, replete with gilt-edged paintings and golden light-stands, a dazzling chandelier and a full-size poker table. Three seats were occupied, two by barely clad females and the other by Mattheus himself. Alicia recognized him from the pictures they'd looked at.

Pushing through, Mai and Kenzie ran with their heads down, guns out. Three guards were standing inconspicuously around the edge of the room. Mai shot one and Kenzie another. The third dived to the floor, but Kenzie leapt atop the poker table and shot him before he could react.

Mattheus, if anything, allowed the edges of his mouth to curl in amusement. "Do you know who I am?"

"Go." Alicia waved at both women. "Get out of here."

Mai grabbed hold of Mattheus's seat and spun it so that the crime boss was facing her. Kenzie ran over to watch the door and Alicia picked up a discarded weapon.

"I will not talk." Mattheus laughed. "You will get nothing from me."

Mai smiled, then jabbed her knuckles right between his eyes. "Stop talking, idiot. Now, give me your finger."

"Wh . . . what?" Mattheus's eyes leaked tears and his chest heaved.

"Steady on, Mai," Alicia said.

Mai took hold of Mattheus's wrist with an iron grip and planted it down on the table. Then she squeezed it around a fresh glass, making sure she got a good set of prints. By the time Mattheus knew what had happened the deed was done.

"I will kill you all for this."

Mai handed Alicia the glass with care and watched as it was wrapped inside several black napkins with the name *Mattheus* emblazoned across the surface.

"We good?" Kenzie called from the door.

"We're good," Alicia said.

Mai punched Mattheus twice more and then watched him slither unceremoniously under the poker table.

"After you, girls."

Drake waited impatiently for the safe to be loaded onto the van, then grew irritated and started pushing it from the back. Luther dragged it from the front. Drake fired three more shots into the wrecked office. Finally, the safe crossed the threshold and Luther slammed the sliding door closed.

"Go!"

Drake jumped back behind the wheel, switched on the lights and gunned the engine. The road ahead illuminated brightly, blinding him for a second and also the lone guard that was running toward them. Drake winged him with the van, ducking as a shot was fired, and heard a side window smash. Luther yelled at the back, still trying to get the safe secured to the floor bolts so that it wasn't rattling all around the metal floor.

Drake drove up the narrow street, then switched the lights off as he reached the main road. Easing out, he turned right and drove away from the nightclub, sending Luther a look that was a mix of elation and worry.

"Just waiting for the women to call now."

"Yeah," the soldier said. "I sure hope Mai's okay."

"Alicia too," Drake said. "Even Kenzie?"

"Yeah, yeah, them too."

Drake proceeded toward the rendezvous point, conscious that the women should already be waiting. Four minutes later, when he pulled up, the area was entirely devoid of people.

"Shit." He looked back toward the city streets. "I think they could be in trouble."

CHAPTER TWENTY FIVE

Alicia led the way, edging the curtain aside and peering into the nightclub's interior. Amazingly, many figures were still dancing, although the herd had thinned. Lights continued to flash to the beat and the bar served drinks to the hardy and the foolhardy.

Alicia wiped sweat from her brow. "Idiots," she said. "Don't they have anywhere better to be after a shooting?"

"Guards?" Mai asked demandingly.

"Yep. Two at the right, two at the left, one by the bar. All with their fingers in their ears. It's a bull pit of confusion right now, but pretty soon they're gonna catch on."

"The explosion has distracted them," Mai surmised. "And probably fear of their boss which, perversely, is working against him right now."

"Nobody wants to report the bad news," Kenzie said. "I remember it well."

"Clock's ticking," Mai said. "Move."

They slid carefully out onto the dance floor, edging their way to the right where the mini-stages were set. Sparsely occupied now, Alicia could see the sweat glistening on the silver poles, spattering the floor and a whole gallery of different brand bottles lying around—lipstick encrusted, peeled, some even broken with jagged edges sticking straight up.

Several men and women danced to their left, moving with more abandon now they had more room. The bar staff stood around looking bored. Only a bouncer, stationed close to the exit, saw them approach.

"We gotta get outta here," Alicia drawled, trying her best to appear nine-tenths drunk. "It's been a long night."

"You came out of the back room?" The man was broad chested, with heavily muscled arms. For now, he was ignoring his earpiece.

"Yeah, everyone had too many alcopops, mate."

"The Man usually calls to say you can go," the bouncer grunted. "Wait there."

Alicia's eyes flashed. "To say we can go? What the hell does that mean?"

The bouncer held up a finger, which drew Alicia like a moth to a flame. Flexing muscles, she was about to explain her physical point of view to the man when Mai put a hand on her shoulder.

She whispered, "Let's see what he says."

Alicia held back with an effort. The man soon finished and then unhooked a two-way radio from his belt. "Figures approaching outside," he said. "Not cops. Check it out."

Alicia wondered if it might be Drake and Luther, but didn't have time to think it through. The bouncer acknowledged them once again.

"You will have to stay inside," he said, offering no other explanation because, in this nightclub, he didn't have to.

Alicia knew they had to take their chances. "I don't think so, mate."

The bouncer frowned. "I said—"

"Go on," Alicia leaned into his personal space, "I dare you. Raise that finger one more time and see where it ends up."

Mai and Kenzie backed her, stepping to each side. This would be easy. The bouncer stared at all three of them and then beyond them, eyes widening.

Alicia sensed it was coming before she heard it.

Mattheus's voice: "Stop those bitches! Stop them now!"

Alicia kicked out, stunning the bouncer who folded quickly. Kenzie pushed him further to the floor. Alicia yanked the exit door open. Mai was right by her side.

A gunshot rang out and a bullet struck the frame above their heads.

"Do not move any further. Or at least one of you will die."

Alicia weighed the odds. She could make it; probably Mai too. But Kenzie was at the back and would get shot first.

This was no joke. Alicia halted and raised her hands, turning back to the dance floor. To her right Mai did the same. Kenzie was already facing Mattheus. Across the dance floor the black-haired man stood, face bruised where Mai had punched him and nose red with encrusted blood. By now, the remaining revelers had gotten the message too and were clustered around the outer walls, trying to appear as unobtrusive as possible. Alicia saw guards at every side and more emerging from the back, where Drake and Luther had relieved Mattheus of an entire safe.

The crime boss waved at them. "What has been going on in my club?"

"A burglary, boss," one said. "We have men searching for them now."

"What did they take?" Mattheus's voice rose an octave, making several guards flinch.

"The . . . safe," came the quiet answer.

Mattheus glared in disbelief at first, but then, quickly, his face grew intensely red. "You call that a burglary? My entire safe? Missing? You should shoot yourself quickly, idiot, and save me the trouble."

"See," Kenzie murmured. "Always kill the messenger."

Mattheus's head whipped toward them. He started walking, holding out a hand which was hastily filled with a small 9mm Beretta. "Her." He pointed at Mai. "I want her first. I want her to suffer."

The guards crowded forward, surrounding them as they drifted to the center of the dance floor with its still-flashing lights and music beat. As if by good fortune one of Alicia's favorite songs started playing, *I Like The Way*, by the Bodyrockers.

She caught the eyes of Mai and Kenzie. "Three minutes to the end," she said. "Let's make 'em count."

As the beat kicked in, Alicia smashed the nearest gun out of its holder's hands, sending it skidding across the floor. She grabbed another wrist and broke it, letting the gun fall. Mai and Kenzie pounced to either side, the Japanese woman leaping into Mattheus's arms as if he were a long-lost friend.

The movement certainly shocked him. At first, he linked his arms, grabbing her, then realized his error and tried to let her fall. The gun useless, Mai brought her forehead smashing down into his already broken nose.

The scream drowned out the Bodyrocker's chorus for just a few seconds. Alicia's lips moved as she sang along, using the throbbing rhythm of the song to guide her movements and fire her adrenalin. A shot was fired, the bullet passing between everyone. The bouncer at the door waded in, only to find himself dumped very quickly onto his face, now becoming the bowling ball in Alicia's strike at the oncoming guards. Several went sprawling over the rolling bulk. Bones broke. Those that remained standing aimed at the women and prepared to fire.

But Mai managed to shove Mattheus in the way. Terrified, the guards held off as their boss staggered between them. Mai was riding his back, careful not to let him fall since he was their only shield. Alicia spun in time to the musical pounding, tripping one guard, pocketing his weapon, then rising to punch directly under the chin of another. The disco beams flashed bright red, green and blue strobe lights flickering through the half-dark. Guards crawled around the filth-encrusted, sticky floor.

Mattheus bucked Mai again and again, finally managing to dislodge her by falling to his knees. Blood poured from his nose. He came around but Mai felled him once more, at the same time dealing with another guard. All of them were down now, or trying to stand. Alicia knew immediately that they couldn't hope to flatten them all, not simultaneously. There had to be another way.

Unfortunately, four were already on their feet. Two more were finding their guns and another was rising with a Glock to hand. Alicia heard the song coming to an end and saw her life about to expire with it. Mattheus was on his knees, a rictus of a grin stretched across his face as he saw most of his guards still in the fight.

"Revenge," he blurted. "I want—"

Alicia didn't hear the rest, launching herself headlong at three guards. Two staggered but the third remained upright, carefully focusing the short barrel of his gun upon her.

Ah, crap . . .

All hell erupted around her. Windows blew inward, shattering to fragments. Frames and even block work followed as one wall was battered. Revelers fell dead and wounded, bleeding on the floor. Alicia was struck by flying shards of brick, the lethal ragged edges drawing blood from her cheek. Kenzie was knocked to the ground, her head bloody as a brick-sized chunk struck her skull. It soon became clear that unceasing firepower was being used to gain entry to the nightclub.

Tempest, was Alicia's only thought. They arrived late but they arrived in force.

Hooking Kenzie underneath the armpits, she dragged the struggling Israeli along the debris-filled floor, pushing guards out of the way as she went. Two were dead, others injured. Mattheus was groaning, rolling in the scattered remains of his empire and his employees. The bar was being destroyed, glasses dancing and breaking, large capacity bottles of spirit exploding and pouring their contents out onto the floor.

Alicia crawled faster. Mai pushed Kenzie from behind, pressing her haunches hard to encourage her to go faster. Kenzie groaned and tried to keep her head still as her body slithered under no volition of its own.

They snaked and scrambled their way past the bar and through the door marked *Private* that led to Mattheus's back rooms, aware of a brand new exit. Alicia saw rooms to left and right, dens where drugs were prepped and money laundered. Where porn was distributed and computers hacked. She took the opportunity to scream at all the occupants, sending them into panic and hoping they would never return.

Behind them the nightclub took more heavy fire; the lights crashed to the floor and the music finally died. Men with machine guns jumped through the new entrances and fought with the remaining guards and Mattheus.

Mai threw the glass, still in its protective wrapping, to Alicia. "I'll block the way."

"Dammit, Sprite, it's bloody broke."

"Well, you try riding bareback on the shoulders of a Greek crime boss whilst trying to bludgeon him to death. See if you can keep your tumbler intact."

Alicia lifted Kenzie and soldiered on, knowing they still had Mattheus's fingerprint even if the glass was broken. Mai dragged desks and dumped computers in their path and then set it all alight.

"Go, go, go," she said, following them out into the dark alleyway where Drake and Luther had worked earlier.

"Which way?" Alicia asked.

"Into the dark," Mai said. "You should know that by now."

CHAPTER TWENTY SIX

As dawn rose, the team regrouped atop a small hill overlooking a vehicle scrapyard. The van stood hidden beneath overhanging trees, its front end concealed beneath brush and branches that Drake and Luther collected. Through phone calls they had directed the women to them and waited until the team was reunited before allowing themselves a single moment of respite.

Drake nodded as Alicia walked up to him. "Looking good."

"Bollocks." Alicia punched his arm and wiped her face. "I look like I barely survived a terrorist attack, which is what we did."

"Yeah," Mai said, a step behind. "But it is better than your normal look."

"Where's the safe?" Kenzie asked, sporting a new bandage across her scalp. "And for that matter—where's the van?"

"Close," Luther grumbled, watching Mai. "Is everyone okay?"

"I am." Mai smiled. "But it was close. We were running on good luck there for a while."

Kenzie glared around. "Oh, I'm fine thanks."

"Good." Drake led the way back to the van, confident they were alone as a golden glow of sunlight spread across the eastern horizon. They could easily see the single road twisting away for miles in both directions and had a good view across the fields. The scrapyard below wasn't open for business yet. Thessaloniki itself lay three miles away and out of sight.

Drake ducked under the tree cover and slid back the van door with a loud crunch. "Let's see what we've got. Do you have Mattheus's prints?"

Alicia handed over the broken glass. "Mai broke it, not me."

Luther intervened. "I have a few shaped charges left if the glass won't work."

"This requires finesse, Luther, not brute force."

The bald man looked disgruntled.

Drake, with Luther's and Mai's help, finally managed to get the safe open by using a large piece of broken glass with Mattheus's unblemished fingerprint. The iron door swung wide to reveal its dark innards.

Drake peered inside, holding a flashlight due to the darkness of the van's interior under the overhanging trees. Three shelves held various useful items including weapons and ammo, an assortment of expensive chocolates, jewelry and two laptops. The shelves were high up and bunched together because the entire lower area was taken up by the Waters of Neptune.

It was a beautiful artifact, about three feet high and, as they had come to expect by now, entirely black. Neptune sat at the crest of a wave, holding her trident in her left hand, with sculpted waves lapping over her feet. The base was a flat piece with an undulating surface, fashioned to look like a rolling sea.

"A weapon?" Luther asked. "I don't see how."

"It'd hurt if it bonked you over the head," Alicia pointed out. "Maybe this one's just an artifact."

"Or," Drake said, seeing something for the first time, "could it be the substance these relics are made out of? Or the rare element inside?"

Luther nodded, handling the Neptune object with care. The three-foot-high piece looked quite small in his hands.

"Let's pack it away." Drake pulled away. "Along with whatever else we can use at Mattheus's expense. We won this round but Tempest are getting pretty damn close."

He walked back to the knoll of the hill and sat down among the overgrown stems of grass. Alicia came to sit by him and Mai stayed with Luther. Kenzie went to find some water to cleanse her wound. The land all around was silent and still, except for the pleasant breeze in the air. Drake took a moment to be with Alicia with no outside interference to pressurize them.

"Hanging in there, love?"

"Considering the circumstances, I'm hanging in there quite well."

Drake remembered vividly the moment she'd decided to stop running. "Understood. We're running again, I know, but not for long."

"Can you really believe that?"

He had to. "It keeps me alive, sane and hopeful. Memories can't be changed, but the future is ours to shape."

"I think we need a rest."

Drake studied her, wondering if she meant right now or in their near future. He thought about all they had accomplished and couldn't see any obstacles to a vacation.

Apart from Tempest.

"Once this mission is done," he said. "And successful. Once we're legit again, not being hunted, there are no unresolved issues. No unsettled debts. We can kick back, if you like."

"Didn't we try that once before? I forget."

"You know what I mean. Beat Tempest and then we're clear. What else could possibly happen?"

"Don't say that!"

"I know, I know, but it's not like the worst, most vengeful enemy of our careers is just around the corner, is it?"

"Kovalenko is dead."

"The Blood King? Yeah, I know, I was there. What I mean is—there are other teams capable of doing what we do. We have no personal investment and I'm pretty sure nobody can say we didn't do our bit."

"I don't want anyone else to die," Alicia said quietly.

Drake saw the hard veneer temporarily lifted and placed an arm around her shoulders. "Me too."

"Even Mai," Alicia added gruffly.

"Oh, I know. And Kenzie?"

"Maybe a little wounding. Nothing too bad."

"Time to heal, then?" Drake picked up her earlier thread of taking a break.

"Time to live," Alicia shrugged, "a different life."

"You know?" Drake scrunched his eyes up as the sun rose higher. "To do that—we'd have to leave the . . . team."

He had almost said the word "family," but changed his mind at the last moment.

"Shit." Alicia playfully slapped the hard ground. "They'd all bloody die without us."

"When this is done," Drake said. "Nothing else will be coming for us."

Alicia looked at him for a long time, and he thought he saw a question in her eyes. They both felt it—the hollow ring to his words—but only in their bones.

"You think something's coming?" Drake asked. "Something from the past, don't you?"

Alicia looked away. "I have a feeling, but it's probably nothing, just my anxiety talking. Being on the run and then tracked by a Special Forces team doesn't help."

Drake nodded, joining her in silence, unable to shake the exact same feeling. Even if they did manage to destroy Tempest, was the worst still to come?

Mai sat apart, studying the fields and ensuring she was weapons-ready. She'd heard Luther make the call to Cambridge and knew they were waiting to learn the location for the artifact's hand-off point. She sat for a while, eyes closed after she'd finished her work, letting the sun warm the left side of her face. It was easy out here, simple. Part of her wanted that minimalism and a way out of the world she had inhabited for as long as she could remember. The real enemies were all gone. Her parents safe and living a clean life. Her sister with Dai over in Tokyo, the two of them as safe as anyone could be, moving toward a promising future. The dead still haunted her though as, she assumed, they did everyone that had lost a parent, to someone that had killed a mortal enemy.

Beyond Drake though, she'd never come close to finding a real, solid partner. The knowledge weighed heavily on her. Their split didn't worry her—she had only been doing what she needed to do at the time. So, the whole Drake and Alicia thing was immaterial. It had happened—move on.

Tears sprang into her eyes, not for all the men and women she'd killed but for those that didn't deserve it, and those she'd cared for. The thing is—life didn't care whether she enjoyed it or not. It was up to her to make the good times, and make them memorable.

As thoughts of Grace flowed around a happier outlook she felt the presence of someone beside her. She looked up, knowing already that the shadow would be huge.

"Mind if I sit?"

She nodded, and the enormous soldier sat himself down. They didn't speak for a minute, gauging each other's mood, but then Luther offered a thoughtful subject.

"This team," he said. "I'm still trying to get my head around it. Some of you are friends, some are enemies, but then you'd die for each other. And has everyone slept with everyone else? 'Cause that's just bizarre."

Mai laughed. "This isn't an American sitcom, Luther. We've been together a long time, been to hell and back. This team was forged in fire, literally in the tomb of a god. We're enemies and friends, united and conflicted at times. We are a family, however that sounds. You live and breathe and fight with someone long enough—" she paused "—you form the greatest bond."

Luther shifted. "I get that. I'm a soldier. I can't forget some of the things I've seen but I can use my better memories to overcome them. War will never end, but as soldiers we can make all the innocent lives we touch a little better."

"And how about other lives?" Mai asked impulsively. "Can you make those better too?"

Luther looked anywhere but at her. "I can try."

Mai reached out a hand. "Then . . . try."

"Soldiers, eh?" Luther let out a noise that was half grumble, half laugh. "When it comes to personal, we don't have a clue."

"Depends what you start with." Mai smiled again. "Let me know."

And for the first time since she'd met him, Luther looked unsure.

A number of phone calls later, Drake announced there were two choppers inbound. One, to collect the Waters of Neptune; the other—Hayden's recently arrived team who were flying out to them. Within half an hour the artifact was winging its way covertly to London and the entire SPEAR team was reunited. Drake tried hard not to appear overly happy to see Dahl, but when the Swede grabbed him in a bear hug he held on tight.

"Well met," he said, meaning it.

"And you, my friend. We have a lot to catch up on."

So, they sat like carefree companions as the sun soared higher, and each told their stories. Kinimaka had brought a bagful of food and bottled water, and shared them out equally. Hayden related their train exploit and Dahl threw in the garnish. Five weapons collected so far and they were still behind Tempest. Kinimaka spoke of the new list of weapons and how the Gates of Ishtar were claimed to be "practically unobtainable." They wondered aloud where Tempest were at and how many weapons they might have seized.

"We're of the mind that it's the weapons' material Tempest want," Mai said. "Or the element within."

"Makes sense," Hayden agreed. "Why the hell didn't I think of that? Anyway, Lauren and Secretary Crowe are doing their best in DC. Crowe helped get us out of the country."

"Any news on the other disavowed Special Forces teams?" Drake asked.

"Not yet. Clearly, they don't know who to trust."

"If we could find a way . . ." Drake let the rest of the sentence hang, thinking hard.

"Whitehall could do it," Dahl said. "Think it through. They're connected everywhere, even helping us all over the world at the same time as storing the weapons and preserving our cover. Give them the job."

"To say what exactly?" Alicia played devil's advocate. "'How about a play date?'"

Drake tended to agree. "She's right, in her idiosyncratic way," he said. "First, we need to come up with a strategy. But first, let's give Whitehall the heads up."

"We learned a little more about the terrorist training camps that Tempest is creating," Hayden said. "They're run by mercs, hand-picked, and are basically a double-bluff. Recruits are fed the usual beginner shit, half-brainwashed, and introduced to several 'father' figures, who will be their handlers. They're then put to use, around the world, doing Tempest's dirty work. Stealing. Killing. Covering missions up beneath the general veneer of terrorism. With every passing day, they become stronger."

When Dahl saw Kenzie again he smiled tentatively, unsure how to greet the woman he'd hurt. She'd wanted more than he could give; but she knew that. She'd known Dahl was married with children. And still she kept coming.

I did the right thing.

So why did it feel so wrong?

Their relationship had soured badly and even now, he wasn't sure why Kenzie remained with the group. Privately, he thought it was for just one reason—a reason she'd never, ever reveal.

Kenzie wanted to belong to something good, doing something good, with the right people.

Dahl felt the same, and wanted her to stay. But he couldn't see how she could get past the problems she'd wrought between them. Whilst it was true they'd had barely a moment to speak since their own clash—where Dahl told her he would keep fighting to stay with his wife—nothing had really changed. She still resented him.

Now, as the group made their decisions, he became aware that she was sat behind him. It was a perfect sunny day with no pressure. Who could stay angry on a day like this?

"How are you?" He turned slightly.

Kenzie stiffened but said nothing.

"That bad, huh?"

"What's the point of answering?" she bit back quietly. "As if you really care."

"I care," he said truthfully. "Just not like you want me to."

"Oh, don't flatter yourself. That ship already sailed. You're just another grunt to me now."

"Is that what we all are?" Dahl asked.

"Pretty much."

"Then why do you stay?" He hadn't meant to force it, to push the sensitive part too much, but Kenzie seemed to have a knack for pushing all the wrong buttons.

"Y'know, I'm wondering the same thing."

Kenzie walked away and leaned up against the quietly ticking chopper. Dahl saw a single chance then, an opportunity to walk up to her and try to make it better. It would take truth, honesty. It would take a huge effort.

But all too suddenly, it was time to go.

When Drake rose, Yorgi was suddenly by his side. The young Russian's fists were clenched into tight balls and his lips were white with worry. It appeared that Yorgi had something to say and Drake had a very good idea what it would be.

"When you told us what happened to your family, why you killed your parents, I wondered if that would change you."

Yorgi looked grateful for the easy opening. "It is not a change," he said, the stress thickening his Russian accent. "But it has strengthened my resolve. You know what I must do, don't you?"

Drake nodded quickly. "I saw it in your eyes, mate, even as you told the story. It's not over, is it?"

"No. It is not."

They walked together toward the waiting chopper, taking their time. Alicia stayed to Yorgi's left, listening intently.

"I have to return to the graves of my kin," Yorgi said with quiet passion. "I cannot just leave them out there, unmarked, lost in that icy wilderness forever."

"You don't have to go alone, mate," Drake said. "We'll go with you."

"No," Yorgi said. "This is for me. I did not come to this decision lightly, either. I told my story—it seems months ago now—and I have struggled ever since. Now I know I must go back."

"With us." Alicia pressed her words upon him. "Together. We're a family, Yogi. You know that."

The Russian smiled at the perennial nickname. "At least you have stopped calling me a girl."

"Well, only for today."

"Then, that is better. I will return to Russia tonight. I have to go."

Drake fought all the protestations, all the offers of companionship. Sometimes, a person had to do something by themselves. It was the only way to overcome the old demons.

"Just keep in touch," he said softly.

"And never forget we're here for you," Alicia added.

Yorgi turned away from them, tears in his eyes. "I never will," he said. "For as long as I live."

CHAPTER TWENTY SEVEN

Karin Blake almost instantly regretted her decision to infiltrate FrameHub.

They were a small bunch of supergeeks that had managed to take control of three countries' weapons systems, making two of those countries fire upon each other. They were lethal, super-intelligent and wholly uncool. Self-proclaimed gods, they were connected through a computer to everything that held a microprocessor, and some things that didn't. They used ridiculous code words for names and held the belief that knowledge was power—so they intended to gain infinite knowledge. Currently, they comprised of eight members and wanted Karin for their ninth.

Based on her old reputation.

Karin was a soldier now, a newly trained deserter to be precise, and she'd brought her two almost identical colleagues along—Dino and Wu.

All well-trained and eager to fight, they went to Egypt with one agenda and came away with another. This confused Dino and Wu, but it was Karin's party. Always would be. They respected and looked up to her.

Their lives, under her leadership, looked good, hungry and full of potential.

They had no idea what was coming.

For now, Karin had said goodbye to Drake and the team after the Great Pyramid battle, tucked her main agenda away for a later date, and turned to rooting out the terrible, destructive organization that was FrameHub before it caused death and agony to any more innocent lives.

She returned their invitation email, hinting that she might be interested in talking. She returned another, then jumped through some hoops proving she could crack an easy code—for her—over the Internet.

This allowed her into a secret web-room.

There was more progress, by the day and then by the hour. They really wanted her. Dino and Wu got bored very quickly, unused to sitting around with no clear plan in sight.

"I have to get inside first," Karin told them constantly. "That's how this works."

"They're geeks, Blake," Dino reminded her. "Let's just take 'em out."

"Now that'd look very embarrassing, Dino," she said. "When they take you out. You don't get it. They're into everything. The best thing you can do is to not figure on their radar."

Dino laughed. "What are they gonna do? Fry me with a cash machine?"

"How about hijacking a self-drive car to run you down? Using stop lights to make a van swerve into your path? Something easier—like using one of the army of mercs they employ?"

Dino jumped on that. "So you're walking into a joint guarded by a merc army? No way."

"No, no." Karin fought to remain calm. "It's not like that. FrameHub work out of a bloody basement. They trust nobody, not even their own mothers. They have only themselves. They're millionaires with no interest in cash. Entrepreneurs without vision. Travelers without the merest ounce of wanderlust. They live, breathe and eat computer data and find it hard to venture up—up into the real world. Only I can get close to them because I . . . I used to live in that world."

Dino didn't look impressed. "You? A fucking geek?"

"Yep."

"What happened?"

"Life happened, you asshole. Shit happened. And don't judge. Everyone needs to find a way to deal with their issues. Some are different to others, that's all. But FrameHub, they took it way too far."

"All right. You go first. We mop up. That's all you had to say." Wu was always to the point.

Karin tuned them out and thought back to the days when she lived with and loved her mainframe, when the lights flashed only to the transfer of data, and the whirring hum of a working computer in mid-hack was the sweetest sound in the world.

Be the old Karin, not the new Karin.

Time to go retro.

And now, seated in a big basement that stank of stale sweat, hot electricity and candy, she reflected on everything that had happened during the last few days.

First, they met in a busy coffee shop in the middle of town. She sat, sipping a vanilla latte, for thirty minutes after the agreed time, assuming they were verifying her identity before approaching her.

Then, one man—a young, spiky-haired individual with bad skin and a nervous disposition—approached her.

"I am FrameHub," he said.

"You are FrameHub?" she asked. "I thought there were eight of you."

"We are FrameHub. I am FrameHub." He shrugged. "It's what we say. You are Karin Blake."

"Well, you got that part right at least."

He blinked and stepped back. Quickly she reminded herself: *Be the old Karin.*

"You guys are badass!" she said too loudly. "Supercool, even."

"Do you really think so?" He was peering at her now as if he'd never seen a girl.

"What happens next?" she said to deflect the creepiness. "I can't wait to meet all you guys."

"Are you British, or American?"

"Once from the UK, but I've worked in America for years."

"Right. You're accent's weird."

Like your fucking face, freak! "Oh, right." She managed something close to a giggle. "Cool."

"How old are you?"

"Don't' ya know that already?"

"Yeah, yeah, but you look older."

Something to do with life and love and loss, she thought.

"Tough paper round," she said.

The geek laughed so suddenly and at such a shrill pitch that she jumped and the barista looked over. Karin found it prudent to stick her face in her latte cup and take several swigs.

"We should go," the geek said, looking around. "By the way—I'm Piranha."

Karin kept a straight face. "Nice."

I should win a bloody Oscar for that performance.

But it turned out to be the first of many performances she would have to enact. Old Karin was long gone, but New Karin was forced to locate that echoing, lost voice and use it to move forward. Karin hated it. The good news was—it wouldn't be for long.

Piranha led her to a waiting car. Karin almost pronounced her shock that "FrameHub" could drive, but then found a paper bag being shoved over her head and was forced to clam up, for fear of blowing her cover in a fit of anger.

Forced down in the passenger seat, with Piranha at the wheel, she was driven for approximately forty minutes. This wasn't a large town, so Karin assumed it was to the outskirts, an industrial area perhaps. The sun was largely to her left, so most of the route was north. Once, a whistle hooted and another time a few minutes before they stopped she felt the change in the road as they went over a bridge.

I could find this again. Probably . . .

No matter. The tracker in her shoe would enable Dino and Wu to follow with ease. The problem she faced was disposing of it before they entered HQ. A darkness came over the car and then Piranha brought it to a halt.

"Wait there," he said. "I'll come around and get you."

Scrabbling hard, bending back several nails, she managed to rip the tracker out of her shoe and cup it in her left hand. When Piranha pulled her out of the car she was able to drop it behind her, underneath the chassis. A moment later, Piranha pulled back the paper bag.

"You're incredibly fortunate," he said. "Only eight others have ever see the lair of FrameHub."

Again, her face twitched, but she somehow managed to stare around in awe. The trick was to remember that these hopeless, antisocial nerds were incredibly dangerous and didn't care who they maimed or killed.

That was the trick.

Piranha led her out of an underground car park, through a door marked *Staff Only,* and then down an echoing, concrete stairwell, cold because it led underground. She shivered. Piranha looked up at her.

"Don't worry. The basement's hot as fuck because of all the equipment. It's shielded down here too. Tons and tons of concrete and metal between us and the shitbricks up there."

Karin struggled with that. "Shitbricks?"

"People."

"Ahh, I see now."

The staircase wound for a while. Rubbish and other debris had drifted down here from upstairs and sat in decaying piles. It became dark enough that Piranha had to produce a flashlight. Gang graffiti covered the walls, but was clearly old and flaking away. Many layers of dust covered the floor, marred only by their own footprints.

Piranha forced open another door, the metal creaking against protesting hinges. A square-shaped room lay on the other side, empty, and they crossed to one more door. This one looked to be in the same disrepair as the rest of the place, but Karin spied two well-hidden cameras. From a hidden panel in the wall, Piranha produced a small keypad.

"Our lair," he said grandly.

Killers, Karin thought.

And on the other side, it was exactly as she'd imagined. As she remembered, to be fair, having once been a part of the hacker underground. A big, oblong-shaped room with several alcoves at the far end. A series of desks set out in one long row with banks of computer screens on top. Wires everywhere, snaking beneath the desks and across the floor, ending up in a series of electrical outlets, such a chaos of cables they would never be able to sort it out. Two rows of strip lights hung from the roof, illuminating the place and, set against the wall opposite the computer terminals were more tables full of laptops, three enormous refrigerators, microwaves and a drinks' mixing station.

Everything a crazy, power-hungry geek could ask for.

The first thing she thought to ask was, "Where do you sleep?"

"Back there." Piranha pointed toward the alcoves. "FrameHub never stops. It's twenty-four-seven, so we take shifts, but share the cots back there."

Un-fucking-likely.

Seven faces studied her, eyes wide. She thought about pointing out that FrameHub were not then in fact currently functioning twenty-four-seven, but flashed an open, nerdy smile instead.

"Hi, everyone!" She waved.

Most of them turned away quickly but one, with a little more presence, came over and introduced himself.

"Hey, I'm Barracuda."

"Karin." She nodded. "Karin Blake."

"We should find you a proper name," Barracuda said. "A real one. Think on it."

"I will."

"Anyway, we have to vet you first. Make sure you're acceptable to FrameHub."

Karin sensed trouble as all work came to a standstill once more and every face turned toward her. "And what does that entail?"

"Remove your clothes."

She choked. "I'll remove my clothes right after I remove your face, asshole."

"We have to make sure you're not wired," Barracuda protested.

"So . . . wand me."

Now Barracuda looked decidedly embarrassed. "We don't have one, sorry."

"You're kidding?" Karin looked around the place. "The mighty FrameHub, feared by nations, don't even have a wand? Look here, mate, if I were military or a cop do you think they wouldn't have descended on you by now? It's not like I would need a confession." She gestured at the row of computers.

"Yeah, yeah." Barracuda admitted defeat with a modicum of grace. "It was worth a try."

Karin fought yet again to keep a straight face, but this time it was fury threatening to take hold, not mirth.

"Why don't you show me what you do down here?"

I won't be able to keep my hands from their pimply throats for long.

But she had to be sure they weren't in the middle of something dreadful.

"First," Barracuda led her to a brand-new computer, "you gotta prove yourself, and this is no joke. Turn this on and crack Morgan Sachs. You've got ten minutes."

Karin sat down. "Ten minutes? Not Langley? Not the NSA?"

"We figure you would already have backdoors or worms planted there. I'd give you three minutes tops with government shit. Morgan Sachs is strong, but child's play if you have the right skills. We have the right skills. Do you?"

Karin spent the next four minutes cracking the Wall Street bank, then sat back. "Are we cool now?"

"Wait." An overweight geek reached across her, assaulting her senses with armpit stink. "We can augment our reserves with a bit of that." He glided over hundreds of accounts, skimming small amounts right off the top.

"Subtle," Karin said.

"Most people don't check their statements," Barracuda said. "And many of those that do only look for the larger amounts. Sachs might flag it, but they won't find us."

Karin spent some time wandering the desks, pretending to be impressed at most of the illegal misdeeds being perpetrated there. Some were reprehensible; FrameHub preying on everyday people just for fun, destroying lives at a whim. It reminded her of Tyler Webb and the atrocities he had committed, so it wasn't a surprise when they asked her about him.

"We know you found his trove of secrets," Barracuda said. "So, share."

Karin sought to cement her standing and presence among them by making them wait. She walked over to the refrigerator and used their personal goods to make herself a coffee and a slice of toast. Then, she wandered back over to them, hooking out a chair from behind a desk and sitting down.

"You want to hear about Webb's secrets? Listen up."

An hour later she stopped, sat back.

"Wow," Piranha said. "But we already knew about Tempest. We're not interested in them."

Karin feigned shock. "You know Tempest? How?"

"Because we have a plan of our own." Piranha could contain it no longer. "We're gonna take down America."

The nervous excitement in the room was tangible, electric.

Karin knew right then that she had to discover what they were up to before taking them out. And that meant staying with them.

Damn it.

CHAPTER TWENTY EIGHT

She drew out the remainder of the day, avoiding "beer o'clock" with the nerds and finding several opportunities to siphon off information. They rarely left the lair. They had more than one plot ongoing, but nothing as big as the one they called America. She spent the night with one eye open, lying uncomfortably on a cot and trying to avoid any contact with the sheets. Two others snoozed in nearby alcoves, snoring and talking in their sleep, restless.

The next morning, she roved the basement, storing every scrap of information related to the place, everything from external data storage boxes to plug points. Questions such as: "Do we have weapons?", "Do we have an escape route?", and "Do we have protection?" were asked and answered quickly. Piranha, Manta and Moray showed her what evils they were up to in their spare time and it was all she could do not to tear their heads off right there and then.

Ruining lives via social media, through doctored emails, messages and photoshopped prints. They lived for it, and utilized a points-scoring system to see who wrought the most damage. Their laughter grated on her nerves.

Again, she was called upon to implement a mini-crisis, but fortunately it was nothing that totally affronted her morals and she managed to live with it. Later that morning, after their ten o'clock chocolate break, Barracuda called for everyone to listen up.

"Time to move ahead with the prison break," he said with an excited lilt to his voice. "Initiate step two!"

Some clapped, some hooted, but one—a kid called Pacu—shouted up: "In front of the bitch? You sure, man?"

New Karin wanted to shove the kid headfirst through his own computer screen, and she would have done it—but Old Karin put the op first.

"I've done everything you asked."

Pacu grunted. "Too early, Piranha."

"I'm right here," Karin said. "Not going anywhere. Why not use me?"

"We'll just keep her here until the mission succeeds," another one spoke up. This one's name was Goonch, Karin recalled. "No risk. Then, we know she's one of us."

Barracuda watched her. "You okay with that?"

Karin nodded but then raised her hand. "I'm cool, but we have to get one thing straight."

Eight faces stared.

"The next one that calls me a bitch will get Error 404'd."

The room broke out into laughter at the little nerd joke. Error 404 was usually followed by the words: Not Found. Even Pacu grinned.

"All right, then," Barracuda said. "We're going all in with this one. Opening every supermax facility in the United States simultaneously. Cells, inner doors, outer doors. And we're gonna keep them open. It'll be a total fucking blast!" He cheered.

Karin coerced another smile to appear. "Will you have eyes on that?"

"Shit, of course we will. That's the whole point. Some of these supermaxes are way out in the sticks, sure, but the prisoners will get to the closest town at some point."

"Cool. Where are you so far?"

Barracuda held up a hand. "Soon," he said. "First, we have to initiate Stage Two. The grunt work's already done. Coding, programming, all that cool stuff. But we still need to install it discreetly on their systems. You can help with that, Karin. Shit, what are we gonna call you?"

"Praying Mantis," Goonch suggested.

"That's not a vicious fish, dickhead."

"I know, but it's cool and kinda describes her, don't you think?"

"Too much of a mouthful. How about Payara—the vampire fish?"

"It'll do," Karin said. "How can I help?"

"Like this," Barracuda led her to a terminal. "First we need to embed the code and then implant a common trigger to start it all."

"I can do that. What date did you have in mind?"

"There's nothing in mind," Barracuda said softly. "It's happening in two days."

CHAPTER TWENTY NINE

"Egypt again?" Drake complained. "Shit."

A subdued team flew under the radar in an unmarked chopper, entering Egyptian airspace with the help of Cambridge and an agreeable airfield controller by the light of the half-moon. What made him agreeable, Drake could only guess, but he assumed it came with a picture of Benjamin Franklin on the back.

Without Yorgi, and with Kenzie's support at an all-time low, Drake felt as if he was nursing wounds that he didn't even have. Not yet anyway. He consoled himself with the knowledge that they would see Yorgi again.

Soon.

Hayden regaled them with more than one tale. "The Flail of Anubis is next," she said. "Our sixth weapon, hopefully. This one also comes with a thorny provenance. The government themselves seized it from the den of a relic crook, and then proceeded to store it away in a vault."

Dahl shifted his bulk, squeaking across the hard seat in the big chopper. "If we catch any more of these dinosaurs," he said. "I'm thinking of bringing my own pillow cushion."

Drake groaned. "You choose now to reveal that nugget? Now, when I'm too depressed to fully capitalize on it?"

"Yeah." Alicia nodded gloomily. "Yeah."

"I thought it might cheer you up."

"Nah." Drake sighed. "Feels like I lost a friend."

"Feels like I lost a cuddly toy," Alicia admitted. "Poor ole Yogi."

"He's not dead," Hayden growled. "Get a grip. We'll be seeing him again soon. Now listen—they locked the Flail of Anubis away until the world at large figured out what these weapons could do. They waited. Nothing happened. The tombs were destroyed and the flail was largely forgotten about. It's still there, inside the vault, but we have a couple of major problems."

"Shocker," Drake intoned. "Lay 'em out."

Hayden rolled her eyes. "Egypt is still reeling from the attack that FrameHub instigated—the rockets hitting Cairo. The city and its people haven't recovered, the government are slow to help. The press only fuel the fire, as per usual, to sell copy. The good news is that the vault isn't in Cairo, it's in Alexandria."

She paused, attracting everyone's attention.

"And the bad news?" Luther asked.

"It's stored inside a bank vault—"

"Not bad," Molokai cut in. "You just have to use the right amount of dynamite."

Hayden tried to finish: "Which is positioned across the road from a terrifying situation currently unfolding in the heart of Alexandria," she continued. "Terrorists are holding hostages captive right across the street."

Drake sat up. "Terrorists?"

"Yeah, my thought too. What kind of terrorists, right? Well, they're Tempest's kind. I'm thinking the entire hostage crisis is a ruse. A deception."

"The terrorists make noise over the road whilst Tempest's mercs steal the flail?" Luther said. "I guess that makes sense."

"Full military presence though," Kinimaka added. "Snipers on roofs. MRAP vehicles on the streets. Seems like they're prepared for a war."

"They're taking no chances after Cairo," Smyth said. "And I don't blame them."

"How far into the crisis are we?" Mai asked.

"Good question. Only an hour. One hostage dead unfortunately, but they're talking."

"Stalling," Alicia said.

"Agreed. The area has been evacuated and roped off, but there's still plenty of ways to approach."

"How long do we have?" Dahl asked.

Hayden indicated the creaking fuselage of the chopper. "We're already there. We're landing."

*

The chopper put them down in Alexandria, three miles from the hot zone. They wore big coats over their gear and moved carefully, speeding up only when the roads and streets were clear. They split into three groups, opposite sides of the road and a minute apart. They checked the new comms set up. All was well. Drake moved briskly with Alicia and Mai, Dahl a step behind, all sweating profusely. It felt normal, it felt competent, but it also felt threatening.

As if a creeping shadow of foreboding lay over them. Drake was not one for premonitions, but couldn't shake the feeling that something was coming. Why? Because, finally, after all this endless struggle, the closing stages were in sight. Yorgi was gone. Kenzie was leaving. Mai fancied a bit of Luther. The tables were tipping, times changing. Nothing would ever be the same again.

But not for now.

Together, they moved closer to the bank and the hotel across the street where the hostage situation was unfolding. Cambridge was relating information down the comms line but, strictly speaking, Whitehall's influence in Egypt was unremarkable, forcing them to read between the lines.

Molokai and Luther broke into the back entrance of a ladies' fashion store. Hayden led the way through the storage room into the retail space, ducking behind a big metal arm full of clothing so as not to be seen through the front windows.

Drake crawled among the clothes and peered through.

A wide road and sidewalks separated them from the poorly maintained frontage of a street hotel, signs unpainted for years and windows unwashed. The front door was closed. Police cars lined up outside as if waiting at a drive-thru, but their occupants were crouched behind wheels and doors, guns drawn and waiting. Two large vans could also be seen—Drake guessed at least one of them was a communications vehicle, the other probably concealing a strike squad. The entire area was lit not only by streetlamps but by portable floodlights, giving it a stark, ghostly feel. Drake saw no movement at the hotel's windows.

"Still negotiating," Hayden reported.

"The only question," Luther said. "Is will they kill the hostages to cover up Tempest's attack on the safe, or to cover up their escape?"

"Both," Mai suggested. "They have eight hostages."

"But Egyptian SWAT will go in at the first loss of life," Molokai said. "They have to."

"Maybe we can diffuse it all," Kenzie spoke up, "by finding the flail first."

"Listen," Hayden said bluntly. "What is happening to the hostages is not something we can influence. Or change. And you can bet your butt that no Egyptian SWAT team is gonna accept our help. So, it's on with the op, no questions."

"I've bet my butt a few times," Alicia said wistfully. "Always lost." She looked around. "Maybe I wanted to."

Drake removed the hem of an electric-blue skirt from his shoulders. "Thanks for sharing," he said. "The bank's on this side then?"

"Next door," Hayden said. "The vault is one floor down. Are you ready?"

Kinimaka struck and then caught an entire arm of clothing one second before it fell to the floor. "Wait. What if they're already inside?"

Molokai grunted. Luther explained. "We want them to be inside, Waikiki. We ain't got any other way of getting in without making the noise of a thunder god."

"Waikiki?" Kinimaka frowned. "I'm from the North Shore."

"Even better." Luther crawled out of the racks of clothing. "Follow me, North Shore. Strictly speaking, my own tendency would be to come at this big, blast this mother out of the water, but I fear for those hostages. Let's not make it worse."

Drake was surprised at the big warrior's low-key thinking. "Lead the way."

Dahl appeared alongside him, wearing the electric-blue skirt like a headdress. "We following the god of blood and war now?"

"Sorry, mate, I can't talk to you looking like that."

"Like what?" Dahl was unaware of the accoutrement.

"Like a pretty Disney princess." Alicia pulled the material tight around his ears and blew a kiss. "Princess Torsty."

"Fuck off."

"That's more like it. C'mon."

Retracing their steps, they approached the bank's rear entrance. Molokai reached it first and held up a closed fist. Drake joined him at the front. The sides of the bank jutted out from the main façade, forming a pillar from behind which they could peer. The bank's rear doors had been breached but no alarms were ringing. A guard lay dead on the floor, just inside, surrounded by a pool of blood. Somehow, they had made him open the door.

Drake knew there were hundreds of ways to coerce a guard—from threatening to kill a passerby to abducting a family member. No scenario was out of the question for Tempest. The inside of the bank was well-lit, seemingly empty apart from the dead guard lying behind his desk, and open-plan all the way to the front.

"It's tricky," he said. "We'll have to be careful the street cops don't spot us."

They established the location of the vault and its access stairs through Cambridge and then made ready.

"If they're already down there it's gonna get noisy," Alicia said.

"Then bring your ear muffs, honey," Hayden said, breathing hard. "'Cause Alexandria's about to get real loud."

CHAPTER THIRTY

Hayden wasn't wrong.

Chaos and bedlam fell upon them, almost as if Luther himself was a jinx, attracting a turmoil of death and destruction. Drake pushed open the rear doors and then Cambridge was shouting in their earpieces, warning them that Whitehall had intercepted a communication from the bank with the message: Engage.

The noise began. Drake heard and saw what happened next as an elongated moment in time, a slideshow of dreadful events. First, the terrorists struck hard. Windows across the entire second floor of the hotel burst out amid flames and a roar of detonation. The cops outside ducked, yelled and the vehicles rocked as glass and debris shattered down among them. A second explosion soon followed.

At the same time there came a muffled whump from directly below. The mercs were blowing the safe.

And then, as the SPEAR team crowded past him, the bank's highly polished, white-marble floor partially collapsed right in front of them. Cracks appeared at first and then a rough hole the size of a Smart car just fell away.

"What the—" Alicia approached it.

Drake went with her, equally perplexed. They waited a moment, staying low so that even their silhouettes wouldn't be seen from the outside. Kenzie had a genius moment and switched the interior lights off at the precise moment of the second explosion.

"I think they cocked up down there," Alicia whispered.

Drake peered into the hole very carefully, allowing his eyes to take in the scene half a meter at a time. A wall had been blasted apart, its edges now standing ragged and damaged. Within that wall stood a wide door with a gray wheel at the center, the entrance to the vault. The door was unmarred.

"They totally screwed the pooch," Alicia said. "Backward, forward, and upside down. Shit."

Two mercs lay dead on the floor, another wounded. Four more

stood around scratching their heads. Drake heard noise from outside the bank and saw the Egyptian strike force jumping out of the van and storming the front of the hotel. Cops drew beads on the windows with their guns. Fires raged. The street was a wreckage-strewn battleground.

"I hate that we can't help," Dahl said.

"That's what we're trying to change," Hayden answered, looking down. "Are they trying again?"

Drake saw that they were. "We should retreat," he said. "Fast."

Seconds later a lesser explosion could be heard across the road just as a slight blast came from below. Drake covered his ears, being close, and prayed that the entire floor wouldn't collapse. By the time he looked up a chorus of cheering started to ring out from below.

Second time lucky.

Maybe not.

He sprang forward, gun up, the rest of the team at his side. They reached the hole seconds later, just in time to see the four men below pulling open the vault door. One slipped inside whilst the others stood guard near the descending staircase.

Drake looked from the staircase to the hole. Dahl crawled up beside him. "Whaddya think, Yorkshire Terrier?"

"I think we should throw you over first, then use your belly as a soft-landing pad."

Dahl grinned. "How about we all go together?"

"Oh, no. I . . ."

But then Luther and Molokai were alongside and grinning all too familiarly. The Mad Swede had them hooked. With barely a pause the three men arranged themselves around the hole, giving first dibs to Dahl, whose idea it had been.

"See ya downstairs, Yorkie," Luther said.

Drake groaned. Now even he was saying it.

Dahl leapt in first, knees tucked in, holding his weapon carefully as he fell through the air. Molokai and Luther were right behind him. Without an instant of pause Drake and Alicia followed them.

The room below became very crowded.

Dahl smashed down onto the shoulders of one of the four

mercs, grinning, using his incredible strength and the descent to knock the main out cold. Not even a whisper escaped the merc's lips as he fell.

Luther and Molokai hit next, the former able to bring an elbow crashing down on the back of another merc's neck. The blow was staggering, devastating. The merc went instantly limp and crumpled without knowing what had killed him.

Molokai came down last, landing close to the center of the vault door itself, looking inside. Two mercs remained standing and both were in there.

Drake hit the floor just as Molokai ran at them.

The mercs were at a total disadvantage, not only because they faced this devastating, throwback, fighting machine clad in dusty scarves. The tallest held the Flail of Anubis; the shortest held the large metal container that had housed it.

Molokai attacked the shortest, striking whilst his arms were occupied, a blow to the stomach and the head. Drake darted around him, raising his gun.

"Don't move."

The merc hesitated. His gun rested on the floor between his legs. Molokai looked up from the merc he'd just destroyed.

"Make a move for it." The feral growl was a death knell. "I dare you."

Drake sensed the others behind him at the door. The merc let the head of the flail hang—it was a thick rod of iron, the black surface inlaid with archaic patterns, a chunky chain leading to the lethal metal head where a cluster of blunt spikes jutted.

"You gonna attack us all with that?" Smyth laughed. "Good luck."

The merc sensibly relented and Drake made sure he lived, securing him in the vault. When the man protested Hayden crouched down before him.

"What did you expect? A ticket to the cinema? What can you tell us about the men that employ you?"

"Man called Tilt employs me," the answer came grudgingly. "Twelve of us. I don't know who employs him. He just calls 'em 'the bosses.'"

Drake had expected standard practice among criminal enterprises. This merc's "bosses" would be yet another shield of disassociation before they approached the layer that was Tempest.

"Is he here?" Alicia looked around at the dead bodies—some from the botched explosion, others at the hands of Dahl's mad antics.

"Nah, he's up top. Waiting for the artifact."

Kinimaka leaned over the merc, his bulk the shadow of a mountain descending. "Why do they call him Tilt?"

"He got vertigo issues. Something wrong with his inner ear."

"We should go." Hayden turned away. "This goon can't help us any further."

They marched out of the vault, leaving the merc to his own devices, and climbed the stairs back to the first floor. A quick check through the front-facing windows showed the street outside still in chaos, the hotel opposite on fire, its brick fascia cracked and crumbling. Police and military dashed back and forth, and the roadway was full of vehicles. They could see blue flashing lights washing over the windows, and approaching ambulances.

"Go," Hayden said before they could dwell. "Don't stop."

Quickly, they filed up out of the stairwell and through the bank's rear doors. Mai carried the flail, wrapping it in her coat as she moved. Kenzie was the last to leave.

Outside, the Alexandrian night was dry and warm, with a light mist of sea spray in the air. They took a route leading away from the bank, mostly traveling in darkness. It would be a short run back to the waiting chopper and then . . .

Drake counted the weapons off in his head, surprised.

The last weapon was the Forge of Vulcan, which was next on their list. A sense of urgency crept among his thoughts—reminding him they hadn't managed to contact the President yet, they were still fugitives, and Tempest still busy creating a significant camp full of terrorists and seizing more ancient weapons.

For the material it was made of? Perhaps.

If that were the case, no single government should be allowed to possess it. He wondered for the first time if Cambridge and Whitehall were aware of its significance.

Cynical? Yeah, but that's how we stay at the top of our game.

A mile-wide, tree-lined park, replete with skateboard ramps, swings, a climbing-frame and hard benches, marked the place where the chopper returned to. It was emblazoned with the crest of a local firm and would have clearance to fly—yet one more favor from Whitehall. As they approached the area, Hayden called the chopper pilot.

"No reply," she said.

"Maybe he fell asleep," Alicia suggested.

"Anything's possible." Mai wrapped the flail tighter and peered at the darkened windows all around, the empty pre-dawn street and the park that lay a hundred yards ahead. "Try again."

They came closer, now able to make out the chopper's bulk as it waited inside the park, shrouded by trees. The silence was eerie, and the presence of so many windows unsettling. Drake reached the gates, finding them wide open.

"I think we need to take this—"

He never finished. From out of the shadows came the rest of Tilt's force. No shots were fired; there were too many houses and civilians behind darkened windows for that, but eight men rushed at them so suddenly it was all they could do to defend themselves.

Drake, unbalanced, staggered to one knee as a large merc shoulder-charged him. Dahl resisted a similar attack but still retreated. Mai rolled clear and Alicia backed into the metal railings that surrounded the park. The others were similarly beset, barely managing to dodge blows, knife thrusts and knuckle-duster attacks. Their own close-quarter weapons were tucked away or sheathed. Only Molokai managed to reach unerringly into the folds of his scarves and come out with a machete.

Kenzie stared as if he was the world's greatest magician. "Oh, wow, so now I'm arou—"

Mercifully, the rest of her sentence was lost as a merc sideswiped her, sending her sprawling to the hard ground. The same merc jumped on top of her, trying to pin her down. Drake, off balance, fought his attacker hard. It had been a shocking rush of men; the team only surviving several knife attacks by experience and reactions alone. No words were spoken. Three of his friends were on the floor. Alicia was pinned against the fence. The mercs fought hard to keep their momentum going.

Drake pulled his knife and fenced an attack away, the blades striking fiercely. Turning, he managed to unbalance Alicia's attacker even as he fended off one more strike from his own. Kenzie rolled her head as a knife flashed down. It missed by millimeters, the point sparking into hard concrete. It went back up and then down again, Kenzie saving herself by reaction alone. Now though, she was able to bring her arms up between their bodies and force the knife-wielder to reposition.

Luther met a second charge by stepping swiftly back then bringing his head down onto his opponent's forehead. There was a sickening crack and the man fell comatose, a rag doll, possibly even dead.

The SPEAR team were recovering already, and less than a minute had passed since the initial attack. Sixty seconds was a long time in a fight, especially hand-to-hand combat. They weren't unscathed. Kinimaka had taken a knife in the back, right where his spine met his tailbone. Saved by the stab vest, it had still hurt tremendously and it was all he could do to fend the merc off before a second blow to the vest made him roar like a cornered bear. Smyth had also taken a vest-blow, then grabbed his opponent's wrist and tried to nullify the weapon.

Mai let the Flail of Anubis fall, waited for it to wrap itself from her jacket, and then swung it at the nearest head. The heavy steel ball flew up under a man's chin, snapping his head back and breaking bones. It came around again, swung by an expert, smashing his jaw from the right and then his temple from the left. Mai moved on to the next. An overhand swing planted the spikes in a man's scalp, and then became a sideways wipe into another's cheek. The swinging flail put the SPEAR team back on top.

Then Drake's opponent held out a hand and a cellphone. "Listen," he hissed. "You have to listen to this."

The mercs stopped their onslaught, panting. Drake started at the man and the phone. Hayden helped Kinimaka to his feet.

"I'm sorry," a voice said. "They have me."

Drake didn't recognize the voice at first. Hayden frowned.

Mai spoke up. "It's the chopper pilot."

Drake stared into the darkness of the park. The chopper sat in a pool of solid darkness, thirty meters away, but as he watched, somebody shone a flashlight onto the face of the pilot. No other figures were visible but the threat was clear.

"We only want the flail," the merc said. "Give me the flail and your pilot lives."

Mai didn't hesitate; just walked forward and handed it over. The mercs melted away, sliding back into the darkness.

Hayden started walking toward the chopper. "Not good," she said quietly. "They planned this as a redundancy. If we didn't know before, we can be damn sure that Tempest know we're in the hunt for the weapons."

"So what do we do next?" Kinimaka asked.

"We beat the bastards to the last one."

CHAPTER THIRTY ONE

The chopper dropped them in Port Said, at a location close to the military museum. El-Montazah Park was quiet in the early morning, enabling the team to slip away and find a hotel, before dressing in civilian clothes and heading out for a long-overdue breakfast. They couldn't hide their bruises, but they did manage to pass for seasoned tourists.

Almost, Drake thought. In reality, soldiers weren't hard to spot.

Seated at the back of a small eating house, they ordered pastries, hot drinks and bottled water. A decent amount of privacy was afforded them as the team sat back to relax and rejuvenate.

"We lost the flail," Hayden told Cambridge over the phone. "Stand your Egypt team down."

The SAS captain didn't question them. "You can go straight to the final weapon. Lauren Fox and Secretary Crowe are making headway in DC. Their plan is sound—it's just a matter of waiting for the right time to execute it now."

"Great," Drake said. "And on that other, personal, matter?"

"Yes. Your friend Yorgi touched down aboard a Boeing 747 last night, landing in Moscow. He rented a car and then found a hotel on the outskirts of the city. He's safe, but we'll keep watch."

"No problems?"

"No . . ." Cambridge's tone made Drake sit up.

"What is it?"

"Honestly, I don't know. It's nothing to do with Yorgi, but something massive is brewing. I hear it in the chatter we listen to. In cell communications. Through informants. Everywhere. It's all unsubstantiated. Do you remember when the Blood King attacked the President in DC? Before that, the terrorist and merc chatter went through the roof. Well, it's happening again. Right now."

"Not connected to Tempest?" Hayden asked.

"No. The chatter there is immense, yes, but it's relatively open channel, centered on just a couple of areas in the world. But this . . . this is so deep and dark, it's scary."

Scary? Drake didn't like the sound of that.

"DC was a bad time for us," Drake remembered. "For all of us. This only reconfirms that we need to get our names cleared fast and restart business as usual. We can't be left in the dark for something like that."

Mai sipped water. "Can I ask if there's a reason you mentioned this in the same breath as Yorgi?"

Cambridge sighed down the line. "Yeah, yeah, it seems to be originating from Russia."

Drake knew they had many enemies over there, but Kovalenko was dead. So were many others. "Let's find the last weapon," he said. "Before worrying about ghosts. And where are we with the Syrian terrorist camp and disavowed teams?"

"Ah, well there's some good news. We have a plan for contacting all the teams and trying to get them to work together. We're proposing a series of code words, and dispatching locals to meet up with each team. You guys were right—there are dozens. Hundreds of men and women. We've established our neutrality with extreme difficulty through already implanted code words— phrases recognized by each team and put in place at training level. We still have a few friends at places like Fort Jackson, Fort Knox, Benning, Sill; that kind of thing."

"Good idea," Dahl said. "A soldier's mindset is established at training level. Throw a few old idioms at him—known only to the men that trained him and those that struggled with him—and he'll sit up and take notice."

"It worked," Cambridge said. "We're developing a strategy to bring them all together."

"Where are they all?" Luther asked.

"Scattered," Cambridge said. "Mostly across the Middle East. Egypt. Syria. Afghanistan. Iran. Iraq. Anywhere there's conflict in Eastern Europe."

"I know we lost it," Alicia said. "But what's the significance of the Flail of Anubis?"

"Sure, I had a whole speech prepared for when you handed it over. Anubis was the Egyptian god associated with mummification and the afterlife. Of course, he's associated with

the quintessential depictions of men with dog's heads and the like. He was one of those that determined whether a soul would be allowed into the realm of the dead. He's one of the most ancient of gods, and also one of the most famous—but plays practically no part in any Egyptian myths."

"Didn't they also depict him as a jackal?" Drake asked.

"Yes, he's had many different roles through the ages. Highly revered though."

"And do we have any idea where this flail might be taken?" Luther asked. "And, whilst we're asking—where all the other weapons are being stored?"

"That is a good, fresh angle we're trying," Cambridge said. "Tracking the weapons, as you say. But the short-range devices we have are limiting. It's difficult to keep track. At the moment, by backtracking events from all around the world, we're pretty sure the weapons are being sent to the United States, and that there are over twenty of them."

"Events?" Drake asked. "Not all terrorist, please?"

"No, not all," Cambridge said to the team's relief. "Nothing on the scale of the train episode either."

"I really think you should start analyzing the weapons that you have," Hayden told him. "The only way to beat Tempest is to get a step ahead of them. Lauren and Crowe are trying in DC. I believe you can do the same over there. What's so special about these weapons?"

"Another good idea," Cambridge acknowledged.

"It's the coffee." Alicia finished off her third cup. "Strong and black over here with a mega-caffeine rush."

"Just what I need," Cambridge said. "I'll be in touch soon but, for now, I'll send you details of the Forge of Vulcan."

"Easy one?" Drake asked hopefully.

"No, it's the toughest yet. I was half hoping Tempest might get to it first but, as you say, perhaps they're leaving the hardest and most dangerous artifacts for last."

"We're on it," Hayden assured him. "And will report back. Oh, and Cambridge?"

"Yes?"

"Use more resources to discover exactly what this 'big thing' emanating out if Russia is. Y'know, just in case we all survive and get back to America. I don't wanna end up stuck in the middle of another blood vengeance battle again."

CHAPTER THIRTY TWO

The Forge of Vulcan was not only dangerous to reach, it was going to be intensely dangerous to get close to. The area lay close to an IS stronghold. Cambridge didn't add it to his report but Drake knew IS emerged from what had been al-Qaeda in Iraq, which was formed by Sunni militants after the Western invasion in 2003. In 2011 IS joined those fighting against President Bashar al-Assad in Syria, where it found comparative safety and hordes of weapons. Drake also knew that over eight hundred people had traveled from the UK to join the conflict in Syria and Iraq, with just under half returning since.

But what would they return to?

He couldn't know that, so locked the question away. Refugees was one of the main issues with this war, over five million fleeing Syria and three million fleeing Iraq. Even the battle for Mosul itself led to in excess of one million people fleeing their homes.

The Forge of Vulcan lay in Syria, within walking range of one of IS's last bastions. The area was intensely guarded up to IS standard, which was to say incomprehensible to most. The cave system itself might even be in use.

"How did the forge end up in an IS fortress?" Alicia asked.

"The militant group discovered it whilst ransacking and destroying people's homes," Dahl read aloud, since not everyone could crowd around Hayden's laptop. "An archaeologist's perhaps. It may even have been stolen from Europeans working here—the land of Syria still lies at the heart of archaeology."

"I don't understand how we know it's there," Kenzie said. "If a team got close enough to use the tracking device why didn't they just go in and get it?"

"That's the interesting part," Hayden explained. "Apparently, it's being advertised for a huge sum of cash on the dark web."

"Part of me wonders if it's worth risking our lives for," Alicia said. "But then the other part assures me that the forge will be the deciding element in Tempest's plan. It's Sod's Law."

"Agreed," Drake said. "And the forge is bigger than the others—containing large amounts of material. Knowing Tempest, they'll just buy this thing."

"They wouldn't trust IS," Kinimaka said. "Don't forget who Tempest are. CIA, bankers, businessmen, judges. They know how deals can fail."

"And all we know is it's inside that cave system?" Drake pointed at the screen.

"Deep inside," Hayden said. "The device barely got a read."

"We'll need to be fully, utterly loaded," Luther said with relish. "More weapons and ammo than Fort Bragg. We get among that army . . . our chances drop by the second."

Hayden nodded. "And we'll need to be HALO'd in. Dropped from four thousand meters right on the edge of their camp," she said. "It's gonna be tough."

Luther eyeballed her. "Tough?" he repeated. "Spec ops eat this shit for breakfast. Sure hope you can keep up, Team SPEAR."

"We'll do our best," Drake replied without emotion.

"Are you kidding?" Dahl said, grinning. "It's party time. Not only are we gonna HALO together, but we get to stick it to IS too. That's bucket-list stuff right there, folks."

Not entirely certain Dahl knew what bucket-list ideals really stood for, Drake looked at the assemblage. Mai, with all the demons of her past laid to rest and now probably unsure of her next step. Her proximity to Luther showed it might be right there. The big warrior himself, unable to curtail his glee at the prospect of a new battle, a warrior at heart and probably incapable of settling down. Kenzie, teetering on the edge of everything—fight or flight, good and bad, struggle forward or fall back. Drake was sure she would leave. Meters away and unmistakably apart, sat Dahl, a man on hold, kept in suspense until he could return to reclaim the family he loved. Then there was Hayden and Mano, skirting around the edge of a new relationship but neither wanting to spoil it by trying too hard.

Smyth . . . waiting for Lauren. Waiting for a miracle, it seemed.

Molokai was a mystery. An anomaly to the group. Drake couldn't read him at all, and wondered if it might be better not to look at the man's past.

And that left Alicia and himself. Honestly, where were they? Their relationship was stronger than mountains, their bond tighter than a death grip. But where were they going? From one skirmish to another, one mission to the next.

Alicia was right. Some R&R was long overdue.

"I guess we should get on with it then." Alicia brought him back to the present by whispering in his ear.

"Eh?"

"Hay just told us to meet outside the hotel in thirty. That corresponds to twenty minutes shagging time. C'mon, better bring your A-game, Drakey."

"Shouldn't we conserve energy for the . . . you know . . . humongous battle we have coming?"

"Nah."

"Shouldn't we be gathering our weapons?"

"I'm only interested in one weapon right now."

"And later? If we save the world?"

"I might let you go on top."

"Aw, thanks."

As they climbed the stairs to their room, Drake thought about their relationship and how they needed some real time together. Do people find getting time off together this hard in the real world? He wondered.

But then they were walking down their corridor and Alicia was already disrobing.

"Whoa, your panties say 'come and get it' on the ass."

"I know. I bought them for your sake when I remembered you're so fucking slow on the uptake."

"Awesome." Drake threw her onto the bed. "How about leaving 'em right where they are, love?"

CHAPTER THIRTY THREE

Karin Blake endured another night and day with the FrameHub geeks, learning what they knew, stealing their secrets and their code with her eidetic memory, trolling their open jobs, their assignments and personal projects, suffering their corner-of-the-eye stares every time she got up to walk to the water cooler or the refrigerator, tolerating their terrible and often deplorable jokes.

It wouldn't be bad if they were ultimately harmless. Then she could bear their smutty remarks, their smaller, low-key hacks, their relatively undamaging social media shamings. She could even overlook all eight of them peeking at her—and using the internal cameras—when she dressed for bed. In part, she understood all these things—they were males under thirty that had never lived with a woman before and sure as hell never touched one. At first, she wondered if organizing a wild party with beer and hookers might cure them of their afflictions, but then she began to look deeper.

FrameHub were evil, perfectly defined by malice. The softer machinations worked atop deeper intrigues, each one more distressing, each one hiding a further layer of depravity. They did not care who they hurt—and they trolled the dark web for the worst immoral sins.

She gave up all hope in them as their supreme moment ticked inexorably closer. The prison break was on schedule, ready to green-light. Karin had never seen such a wicked glow in men's faces, not even in the expressions of the worst mercenaries, warlords and crime bosses she'd come up against. In short, they wanted every single human being to suffer—man, woman and child—and intended to create countless, unending scenarios to make sure that happened.

Karin used a dead drop account to message Dino and Wu. It was part of her routine to check the account every hour for incoming messages relating to her hacks, and FrameHub accepted it after the first day and stopped checking.

Now, they had twelve minutes left.

Karin looked over Piranha's shoulder, getting deliberately close. The kid couldn't concentrate and kept breaking off to smile at her. Time ticked by. In an ideal world she could probably take all eight of these assholes out herself, but army training had taught her to rely on trustworthy backup. To wait for it if possible.

Having tracked and then followed her on the way down here, Dino and Wu would arrive at this very spot in . . . six minutes.

She clamped a hand on Piranha's bicep. "Wait, is that San Quentin?" She nodded at the quickly scrolling list.

"Yeah, why?"

"My old boyfriend's in there." She laughed. "Wow, I could tell you a few stories about us two."

Sixteen eyes locked on. "Like what?"

Three minutes.

Karin wandered across the room to pour a coffee, deliberately taking it slow. She knew they'd be watching. "What's left to do, Piranha?"

"Upload the virus. Launch the code. A few seconds after that—" he made a whooshing sound "—doors opening all across the homeland. Special doors."

"Drink?" she asked. "How about a beer? Let's toast and then we can get down to party."

Several expressions of interest crossed the gathered faces, but Goonch wasn't about to be delayed.

"Cool, cool," he cried. "But let's press the button right now! I can't wait to see what happens to the guards, and when they reach the first few towns!"

Karin strode over to his workstation, planted her hands on his shoulders and then used his seat to swivel him around. Her eyes were two inches from his.

"You can't wait to see who they maim or murder first?"

Goonch nodded, breathing the stench of garlic mixed with candy into her face. "We are FrameHub," he said.

"From now on," she whispered, "you should consider all your systems crashed." She had hopefully uttered the last geek-line of her life.

An explosion ripped the door off its hinges; the metal rectangle spinning like a dice into the room. Goonch stared with wide eyes whilst the other geeks all threw themselves onto the floor. Karin had been expecting it, but shielded her face for a moment before throwing the contents of her cup at Goonch's face. The boiling hot liquid scalded. Goonch screamed, tipping over and hitting the floor with a crash. Dino and Wu darted into the room, semi-autos raised. Karin paused for a moment as Dino threw her a weapon.

Piranha jumped up, reaching toward a desk drawer. Barracuda and Manta did the same. Moray stayed with his head between his hands, ass in the air. Another geek made a break toward the open door.

Karin turned the barrel of her gun onto Goonch. "You wanna know who's the first to murder?" she asked. "I am."

She squeezed her trigger twice. Goonch's face exploded and he lived no more.

Karin ran over to Piranha's computer just as Dino and Wu yelled out for the geeks to stand down. Karin shouted without looking up.

"Kill 'em," she said. "They're only ever going to be trouble in the real world."

"Wouldn't it be worse for them in prison?" Dino grinned.

"No," Karin said. "I've seen what they can do and what they are doing. The best they deserve is a bullet to the brain, Dino. Just do it."

Karin focused on closing Piranha's program down. It took several minutes, careful keystroke after keystroke. She was aware of Piranha pulling a handgun to her right and Dino sweeping in to disarm him. Closer still, Wu smashed Manta across the brow, sending him reeling into the banks of machines, and then lifted Barracuda by the collar, preventing him from reaching his own small gun.

"You weigh nothing, boy," Wu said. "How you like flying?"

He hurled Barracuda overhead, throwing him at the floor. The geek hit hard and then skidded further, face scraping across rough concrete. Karin still hadn't heard a gunshot. To her left, three other geeks stood bolt upright, unsure what to do. When one yanked out the drawer of his desk, Karin stopped what she was doing and shot him in the chest. The feel of his blood spattering across their faces made the others retch violently. Karin took a little while longer to finish what she was doing.

Piranha, with no weapon, ran at Dino. The soldier should have shot him then and there, but elected to bash him across the head with the butt of his rifle gun instead. Piranha went down. Karin stepped away from his computer.

She lined up her weapon and opened fire, destroying the monitor, the hard drive and everything attached to it. She glanced over at Wu.

"The storage cabinets are back there," she said. "Go fry 'em all. And I mean comprehensively. Bullets and fire, Wu."

"We're not handing all this in to the authorities then?"

Karin regarded him as if he were mad. "Don't be ridiculous. Not counting all the private shit these assholes have hacked into and stored, there are dozens of active enterprises happening here. I wouldn't bet on any authority not sifting carefully through them, would you?"

"No," Wu admitted. "No, I wouldn't."

Karin turned back to the main room. The geeks to the left were still retching, white faced and terrified. Dino had Piranha by the hair, holding him upright, and pointed his gun at the rest.

Karin strode over to them. "I thought about this," she said. "I honestly did. I tried to see the good in you. I tried to imagine you didn't know better. I even tried to see if some of you were being coerced, which is why I checked all your jobs. But it just isn't there. You're all like-minded. All the same. Nobody can help you."

She raised her semi-auto, training it on Moray and Manta, with Barracuda cowering behind them.

"You are FrameHub," she said. "Think on all the civilians those missiles murdered. All the families you destroyed. Think on the irony of this—how many will be saved by killing you?"

Karin had no compassion left. In her life, she'd already witnessed the worst, seen loved ones die, murdered at the hands of a madman. Whatever dregs of kindness she had left would be saved for those that deserved it.

The gun bucked in her grip. She held tight. Bullets riddled three bodies, made them collapse bleeding to the floor. Behind them, computers shattered; wires, plastic boxes and broken glass dancing across the wilting desks. The wall billowed plaster dust where the lead finally came to rest.

Piranha screamed. Beside him, only two others remained—Stingray and Bull—and their blood-stained faces ran with tears.

"So," Karin said. "How do you like me now?"

"Wait," Dino said. "This is cold blooded murder."

"What did you think you signed up for? Our original agenda was to kill Matt Drake."

"He's a soldier. They all are."

Karin shook her head sadly. "So are these wankers," she said. "But you don't see it. Why? Because they're young and inexperienced? Because they're not firing bullets? Their fingers, Dino . . . their sticky fingers can do more damage across the world in sixty minutes than your trigger finger can do in a month. Do you understand?"

Dino frowned. "But—"

"Shit." Karin shot Stingray through the head. "They were loving every second of the damage they did. Right here, right now." She shot Bull through the head.

Only Piranha remained.

"Cowardly, emotionally deficient psychopaths with no morals," she said. "Delighting in the slaughter that they wrought."

She pressed the cold barrel right up against Piranha's head.

"Excited to their core. Emotionally. Sexually. Physically." She started to squeeze the trigger. "By the misery and the pain of others."

The last bullet echoed sharply through the suddenly silent room. Piranha's body made a sickening wet flopping sound as it struck the floor.

She stared Dino in the eyes. "Thanks for helping."

Carefully, he inclined his head, clearly not completely on the same page. Karin checked on Wu. "Let's go. Now that FrameHub are out of the way, and their evil nullified, we can complete our agenda."

"That hasn't changed?" Wu asked.

"No. Why do you ask?"

"We've been there. You had a chance. I thought . . . maybe you'd had a change of heart."

"Everything I did since joining the Army has been with this goal in mind. I explained that and you still came. If you don't like it you can walk away, but now we go to finish this."

"And nobody else knows?" Wu asked.

"Nobody. Don't worry, we're safe."

Dino was staring at Wu. "You know that, man. You've been with us at every step."

"I like reassurance."

"What you need is a mother."

"My mother died when I was six."

Karin didn't want to get into it. FrameHub were officially shut down and she didn't feel an ounce of regret. The world was a hard place. If you faced it head on, messed with it, you deserved whatever harsh fate came your way.

The world is better off without them.

"Let's leave these bastards to rot."

Dino and Wu made ready. Karin grabbed anything she owned and a few items she could see that were of value. They relieved the dead of their cash simply because they needed it no more. Karin did have access to funds, but was always aware that, in the game she was playing, the need might arise for even more. Most of FrameHub's valuable information was stored away in her memory.

Dino headed for the door. "C'mon. We can make contact with SPEAR up top."

Karin followed, but then her phone rang. When she fished it out the screen read: *Unknown Caller,* which wasn't surprising in their line of work.

"Hello?"

"Is this Karin Blake?"

"Who wants to know?" The voice held a heavy, thick accent she recognized as Russian.

"You don't know me, Miss Blake, but you will. We should meet, because we have the same goals."

"Who is this?"

"Someone planning something very big. Worldwide. Devastating. They destroyed my legacy and I will have my revenge."

"They?"

"SPEAR. Drake and the rest. Even that sniveling weasel you call President. Plans are in place, but they don't know I am coming."

Karin couldn't help the hollow fear that started to churn around the pit of her stomach. "Who are you?"

"Meet me." He reeled off an address. "Meet me there and let me show you. Bring your companions. You will be safe, for now."

"I'm not meeting you. I couldn't possibly trust you."

"Of course you can, Miss Blake. My machinations will not begin until SPEAR have finished with Tempest. I want their full attention."

"So you're saying Tempest are a hindrance to you too?"

"Let's just say I want them out of the way. Then . . . the day of death begins."

"That's a bit corny, bro," Karin tried to bait the man.

"Corny? I do not know. I do know that your only chance of survival during the coming weeks is to meet me."

Karin sighed. "You're fucking up my timetable here."

The man gave her a date and time. "If you don't turn up you will be the first to die."

The phone went dead. Karin stared at it for a minute before including Dino and Wu in her thoughts. "You hear all that?"

"Sure. Just another psycho." Wu shrugged.

"Really? Then how did he get my number? How did he know we'd just finished here? How did he know our agenda? And, if there's a threat to SPEAR, there's a threat to the world at large."

"SPEAR won't go down easy," Dino said.

"Not just that. He mentioned the President too. This could be huge."

"So, you wanna meet the psycho?" Wu said it as if resigned. "Of course you do."

"I think we have to, guys."

Dino shouldered his weapon. "Best get moving then."

Karin didn't look back.

CHAPTER THIRTY FOUR

The HALO jump should have been exhilarating, a heady rush from beginning to end, but Drake barely felt it. Risk lay everywhere, from the size of the team jumping to the chances of being spotted from below.

And then there was the landing area.

Close to an IS stronghold and a mountainous ridge, they were trying to come down as close as was reasonably possible. Drake had never seen a team so tooled up; they were literally burdened with weapons. Enough to win a war.

It might come to that. Luther had been grinning from ear to ear.

Drake landed and rolled, catching his hip on a rock but coming away with nothing more than a nasty bruise. The others came down one by one, pitch black their ally, stiff chutes guided by GPRS. Despite more bruises and scrapes the team came together in a reasonable mood.

"All quiet?" Mai whispered.

"We're a few miles from the town," Drake said. "You see that ridge over there?" He pointed at the horizon where an uneven line was outlined against a silvery sky. "That's our target. We need to be there before first light."

They moved out. The air was cold, biting even, chilling Drake's blackened face. They couldn't help but make a small amount of noise, weighed down by all their gear, so they took it easier than normal and stayed low. Underfoot, the ground was hard-packed and uneven. Drake heard no sounds drifting along on the slight breeze that scoured the desert. They could easily have been alone.

Very soon, they found they were far from it.

Dahl, ranging to the left, came across a man seated next to a battered-looking rifle. The man didn't see Dahl at all, but his eyes grew wide when the enormous shape loomed over him. He opened his mouth to scream.

Dahl jabbed a knife into his throat to stop any sound, and caught the fighter as he fell. Then, steadily, he laid the man down next to his unused rifle.

"Guard?" Drake asked through the comms.

"Think so. We'd better range further to the right if they have sentries this far out."

They followed the Swede's advice and moved ahead with extra care. To be sighted at this point would be ruinous, terminating the mission. An hour passed as they moved light-footedly through the oppressive gloom, danger to every side. No unnecessary words were spoken; no observations raised beyond terrain and destination. Finally, they reached a ravine and allowed themselves ten minutes respite after sliding carefully down to the very bottom.

Drake shifted close to Alicia. "Not long now."

"Yeah. You want chocolate?"

"Hell yeah." Through the years it had become a tradition whenever they could possibly manage it.

"I'll take some of that." Dahl was beside Alicia.

"You ready with that tracker, mate?" Drake asked as he chewed.

"Ready and willing," Dahl said.

Drake checked his watch, then clicked the comms. "Move out, folks."

Another thirty minutes and they were approaching the foothills. Here, Drake saw several campfires dotted around the folds of the lower mountain and some small structures that looked like tents. The trouble was, they stretched all around the wide, rocky base.

"I'm guessing it's some kind of overflow," he presumed, knowing the reason didn't really matter. Knowing wouldn't clear the obstacle.

"They're not so close together," Luther said. "We can go straight through."

Drake winced, positive now that Luther was looking for an excuse to start using the hardware. The trouble was—he was right, and dawn wasn't too far away.

With great care, he crept silently over the nearest rock, then used leg muscles to ease down the other side. Skirting the closest fire, he embraced the shadows, checking every footstep, every rough obstacle. A figure lay wrapped in a blanket next to the fire, snoring loudly as they came closer. Drake held his breath, but slipped past without bothering the man.

And into the second small camp.

Like the first, it consisted of a small fire and a tent, but this time there were two figures sleeping outside—both women. Their faces were blank, pointed up at the stars, their chests lifting and falling gently. Drake stepped across a narrow crevice before negotiating a slight slope on the other side. The tent rustled suddenly, its outside bulging. Drake froze, HK ready, hoping it was just a man turning over in his sleep.

It was. A moment later they continued, stepping into the third camp. Here they could circumvent the main area by hugging a wide ravine that curved up alongside it. The ravine ended in a paddock full of horses, however, and they were forced to double back.

Carefully, they chose another route.

Forty minutes passed. Drake kept an eye on the eastern horizon, which was definitely less dark than it had been twenty minutes ago. Up ahead, the mountain loomed, but not quite as daunting as it first looked. They knew they were climbing the correct side, and that the cave entrances were approximately one hundred meters high.

"Slow down," Drake said. "We're here."

Out of the darkness above, a yawning entrance appeared. To their right another camp had been made, and Drake could see figures starting to stir. Out here, they had no idea what awaited them inside.

"Now or never," he whispered. "Move it!"

Without hesitation, the entire team dashed inside the mountain.

CHAPTER THIRTY FIVE

The darkness was infested with rats.

Only these rats wore desert clothing and carried guns. They had nothing but murder on their mind, rebels until they died.

At first, the blackness inside the cave was overwhelming. Illumination came from the infrequent lanterns that had been hung around the rock walls. It was clear there were others inside from the moment they entered the complex.

Echoing conversation, a low bleat of laughter, and rough words came from several adjoining passages, making it impossible to check who was where. The team moved a step at a time, passing archways and ragged holes in the rock walls that led through the complex. In one corner they found three men fast asleep, in another a pair of manacles attached roughly to the rock with heavy pins. Bits of clothing lay all around but no sign of a body. The team sobered even further. Darkness pressed in at every opportunity.

Dahl aimed the tracker signal in front of them as often as possible. Occasionally they had to branch left or right, but soon found a path that led down. The way wasn't without its peril either. Three times the group were forced to split up and hide around alcoves or jutting walls as fighters came past. From what Drake could see they were a ragtag bunch, undisciplined and quiet, solitary and lacking enthusiasm. They walked without observation, many looking down at their feet.

Of course, they would never expect an enemy in here; the place they'd frequented for years. Still, their complacency lent increasing hope to the team

If we can get down, we can get back up. Safe. Free.

Drake stifled his building confidence as Dahl came to an abrupt halt. The Swede pressed instantly back against the wall, making those behind follow suit. Slowly, he clicked the comms button, whispering, "Passage opens into a chamber ahead with four exits. There are four men playing cards right at the center, heads down. No way past."

Luther was first to react. "Knives."

Again, the big man was right, but the warrior's lust betrayed him as he walked up to Dahl. Molokai was at his back. Kenzie was right behind him, trying to restrain Smyth.

"Sooner we get this done, the sooner we all go home," Smyth growled.

Drake let Luther have his head and covered the path they'd already trod. Mai had been ranging back there to check nobody was following and now appeared.

"All clear."

Luther's voice filled his ears. "We're done here. C'mon."

Past the chamber and down they went, further and further. Luther and Molokai had concealed the bodies in a place they said would not be found until decay set in. The cave complex was vast, but not hard to navigate. All they needed was a downward slope and Dahl's GPR device.

"Is the signal strengthening?" Kinimaka asked once.

"Steadily," Dahl replied. "Too bloody steadily."

It meant the artifact was far underground. Little by little, step by step, they fell deeper and deeper into the bowels of the earth.

"How heavy is this thing?" Hayden asked as they walked, seeing fewer and fewer enemies now. "I'm worried about carting it all the way back up."

"I will do that," Molokai said.

"No," Drake stepped in. "Let's gauge the weight first."

"I will carry it," Molokai said again in a stern voice.

"Leave it." Luther tapped Drake's shoulder. "He's a beast."

The Yorkshireman regarded the mammoth soldier that spoke. "Riiight, okay then."

The hours passed. What appeared to be a raiding party came running up from below—four men wearing dusty, drab clothes wrapped every which way and carrying AK47s. They were primed, pumped up, chattering to each other about some task they'd been set. Drake wasn't good with the language, only catching a third of the words. He considered ambushing them purely because they carried radios, but by the time he'd made the decision they were gone.

Further on, they came to a vast arch in the mountain. Drake saw rushing water ahead—a torrent falling from some place above, passing before their eyes and vanishing below. The underground waterfall filled their ears; its spray touching their faces. Drake found a narrow ledge that ran behind it and stepped on, hugging the wall. Helpful handholds had been cut into the rock, so he clasped them with his fingers, sidestepping along. For once, the comms were absolutely silent as the team used every ounce of concentration for balance. The ledge was no more than a foot wide and, in places, their heels hung over the edge.

The endless flow cascaded so close they could feel its power in their guts. Drake was soaked already. Of course, any confrontation here would end in certain death, but they managed to climb past. The ledge widened and continued along the rock face ahead for a while before descending into another jagged tunnel.

Drake halted for a moment and looked back. A bedraggled group presented itself, equipment dripping, hair plastered down, many wiping their eyes.

The ledge curved steeply and the drop to their left was only too apparent. It wasn't until they entered the new tunnel that the waterfall roar started to die away.

The noise of boots came from up ahead. Drake stopped in his tracks. Walls rose to either side.

"Nowhere to go." He tapped the comms and dropped to one knee, sighting his gun.

Luther appeared above him, sighting another. "Got you covered, bud."

Out of the darkness a man appeared. He seemed to be squinting, unable to believe what stood before him. Drake fired first and then Luther, their weapons fitted with silencers. The barrels barked quietly and the man went down, his own weapon clattering. Drake quickly checked he was alone.

"All clear. Move out."

Ten minutes later they exited the tunnel and entered a wider chamber. Passages ran left, right and straight on, leading down. Dahl's signal was finally starting to glow brighter and become more centered. The Forge of Vulcan was close.

Drake pushed on. The ground in front, wreathed in shadow, descended sharply and then seemed to disappear. Drake assumed it was deeper darkness until he got up close to it.

And felt the draught rushing up.

"Whoa!"

He staggered back, suddenly beset by a rush of giddiness. A deep void lay ahead, just a crevice in the floor: murky, deadly and unexpected.

"Big trench," he said aloud, squinting to make out the far side. "Not good. I can't see shit in here."

Luther took out and cracked a handful of glowsticks. "These will help."

The first he tossed over didn't make it; it barely made halfway. The second hit the crevice wall. The third landed on rock, spinning, and cast its orange glow over their new predicament.

"How far?" Hayden asked.

"Gotta be ten feet," Luther said.

"Fifteen," Molokai decided.

"Well," Drake was scanning the fissure both ways, "the enemy must jump it. There's no bridge. Not even a plank of wood."

Mai and Smyth shone their flashlights around the chamber to make sure. They came up empty-handed, shrugging. Drake looked at the group.

"Anyone nervous?"

Without waiting he turned, sprinted and jumped. His arms wind-milled in mid-flight, the HK smacked him in the cheekbone, and then he landed safely on solid rock, rolling just once for good measure.

Dahl threw him the device, then jumped. The rest of the team came one by one. If there were any nerves none were shown. "Hard as nails," Drake said, grinning as the last man, Smyth, leapt across.

Once more, they descended.

More time passed them by. It was Dahl that said: "Any deeper and we'll be in Hell," but the words sent a shiver trickling up Drake's spine. The Swede was right. The descent felt endless, the vast complex around them crushingly prodigious. With every moment that passed they fell deeper and deeper toward their goal, so far below the earth they'd all lost the will to speak.

Finally, Dahl stopped. "The signal is as centered as it will ever get," he said. "The forge should be just around the next corner."

Drake shook himself, keeping focus, remembering most treasures were usually guarded. "Just don't forget," he said in a light voice. "We're never gonna get it back up there without a plank."

"Ah, the woes of all treasure hunters," Alicia said, upbeat.

"Two would be better," Dahl said.

"Why, one for each foot?"

"We could lash them together."

"Fine. Two planks. Now, are we ready?"

Luther was already there.

CHAPTER THIRTY SIX

Light filled this chamber, spilling from dozens of flickering flashlights set into the walls. Black smoke spiraled into the loftier shadows and was drawn away. The floor was flat, the walls ragged as if hewn by a drunken giant.

Drake saw six men.

One sat atop a pile of dusty old books, disrespectful and uncaring, since he surely knew he was guarding stolen valuables and possibly significant relics. He sat chewing, staring into space, and spat onto the dusty floor as Drake watched. Two more were seated to the far right, passing the time with an old board game. The final three walked among the treasures, picking some up, turning and squinting at them as if evaluating their worth.

"Did we expect this kinda bootie?" Alicia asked.

"Not really," Hayden answered. "But we sure can't take it all with us. Take photos and let others decide. That's the best we can do."

"They're not particularly photogenic," Mai said, gesturing toward the guards. "Shall we move them out of the way first?"

"Get in line." Kenzie rushed past Luther and Molokai, entering the chamber. Padding on silent feet, she lined up the seated man and fired, the gun spitting softly. The noise inside this chamber was enough to make the others glance over. Kenzie ran at the seated two, leaping at the last minute as they fumbled for their guns. She caught one full in the face with a flying boot, bringing her gun around like a club to batter the other on the temple. Both grunted and collapsed. The first's head whipped back against the rock wall. Kenzie concentrated on the second, regaining control of her gun and firing twice at point blank range.

Luther and Molokai kept pace with the Israeli, seeing the other three guards staring over in shock. Two blasts sent two bodies hurtling back, but the third missed as Luther stumbled on a small rock.

The final IS guard dropped behind a heavy chest. Drake could hear him groping around for his gun. The team ducked and Luther bemoaned a twisted ankle. Kenzie crept around from the far side. Molokai chose the other. Drake sighted on the very top of the chest where the head would pop up.

Seconds passed, and then the guard acted. Three shots were fired, all hitting their mark. The results were not healthy for the guard.

Hayden and Kinimaka pushed into the chamber. Everyone fanned out and searched the place, leaving Mai and Smyth to watch out for any unpleasant surprises. Drake opened a safe and a chest, then rooted through a chest of drawers. Alicia upended a shoebox. Hayden found gold bars rolled in sweatshirts and Kinimaka a round carousel stuffed with fake swords.

Kenzie gave them the once over. "Utter trash. You'd die before you drew blood with one of these."

"But maybe precious to somebody," Kinimaka said. "Sentimental."

"I guess."

By now, of course, they knew the color and general design of the object they were searching for. Alicia spotted it first and called the others over. "I found it first. What's my prize?"

"An evening with Torsten Dahl," Drake said, coming across. "Where no doubt you would cook meatballs and listen to the greatest hits of Roxette whilst building flat-pack furniture."

"Sounds . . . different."

Dahl didn't hold back. "Yes, in contrast to the usual fare of battered seafood, Chumbawumba and *The Full Monty*?"

"Doesn't sound half bad," Drake said.

Dahl grunted. Alicia dragged the artifact away from the pile it inhabited. A miniature forge, fashioned in midnight black, with two sides, an open chimney and a rodded grate, it stood quite imposing despite its shrunken size. Vulcan was the god of fire, volcanoes and forges in Roman mythology and was often depicted hammering away on a forge whilst forming the blade of a new sword or the shaft of a hammer. Hayden started rooting around for a canvas bag large enough to cover it, but Luther pulled one from his backpack.

"Always come prepared," he said.

It was barely large enough. Drake could see why this artifact contained more material than the others. It was not only larger, it was denser, the walls and internal design thicker. If Tempest came for this, they would come hard.

"Long journey back," he said. "We'd best get started."

The return was a long, hard slog, testing the limits of even their endurance, but finally the cave's exit loomed ahead. Molokai took the opportunity to rest, never complaining, but sinking down to the floor of the cave with the pack still strapped to his back.

Alicia tried to help. "Let me take that,"

"It's better I do this alone," Molokai said not ungratefully. "My thanks, but I am used to struggling alone by now. It builds character."

Daylight shone outside in all its glory. At first they could only see the skies, which were blue and dappled by white clouds. Drake and Luther edged cautiously toward the edge of the cave so that the landscape opened up gradually below with every step they took. First field and then foothills, then mountainside.

Luther grunted. "Shit."

It was a vision that would haunt Drake for the rest of his days.

CHAPTER THIRTY SEVEN

"We're gonna need more ammo," Drake said.

"You said that before," Mai came alongside them. "But here we are."

Drake allowed her to see what lay before them. "And now?"

"You may be correct."

"Of course. It's a Yorkshireman's birthright."

The plains below were full of IS militant fighters; clumps of them scattered all around the field like fungus on food. The lower foothills were crawling with them, all armed: seated on rocks, standing apart, crouching alongside each other. The mountainside was thick with bodies, making a covert escape impossible.

The worst of it was—over half the fighters had already seen them and the other half were gradually becoming aware.

Luther ducked back quickly. Alicia stared at him. "And how does that help, soldier boy?"

"Instinct."

"Oh, wow, we'd better watch out for that. Make sure it doesn't infect us all."

Drake watched the faces as they turned upward, all focusing on the insurgents that had crept among them. He couldn't count them all, but gauged their number to be in the hundreds. Worse, every single one of them appeared to be carrying a weapon.

"The only way is back down," Kenzie said. "But there's no way out down there."

"We could hold them off though," Smyth said. "Whilst we look for another exit."

"Shit, this complex is vast," Drake said warily. He didn't move, hoping stasis would give them a little more time.

"And those guys will know every inch of it," Hayden said.

"We have no food," Kinimaka said.

Alicia glanced over at him. "Typical Mano."

"Lots of problems," Hayden said. "Any solutions?"

Luther hefted guns in both hand. "We fight our way through like soldiers."

Drake sighed. "Y'know, mate, you're gonna get us killed. With that plan, yeah some of us may make it, but not all."

Luther looked around at the faces. "Your team's oversized anyway."

Drake hoped he was joking. For once, he couldn't see a way out. The caves were vast enough to claim everyone's life. The mountain and the plains were full of enemy soldiers. Their best option was speed, but in what way?

The natives were getting restless. Some were shouting, others gesturing. It was all aggressive. Boots were starting to step forward, guns waved. The charge was coming. Drake had no doubt they would last a while in here; they could protect the entrance and the cave's offshoots, but sooner or later the militants would start to think bigger—explosives and RPGs.

Think or die.

He found himself looking at Dahl and the Swede merely flicked his eyes upward.

Of course.

There was a chance. Drake freed up all his weapons and laid them on the ground. "Two minutes," he said. "Tool up. This is gonna be one of the hairiest things we've ever done."

Dahl handed him the radio. "You want the honors?"

"No, you do it, mate. It was your idea."

Everyone else just stared at them, expressions saying: What just happened?

Dahl made the call and then said: "Eight minutes."

Drake pursed his lips. "That long?"

"It is what it is, my friend."

The gunfire began. Bullets ricocheted from the cave entrance and the roof, shearing off rock fragments. The floor became a good place to live. Drake and Luther couldn't risk looking out, just simply rested their guns on a rocky ledge and fired blindly into the mountains. Behind, Alicia and Kenzie found a safe hide behind a jutting rock, enabling them to keep a better eye on the entrance. Already, Alicia was picking off those that the others missed as they stepped up to partially block out the light.

Already, they were close to being overrun.

"More firepower!" she cried.

They were already on it. Hayden and Kinimaka joining Drake and Luther on the floor, but further back, giving them a better angle. Smyth and Mai covered the cave's rear, where the adjoining tunnels branched off. Between them, they had good coverage. Dahl stayed low to cover Molokai and pick off any stragglers that the others missed.

The noise inside the cave was tremendous, non-stop gunfire. The noise outside was nightmarish, the screams of those dying and the cries of the wounded. Drake saw hard, grizzled face after face looking over him, and had to trust that the others would take them down. Luther and he took turns reloading and then heard Dahl's yell.

"Four minutes."

The enemy came, shouting obscenities that the team didn't understand. They came ready to maim and kill themselves. They came determined to rid this stain from their lands, their homes. There was no respite.

"Shoot!" Luther bellowed. "Fucking shoot!"

Bodies were piling up outside. Mai and Smyth blocked the passageways with the dead. When a grenade came toward her she kicked it straight back, shredding those that she'd already killed. Alicia somehow managed to grab a grenade in the air and throw it backward, further into the cave system before it exploded. Still, shrapnel and cave dust billowed through their space near the exit, rolling out among the attackers and disorienting them.

Drake heard it first: the incredible, timely, beautiful sound of an approaching Apache AH-64 attack helicopter. It housed a two-man crew and a nose-mounted sensor suite for target acquisition. Not that it would need that today. It carried a 30mm chain gun, Hellfire missiles and Hydra rockets. The amount of inbuilt survivable redundancies was mind-boggling, from shielding between cockpits so that at least one pilot might live, to airframe and rotor blades designed to withstand a hit from 23mm rounds and a self-healing fueling system.

Right now, it represented survival.

It came with an identical twin, and a cargo chopper that hung high in the skies.

"How?" Alicia wondered.

Dahl shrugged. "Swedish ingenuity."

Drake choked. "Did you flat-pack them in?"

"I called Secretary of Defense Crowe, through Cambridge," he said. "And asked for an airstrike."

"Damn, then she still has juice!"

"Enough to save our lives."

Already, the militants were turning away from the cave, re-evaluating their attack. Drake was able to glance carefully over the ledge. Huge gray choppers filled the air above, making a beeline for the top of the mountain.

"Down!"

The chain gun let loose; its nightmarish, thunderous release striking down anyone in its path and terrifying the rest. Its deadly course was marked by rock, earth and bodies shooting upward. The SPEAR team didn't lose a second; rising instantly to evaluate their escape. At that moment the other helicopter used its own chain gun lower down the mountain, taking the attention of those gathered below. The scene was one of devastation.

"Cargo bus is hanging back," Drake said. "We're gonna have to hotfoot it."

"There." Luther pointed to a patch of the plain below which was empty.

"Looks good. We ready?"

They gathered and then waited as both Apaches came around again. More 30mm rounds laced the air, destroying everything they touched. Most of the militants were routed, seeking shelter and safety. Only the hardiest, or most foolish, kept coming.

Drake saw two scrambling among the rocks and picked one off immediately. The other ducked behind a boulder. Luther kept him covered with constant fire.

"Go, go." Hayden hurried them out.

The mountainside was a battleground, littered with bodies. The Apaches came around again and again. Hellfire missiles eliminated groups of militants and took enormous chunks from the mountain and the foothills. Earth and rock drifted in the air, in places a visible screen of fine debris.

The SPEAR team hustled from shelter to shelter, finding plenty of rocks to hide behind up on the mountain. The choppers followed their paths above, raining down hell and death onto their enemies. Molokai ran valiantly with the heavy artifact, watched closely by Alicia who helped guide his way. Drake, Luther and Dahl darted with guns up, constantly firing, picking their enemies off or forcing them to duck down behind rocks. Mai and Smyth used grenades from the back, helping to flush out the stragglers and obscure the view from behind. As a complete team, their firepower was stunning.

Drake's boots touched the foothills, the ground becoming less rocky. Finding cover was harder down here, so they moved slower and with precision as yet more missiles flew at the mountain and the plains below.

The cargo chopper drifted toward the empty field.

Constant fire from the Apaches dampened their enemies' resistance, making every person fear for their own safety. By the time Drake reached the base of the foothills and saw the desert plains opening out before him, there was no more gunfire. Still, they all moved cautiously with their weapons. The big chopper touched down gently, its rear door lowering.

"RPG!" Mai yelled.

It came from nowhere, fortunately flying wide of the target. Mai and Smyth spotted a glint in the foothills and concentrated their fire as they ran. There were no more RPGs.

Drake's boots hit the lowered door first. He knelt and turned, gun to shoulder, seeking enemies at their rear. Luther and Dahl were beside him, ranged across the ramp.

"Clear."

The last person ran aboard, jumping at full stretch since the helicopter was already rising. Drake and two companions laid down a hail of covering gunfire.

"Are we alive?" Alicia asked from her place on the floor, staring out of the rear door.

"I certainly hope so," Mai said. "Because you're surely no angel."

"And proud of it."

Drake watched intently until they were out of missile range and the door had finally lumbered shut. Only then did he relax, dropping his gun and taking several deep breaths.

"That was bloody close."

Molokai wriggled out of the heavy backpack, dust mushrooming from his clothes and filling the cabin. "And the artifact is intact."

"Good," Drake said. "Because that's the last one. Where do we go from here?"

Hayden unhooked her satphone. "Let's find out shall we?"

CHAPTER THIRTY EIGHT

All hell had broken loose.

It quickly became apparent that a member of their team ran in the worst of harm's way, fighting for her life. Suddenly everything began to escalate.

Lauren's voice was strained and full of terror, humming desperately down the line thousands of miles away on the other side of the world.

"I'm out . . . I'm free . . . shit, wait."

The whispered fear made Drake bunch his fists, desperately wishing he could help. Smyth was beside himself. Hayden had been trying to find out what was happening for six minutes now, but Lauren was fighting a lethal cat-and-mouse game.

Absolute silence descended in the back of the cargo chopper. It was at rest, sitting on a dark runway in a dark corner of Egypt, just waiting for a call to action.

What next?

They hadn't expected this.

Lauren's breath caught in her throat. There were no words among the team; even Alicia and Kenzie sat in silence and with utmost concern on their faces. Lauren's next comments were barely audible.

"My God . . . they're here."

Hayden gripped the satphone hard. "Stay absolutely still. Do nothing."

There was a shout and a large amount of rustling. A gunshot was heard. Lauren yelled out in shock. More rustling. One more gunshot.

Smyth stood just a meter from the phone, eyes closed tightly, fists to his temples. He said just one word: "Lauren?"

Voices came over the phone, deep and guttural: "Is she dead?"

"Looks like it."

Smyth sank to his knees. Hayden held on to the phone and the open line in desperate hope, but didn't hear Lauren's voice at all. Just some shuffling.

"Better drag the bitch over here, Urban."

Yeah, dispose of it where it belongs, hey Carmine? In the gutter."

The entire team logged both names. Drake knew it was one of those moments when two identities would be forever remembered.

More rustling, and then a dragging sound. Both men were grunting. Drake saw Kinimaka and Kenzie turn away, not needing or wanting to hear what happened next. Alicia's face was set in the hardest mask he'd ever seen.

"Get this fucker warmed up," Smyth growled. "I know where I'm going next."

Both men screamed then as two shots rang out. Drake thought he heard two bodies fall and then two more shots. It was a blessing to hear Lauren's ragged voice.

"I'm okay," she breathed. "They shot me. In the arm. But I'm okay. Faked it, ha ha. That's the one thing I am good at."

Smyth was suddenly on his knees, unable to hide the emotion. Hayden's knuckles were pure white on the phone. "What's happening over there?"

"Wait . . . I have to get clear."

Three minutes later and after a good deal of panting and crunching she was back on the line.

"Goddamn, this hurts. I'm bleeding, but managed to wrap it."

Drake spoke first. "Did you grab one of their guns?"

"Shit, no. I'm friggin' useless."

"No, you're not," Smyth said.

"Look, we're hanging on by our fingertips here. We're not soldiers. They're gonna kill us."

Hayden forced her voice to project calmness. "Are you safe for now? If so, tell us what happened."

"Yeah, I'm bang in the middle of a huge parking lot, in between cars." The New Yorker took a deep breath. "First, they took Kimberly."

Drake tried hard to keep his mouth from falling open. "You mean Tempest? Shit."

"Yeah, they snatched the Secretary and have her somewhere. I don't know what's happened. It was only . . . hours ago. We were planning to grab the President after his speech. I mean, not literally grab him, but Kimberly had organized anonymous press passes for us and it was clear to approach. She used her last favors with those passes, and somebody must have talked."

"They have eyes and ears everywhere," Kinimaka said.

"Anyway, they dragged poor Kimberly right out of the car in the parking lot. Just threw her into a black van in broad daylight. It was . . . horrible."

Lauren's voice was rising. Hayden told her to calm down. They couldn't risk her being heard now. She may have found a good hiding place, but good hiding places were often the hardest to escape from.

"I ran. Luckily, I was close to the press conference so managed to find a place where they wouldn't dare touch me. Hang on . . ."

Drake assumed she was checking the area. The team waited with bated breath.

"We're clear, but I need to get this arm checked. It's on fire." Lauren fought down the panic again, resetting her core. "Look, despite all that, I did manage to talk to President Coburn."

Drake was amazed. "Whoa, you did?"

"Yeah, I got up close and he recognized me. He was familiar with the code words too, which got me a private chat."

Drake knew there was no code word. It was Lauren's way of saving time. In truth, he had no doubt that she would have reminded him of the Blood King's attack on DC and what had happened then. Coburn would have seen it as a warning sign, a cry for help from SPEAR.

"I laid it all out, plain and cold. A few advisors were there too; I couldn't keep them out of it. I spoke of Tempest, the Spec Ops teams they left out in the cold, the weapons of the gods . . . everything."

"Was he responsive?" Mai asked the question on all their minds.

"Yeah. Asked questions. Asked for dates. Lots of stuff."

"Lauren," Hayden said. "How the hell did you end up on the run?"

"When I finished talking to Coburn I stepped away a little and Rick Troy was standing right behind me. You know him—the presidential aide that's part of Tempest. The asshole that's been blocking us this whole time. Well, I grinned. I said: 'Got you, bastard,' and then I told Coburn to act fast as his life was in danger."

"Great," Hayden said. "Just wait. We have a lot to think about."

"Or nothing," Smyth said. "We're going to DC."

All this time, on another line, Cambridge of the British SAS had been listening. Now Hayden gave the floor to him.

"Where are we with the weapons?"

"Tempest are in control, I'm afraid. They have almost twenty god-weapons. They have Secretary Crowe. Lauren is clearly being hunted. And, by now, I'd imagine they have a plan to take the President out if Troy overheard all that. This just got huge."

"Understood," Hayden said, and turned back to the satphone. "You two managed to locate Tempest's hideout, right?"

"We identified where they meet, yeah, from Gleeson's laptop."

Hayden acknowledged every pair of eyes in the big cabin. "We have to destroy Tempest. Immediately."

Smyth pumped the air with a fist. "Exactly!"

"I'm sorry," Cambridge intervened. "It's not quite that easy. Tempest are not alone, as you know. The terrorist camp is now fully operational. It won't be long before they're shipping them out in droves just to cover up what they're planning next."

A deep, difficult silence fell across the cabin. There was no easy answer.

"How many terrorists?" Luther asked.

"Hundreds," Cambridge replied. "At least."

Strike Tempest, or strike their network, Drake thought. *Save Lauren and Crowe and possibly the President or cripple a terrorist army?*

Hayden came up with the plan. "I'm afraid there's no choice. We will have to split up, again, and both teams will be heading into severe danger."

She rose with all the weight of the world on her shoulders. "Say your goodbyes while you can. We split in five. I'll take Smyth,

Mano and Molokai with me. The rest of you will deal with the terrorists."

There were no protests, no diverting suggestions. Hayden was right and had decided their course of action. The team rose and crowded around, making sure Smyth knew he had their support and passing everything they had on to Lauren. Hayden told the New Yorker about a doctor she knew, that might be able to admit her to hospital under an assumed name.

"Get over there right away," she said. "I'll tell him you're coming and work out a code word."

"I will," Lauren croaked. "And guys . . . thank you."

"We'll see you soon," Hayden ended the call, addressing Cambridge.

"So, any thoughts on how five soldiers are gonna take on hundreds of terrorists?"

"That had crossed my mind too," Drake added for good measure.

"Five?" Cambridge laughed. "No, no. How about one hundred Special Forces soldiers. Everything from Navy SEAL teams to Marine Recon, Green Berets to Delta Force. And that's not including the undercover CIA teams and half a dozen more that don't even have names. They're all ready to help you."

"Fuck me," Drake murmured. "Talk about a dream team."

"Never again will there be such a team assembled to defeat a terrorist army," Cambridge said. "I'm bloody jealous of you."

"Stuff of fantasy." Dahl rubbed his hands. "Can't wait."

Hayden gestured at the chopper. "But who goes first? We only have one transport."

"You," Cambridge said immediately. "Because, Hayden, our insiders are already hearing chatter. A Tempest attack on President Coburn is imminent."

CHAPTER THIRTY NINE

Through code words agreed at face-to-face meetings that Whitehall and Cambridge had arranged through old-school contacts, the widespread, cut-off Special Forces teams began to gather in Syria. The agreed meet point was a lofty, abandoned village about a mile from a dusty main road—easy enough to get back onto the main route, far enough away to meet en masse and attract no attention, simple to defend if need be. At first the teams trickled in one by one, but then began to arrive in groups after finding it relatively simple with their skills to slip into the war-torn country.

Leave your ego at the border, was a welcome, flapping sign; the first thing Drake saw as he walked into the village. Somebody had scrawled the words on a dusty gray sheet and hung it between two buildings. With Alicia, Mai, Luther, Kenzie and Dahl he strode up Main Street, getting a feel for the place. They were well-armed and well-fed, ready to depart immediately, and were just waiting for somebody to call a meeting to order.

It happened quickly, as soon as the last team attended the meeting point—a simple desk set up in the street where codenames could be ticked off. When all were present an Englishman of maybe fifty walked up behind them, climbed up onto a rickety wooden chair and called out for some attention.

"I'm not in charge," were his first words. "I'm not your leader, and I'd never want to be. You all know Cambridge? You all know Whitehall? They asked me to speak first so we can come to order and make a plan. Are we ready?"

A general affirmative filled the air.

"Then send your captains forward. Right here and now. We're gonna make this plan and go kick some terrorist arse!"

Cheers erupted and feet shuffled. Drake slipped sunglasses on since the bright yellow orb was beating down hard, causing sweat to pop out along the creases of his forehead. Dahl nudged him.

"Wanna toss for leader?"

Alicia nodded at Kenzie. "You do Dahl. I'll do Drake."

The Swede closed his eyes wearily. "I meant—"

"I know what you meant," Drake said. "But really . . . honestly . . . I think we have a celebrity in our midst."

More and more as they'd moved along with the crowd, as people pressed around them, he had noticed respectful and admiring eyes being turned upon Luther. To some he was a real myth, to others no less than a legend. Drake remembered Crowe calling him the old-school blood warrior. The man that brought hellfire to every enemy of the United States.

He wasn't a man prone to egotism. "I think we have our captain right here." He nudged the big, bald warrior. "Go forward, mate."

"Me?" Luther tried to look modest.

"You're bloody famous, mate. Go for it."

Dahl grabbed Luther's huge shoulder before he could move. "But don't fuck it up."

Luther shrugged and walked through the crowd, joining over a dozen others. First, they divided their hundred or so soldiers into four teams—one for each direction of assault. Aerial recon pictures showed the terrorist camp as it was—five main areas positioned either side of a wide stream—a parking zone, a place for all the tents where the trainees slept, a teaching school, a meeting house and a makeshift town. Nothing was obvious or perfectly clear from the surveillance, but at least the teams knew what they were dealing with.

Four teams then, Drake thought. After that they were keen to allocate four points of contact within those teams—not leaders, they were quick to point out. Luther quickly became the point of contact for the team Drake and his companions became part of. It would be Luther's job to ensure his larger team coordinated seamlessly with the other three.

And then they were ready to move. No exorbitant, intricate plans. They were here to neutralize a terrorist camp and destroy Tempest's worldwide reach. Only Drake and the others there were two attacks coming—the other being at the heart of the secret organization and led by Hayden.

It took some time to maneuver so many men into place, but

with the help of cutting edge comms, and years of training that suited this very purpose, they were ready.

Drake had eyes on the camp. A river ran through the middle, about as wide as a man lying lengthways, flowing rapidly. It filled a natural depression in the ground; the parking area, roughly graveled over, to his left had enough space for three buses and half a dozen cars. Beyond that stood a low building made of metal sheets which they told him was the training shop—the school. At the far side he saw a big huddle of tents, one brushing up against another and a brick-lined well. To the right of that, across the river, he spied the meeting house—somewhere to let off steam, perhaps.

One more set of structures was visible, and the most surprising. To his immediate right they had built what appeared to be a makeshift American town, something small but with the correct decor, even some of the correct brand names. It was for familiarity, Drake realized. Something to help these new recruits feel more confident.

The new team ranged alongside and behind him, performing last-minute checks. The sun was already arcing down the western skies, about halfway now, but better for Drake, since the temperature was dropping. Lying low, trying not to inhale sand, he was staggered by the incredible array of Special Forces soldiers all around him.

"A hundred of us, five hundred of them," Luther said through the comms. "Little fuckers don't stand a chance."

"Make it real," Dahl said. "Be strong."

They would attack simultaneously from four directions, concentrating on four different areas. Luther coordinated smoothly with the other three team controllers and gave everyone a countdown.

"Twenty seconds."

The mind-boggling Spec Ops force took a moment to reflect. Drake, Alicia and Dahl grinned at each other and then found themselves feeling humble, part of a phenomenon, ready to stand alongside a hundred like-minded warriors as part of one of the most critical, heroic armies of all time.

"Go!"

The call went out. Drake started to run, rushing down the slope in a battle charge with Dahl and Mai to his right, Alicia and dozens of others to his left. A kind of greatness touched them. There was no retiring from this selfless bravery. It was everything they were made of.

"The end of Tempest starts now," Drake said.

They hit level ground where the parking area began, hearing gunfire from the south already. Drake was running with his gun pushed snugly into his right shoulder, cautiously scanning the way forward. The air smelled of oil and diesel; Drake saw it in exposed-top drums. The sound of fighting grew louder. Among the buses he crept, drawing ever closer to what they assumed was the school building.

Terrorists lounged among the vehicles. Kenzie shot one climbing down from the front of a bus, rifle slung over his back. Many others that were trying to see the source of the new noise then realized they were under attack.

Drake saw one duck behind the front of another bus, threw himself to the dusty sand floor and took out the enemy's legs. Dahl ran around to finish him. Beyond that, heads bobbed up at the next bus's windows, followed by gun barrels. The attacking force wasted no time. They riddled the windows with bullets, smashing every single one on that side, then threw in grenades.

Drake fell to one knee, fingers in his ears as the bus exploded, detonating flames into the air. Black smoke billowed.

Drake and Alicia were up almost before the shrapnel finished flying, moving closer to the flames to skirt the back of the bus.

The school was up ahead, maybe thirty meters distant. Men were piling out of the only door as if there were a pack of lions inside. Drake saw their play immediately.

"Move!"

Firing hard, they ran at the school. There was still a chance that they could stop most of the terrorists from exiting through the only door. The soldiers numbered eighteen—the remainder were still mopping up around the parking area—and ran in a single wave, an unbroken line of accurate, deadly gunfire.

The escapees fell instantly, still half a minute away from any kind of shelter. The hardiest fell to their stomachs and started firing back.

Drake picked one of them off, his bullet destroying the top of the man's head and making his entire body slump. They fired round after round into the exit door; men slumping down there on top of one another. Windows smashed all around the building as the trapped men sought a means of escape.

"Circle it," Luther hissed. "Custer's Last Stand style."

"You want us to run around this building in ever decreasing circles?" Alicia hit back, off comms.

Luther ignored her, closing in. Those to the left peeled left whilst those to the right went right. They ran around the school, circling it and covering every window. Drake saw two of his own fall, but didn't know their names. Bullets flying toward them were rare—they had timed their attack to perfection—but Misfortune and Bad Luck were bastards that trod everywhere.

Drake dropped to one knee, firing with precision, switching his aim by millimeters every time, picking off everything he saw moving. Alicia and Dahl were at his sides and Mai beyond them. Slowly, they advanced, not still for long. In this kind of battle, movement was essential.

Drake saw four windows along this side and Special Forces soldiers ranged all the way around. Terrorists were starting to stay inside now, pointing whatever weapons they had through the damaged window panes.

"Grenades," Luther said.

They ducked and weaved as they dashed forward, throwing their grenades before they became sitting ducks. Even then an RPG was pointed out of the window, its wielder uncaring about his own safety. Not all flew in through an open gap; some bounced back off the metal structure.

Drake threw himself to the sand and gravel floor, hands over his head.

The explosion was mighty, shattering the metal structure, making its panels collapse outward. Fire shot out in all directions, scorching the earth and anything that stood in its way. A couple of men in Luther's team were singed, but nothing too dramatic. Luther would see them as "enthusiastic." His yell of victory was fired by bloodlust.

"School's fucking right out, boys. What's next?"

Drake rolled and jumped to his feet. Judging by the chatter on the comms the other teams were experiencing more resistance. The parking lot had been cleared, but they had lost four men.

"Major battle over at the tents and the river," Luther said. "Let's go."

Drake still scanned for movement, trusting nothing. Dahl slapped at his own clothing, emitting a cloud of dust. Sand dripped from the folds of his jacket in rivulets.

Alicia reloaded. "No time to pretty yourself up, Torsty. Let's face it—that's a long job."

"Hey, Drake's the one putting the beef on."

They jogged around the remains of the school, feeling the heat of unrestrained flames on their faces.

"Nothing wrong with that, pal," Drake drawled. "Bloody hell, that's a real mess."

Luther stared at the incredible melee between the tents and the river.

"Time to get stuck in, boys."

CHAPTER FORTY

Hayden was feeling lightheaded, and not from the swift flight. Events had spiraled into a fast-moving reel of incredible incident, starting with them arriving back in DC and being shoved into a matte-black, frighteningly quick saloon car. Washington DC was shuddering in silence, it seemed; the city moving along as normal but with an underlying sense of intense fear and violence. Only those few in the know had an idea of what was truly happening, but their uncertainties and their phone calls and their warnings soon escalated around the city.

Hayden recalled being taken from the blacked-out landing strip straight to a private hospital. There they met Lauren and took a precious few minutes to express their joy at seeing her.

Smyth had been beside himself. He ran in, despite all their recent differences, taking her weight from the bed and hugging her close. Hayden had pretended not to see the tears in his eyes and the big smile on Lauren's face.

"Thank you," Hayden said. "Thank you, thank you, for everything."

"Been a long time since Transylvania," Kinimaka said. "You knew better than we did, girl."

Lauren grinned, crushed by Smyth, but not unhappy about it. "I got there in the end, didn't I?"

"Damn right you did," Hayden said. "Coburn, and we, owe our lives to you. How's the arm?"

"It'll be fine," Lauren said. "Eventually."

Hayden saw the tiredness in Lauren's face, the utter exhaustion, and reflected over what she'd been through during the last few weeks. Constant pressure, constant fear, twenty-four-seven.

"Look," she said. "We'll continue this when Tempest are busted. Right now, we gotta move."

Minutes later they had been speeding again in their unmarked car, leaving Lauren behind and discussing a plan with Coburn and his trusted advisors that would end this thing. Coburn had been hustled to safety after speaking to Lauren at the press conference, thwarting Tempest's plan by but a few hours.

"You know where they meet?" Coburn asked.

"We do." Hayden hadn't wanted to reveal it to anyone but the President. There were no second chances tonight. "We can be there in half an hour."

"Agent Jaye, I am still the leader of the greatest nation of the free world," Coburn said. "I think I might be able to rustle you up some support."

Hayden hated to question this man and gritted her teeth after asking: "One hundred percent trustworthy?"

"Six men. Delta. I trained with two of them, and they trained the others. I stand by them."

"Sounds perfect, Mr. President. I forgot you were military."

"Not something you should admit to me, Agent. Can I trust you?"

Hayden knew it was just a small reprimand. "Yes, sir. Let's meet 'em."

"And thanks," Smyth put in. "Thank you for helping Lauren."

"My pleasure, soldier. She saved my life."

"Are you safe, sir?" Hayden asked as they re-routed to a new address.

Coburn chuckled. "I believe that question is moot. Is the President ever safe? Before this very real threat there was another looming. Worse, if you can imagine that. Out of Russia."

Hayden knew the President and many DC officials received constant, credible information of assassination attempts. It wasn't unusual.

But Russia?

"Are you close?" Coburn asked.

Hayden shook herself and checked the satnav. "Five minutes out," she said.

"Then good luck to you all. Bring me back good news, my friends."

"That," Molokai said, "is never in doubt."

*

Hayden knew that Lauren had discovered Tempest's secret lair—a place they called The Chamber—after her incredibly brave final crack at being Nightshade for General Gleeson. The laptop gave them the location and, thanks to Lauren's quick-wittedness, Gleeson never really knew, nor revealed to anyone what had happened. Hayden also knew that Tempest were fully invested now—from killing everyone that got in their way to abducting the Secretary of Defense. When they met up with the Delta team, she made sure they were fully prepared.

"You're SPEAR?" the team leader asked. "I thought there were more of you."

"We're a little stretched right now," Smyth said. "But eager to get this done."

It was just passing 9:00 a.m. in DC. The Chamber was code for a meeting place inside Meridian Hill Park, a small gazebo-like structure where these seven powerful men could meet in person. This had been Tempest's big moment and was now their crisis—it was obvious they would meet up. The question was: When?

They'd been dug in around the area since first light, shivering and cold. Nobody talked, nobody moved. It was only when the obvious form of General George Gleeson approached that Hayden felt the uplift in her heartbeat.

"Strike one," she whispered. "Nobody fucking move."

Two minutes later, Mark Digby drew near from a different direction.

"Strike two." Hayden was already clenching her fists.

"And three." Kinimaka nodded to the west.

"Look there," Smyth hissed with real venom in his voice. "That's Rick Troy, the President's aide; the one that burned Lauren and ordered the kill."

"Just a little longer," Hayden told him. "Then you'll get your revenge."

And in full, she hoped. Each member of Tempest came with more than one bodyguard. The odds were good that the men that tried to kill Lauren were here too.

"Ready," the Delta team leader confirmed.

"Strike four," Hayden said as another familiar face walked up to the brick-built structure and disappeared inside.

Kinimaka aimed a parabolic microphone at the building, listening to their comments through headphones. He gave them a thumbs-up, signaling that he was getting some key information. Of course, they didn't need the extra evidence; they already had enough, but Hayden saw it as several more nails in Tempest's coffin, and nobody could deny them that.

By 10:00 a.m. all the players were in place. Hayden signaled the Delta team that they were ready to deploy. A woman came sauntering along then, walking her dog along the dirt path, making the team hit pause.

"Wait," Hayden said. "No risk to civilians right now."

"Or canines," Molokai added.

Hayden gave him a sidelong glance. "Those too."

The dog-walker vanished only to be replaced by a jogger. Frustration set in. The team waited, primed to go but frozen in place. Another two minutes escaped from the day.

Hayden saw the moment finally arrive and gave Mano a nod which, for her, held multiple meanings; the most important of which was "stay safe." Delta rose before SPEAR, climbing out of the underbrush. Already, they'd established there was no back door. They ran across the grass, shouting, drawing most of the bodyguards out into the open.

Hayden picked off two men, crossed the open greenery, and then ascended a gradual slope toward the front of the gazebo. Two dead bodyguards sprawled out and then rolled down the hill a short way. Hayden hurdled one, sidestepped the other. Delta Force ranged ahead, pinning men down or killing them. There was no respite. The park, the blue skies and the green shrubbery was no longer real for her—life had narrowed down to survival and victory, the unpleasant fall of what might have been a terrible empire.

More shots came from the gazebo as bodyguards hunkered down behind the walls, creating a stand-off. Hayden hit the grass hard, the slope affording her some cover. Within seconds, before she could ask, the Delta leader was shouting.

"Stand down! We will kill you if you don't stand down. Look at your position."

Tempest would be in a state of panic, forcing their armed protectors to get them out of there. Walls would be closing in. Panic in their chests. They deserved all of it and so much more.

A Delta soldier showed their enemies the error of their ways by throwing a grenade. It was hurled deliberately short—a warning blow.

"Last chance!"

Hayden took aim in case they went for a sudden break out. For long seconds nothing happened and then several guns arced through the air, smacking down onto the grass with a heavy thud. Shouts could be heard—Tempest berating their guards and ordering them to fight. But it was futile. The Chamber, as they called it, was indefensible.

Delta ordered the bodyguards out, lined them up on their knees and pointed guns at their heads. Smyth ran forward, ostensibly to help, but Hayden knew exactly what he was doing.

"Lancelot Smyth," she warned. "You stand down right now."

He didn't acknowledge her. Hayden screwed her face up in irritation, but at the same time sympathized with the man. If Urban and Carmine—the two mercs that had tried to kill Lauren—were here, Smyth would take some form of recompense.

Incredibly, it ended as quickly as it had begun. General Gleeson emerged first, hands up, blustering hard, which only made Hayden smile. The others came shortly afterward. Rick Troy, the presidential aide, came last.

Hayden stared at him, the man that had ostensibly made SPEAR enemies of the state. Kinimaka and Molokai spread themselves out, observing every small movement.

Hayden breathed a sigh of relief, her mind turning to Drake and the others for one single, clear moment.

And then it happened; the last act of Tempest.

CHAPTER FORTY ONE

Hayden's mind was in cooldown. The enemy were beaten. Not even the jab of faint worry nagged at her. Later, she understood it was always going to end that way—Tempest could never let themselves willingly be taken alive after all the horrors they'd perpetrated.

Gleeson reached for a gun and then so did three of the others. Troy let a small handgun fall from the sleeve of his shirt into his hand. Another—Hayden recognized Mark Digby of the CIA—threw a live grenade high into the air.

"You think we didn't prepare for this?" Gleeson screamed.

It was the matter of but a moment to line the general's forehead up in her sights. She thought: *I don't care what you think, asshole,* as she squeezed the trigger. Gleeson died instantly, which was unfortunate, falling into another man. The grenade looped lazily down. Smyth moved faster than an exploding firework, shifting his aim to Digby even as the aide leveled his handgun.

Smyth fired first. Digby flew back. Hayden grunted with approval.

The grenade came down as Delta and the bodyguards threw themselves to the grass. It exploded a meter above ground, killing several men. One of the dead was a member of Delta Force, sending a jab of pain through Hayden's heart.

Bodies littered the grassy knoll just in front of the gazebo. Hayden approached the remains, desperate to find at least one still living.

Smyth already had the unlucky felons under close watch. He shifted his eyes briefly as Hayden approached.

"I believe these two are Urban and Carmine," he said. "My Delta friend here showed me the CCTV captures from the parking lot where they attacked Lauren. I'm happy to fire as much lead into them as you require."

The Delta leader was kneeling down beside his fallen colleague.

"My eyes are blurred because my friend is dead. I see nothing, and so do my team."

Hayden's face was mud-streaked, careworn and vicious as she stared at the two mercs. "Where is Secretary Crowe?"

CHAPTER FORTY TWO

Drake launched his body across the wide river, landing with boots firmly in the dusty mud, then ran up the short slope to the edge of the tent village. The chaos was intense here. Terrorists and mercs had been resting, some sleeping, taking a break from the day with the sun at its hottest. Gunfire had roused them and they had come out firing, especially the mercs that were better trained.

Drake launched himself atop a dark-skinned young man, punched him to the ground, the two rolled, crashing into a tent. Alicia fell beside him, struck horizontally by a man that had been flung by another. Dahl's boot landed in Drake's opponent's face, smashing down hard; then Dahl was dragged away by two mercs. Drake elbowed his opponent, drew a knife and stabbed him twice. Then he saw Alicia rise, and looked for Dahl.

The Swede lay on his back, arms scrabbling in mud, as two men struggled to stay on top. One punched his face, the other punched his midriff. Dahl was attempting to roll them off. Drake hooked an arm under the closest man's chin and heaved, crushing the throat at the same time. Alicia went for a flying kick, striking the other man in the left ear with her boot. He toppled clear and Dahl was free.

There was no time for gratitude. Alicia was dragged backward by a huge merc and then that man fell in a pothole, staggering into a tent. The material enfolded them, thrashing left and right as Alicia and her opponent sought superiority.

Drake twisted so hard he thought his foe's head would come off. The struggle didn't last long. Drake left the man face-down, turned and was then hit full in the face with the butt of a rifle. He staggered back, down the slope, a step at a time. Blood ran into his eyes, stinging and blinding him. A knife deflected off his stab vest, and then the butt of the rifle came again, making him think the wielder was out of ammo. In the end it was the river that stopped him.

Boots splashed down in running water as Drake finally

managed to stop backpedalling. The fighter must have launched himself through the air because his bulk struck Drake then and sent him crashing down into the deep water. He fell and rolled, swallowing a mouthful, coughing, thrashing. A hand found his throat, holding it down. Drake struck up twice, seeking soft targets and finding what he thought was a ribcage. The knife was still in his hand so he twisted hard and thrust that up through the water as hard as he could. The blade sank in and the pressure eased, the figure twisting away still with the knife in its body.

Drake surfaced fast, sputtering. Water fell from his top half in torrents.

At last, his vision cleared. He was on his feet now, chest above water, staring up the slope and at the tent village.

Figures struggled everywhere. Shots and screams rang out without relent. Drake saw several comrades struggling, and splashed his way out of the river and back through the mud to the top of the incline. Handgun out, he resorted to point and shoot. Where a merc or terrorist stood in space, Drake shot them. Eight went down and his own colleagues stood or knelt and did the same.

Mercs came at them again, a wave of screaming outlines. More hand-to-hand combat broke out. The terrorists were backing away from every encounter, being herded toward the center of the tent village. As Drake stood among the fallen tents he looked for his friends.

Alicia spun and shot an oncoming merc. Dahl threw a man into a tent so that the material enfolded him, giving the Swede an easy kill. Kenzie held her own against another, using two knives to confuse and strike in tandem, leaving the man defenseless before ending his life. Luther and Mai were almost at the center of the tent mass, at the far end of a path of fallen material and men which, Drake guessed, the two had mostly caused.

Other members of their team fought all around them.

Sweating, still dripping water, bleeding from a dozen wounds, Drake labored through the mass to Alicia's side. He was just in time to stop a merc rising from the floor, gun in hand. Drake picked up a discarded gun and shot him. The Special Forces teams consistently watched each other's backs, always lending an eye for a colleague.

Luther's voice blared through his earpiece. "Team Ricardo has met major resistance in the false town," he said. "Mop up here and move out."

Drake swore. Was Luther implying this wasn't major resistance? Shit, what were the other team up against? He shot a man emerging from a tent with an RPG cradled across one shoulder; kicked out at one more that lay in the dirt, still lively enough to cause trouble.

Alicia spun. "You in one piece?"

"More or less. You?"

"Think I broke a nail on some bell end's tooth."

"Shit, I'm so glad you added that last word."

Again, they were parted. Drake threw a man over his shoulder; then staggered beneath another's heavy blow, finding himself on his knees, staring at bloodied earth. A quick twist and he launched his body to one side, gaining precious seconds. The next attack was stalled, though, as Dahl turned up and confronted Drake's opponent.

Four seconds later, Drake, Alicia and Dahl stood shoulder to shoulder.

"There," Alicia said.

Luther, Mai and a dozen others had converged on the center of the tent town. The mercs and the terrorists were rallying there, showing the last of their resistance. Luther carried a machine gun in each hand, their barrels so hot with constant use they appeared to be on fire. Smoke surrounded the scene. Kenzie launched herself in to it so carelessly, armed only with knives, that even Dahl winced.

"Shall we?"

Scooping up the weapons they needed, the trio hurried across earth that was thick with clumps of matted soil, grass, dirt and blood. The battlefield was laden with the dead and the dying. Drake saw their own men being tended by others. They came at the center to either side of Luther and Mai, seeing mercs falling ahead, unable to shoot in any one direction for fear of an enemy at all sides. Team Luther came from north and south, east and west, routing and devastating the mercenary lines. Every trainee terrorist that Drake could see knelt in the dirt with their hands on their heads—defeated.

Soon, the tent village was captured. Luther ordered men to bind the captives and just a few to stay behind to watch them.

Drake gazed over to the makeshift town, the last and worst area of resistance. Buildings were on fire, spitting flames from their roofs. RPGs fired and grenades exploded.

And of course, it was right where Team SPEAR needed to be.

CHAPTER FORTY THREE

The makeshift town was a war zone but, for Drake, a special sight as dozens of elite Special Forces soldiers fought in conjunction with each other. The mercs were holed up in a diner, complete with red and yellow shutters and lettering, their firepower clear to see as they held off any attempt at assault. The terrorists also sniped from nearby windows—a bank, a coffee shop, a burger joint—recognizable features of American living. Some were heading to the roofs.

Through comms, Luther and the other three coordinators organized their teams. Groups ran through shops and stores, six at a time, sweeping the place clear of enemies. Another team backed them up. Terrorists were allowed to head to the tallest heights of the town simply because world class Special Forces snipers already waited there for them. An incredible pride swelled in Drake's chest.

"Everyone wants the same thing," he said.

"If only it could always be like this," Dahl said.

They had come up against special ops teams themselves—both on the same side yet forced into confrontations. The lines were always blurred.

Not today. Drake listened to the comms chatter as he crouched in the shadows between two structures. It was being reported that the buildings were of inferior design, no doubt through necessity and speed of assembly, and would crumble under heavy assault.

This gave Luther an idea.

When he voiced it, Drake looked to Alicia and Dahl, shaking his head ruefully. "Trust that bloody dinosaur," he said.

"I like it," Dahl noted.

Drake laughed and they backed away, following the lead of every other spec ops soldier in the town. Snipers scurried down from their perches and those that were engaged in combat broke it off as quickly as they could.

The mercs were jeering at the retreat.

Drake frowned. "Not clever."

Terrorists could be seen here and there, sticking their heads up like meerkats to see what was going on. Shots were fired. Drake returned that fire, giving a dozen of their men the chance to run forward, RPGs braced across one shoulder.

They knelt quickly and fired instantly.

The effect was shattering. In all his life, Drake had never seen anything like it. Powerful rockets sped in pairs into every building, detonating on impact and filling the interiors with fire and death. Not one structure was strong enough to withstand the flaming devastation. Drake whistled as six buildings collapsed onto themselves, timbers and spars, bricks and blocks tumbling down together on top of the killers inside, crushing and devastating everyone within. Luther was at the head of the RPG line, the man most exposed, and already loading another rocket into its barrel.

"You gotta hand it to the man," Alicia said. "That worked really well."

"Devastation is his forte," Drake said. "And yeah, he just saved a lot of lives."

"Who would even think that way?" Dahl muttered.

"Quit that," Drake said. "You're just pissed you didn't come up with it."

It became clear that just one building hadn't entirely collapsed; its left side shored up by a rubble of fallen debris. Within, several mercs were still active. They fired now and Luther ducked, but one of his companions was struck in the chest. More bullets flew. Dahl and Drake were best placed to help.

"You got my back?" Dahl asked, already sprinting.

"Always, pal."

The Swede darted around the surviving mercenaries' blind side, coming up around the rear of the building. Drake expected him to leap and run up the collapsed side of it, maybe throw a grenade through a gap. What he didn't expect was for the Swede to run at full pelt smack-bang into the side of the fragile structure.

"Always the bloody show off."

Dahl's sheer momentum shook the entire shop, shifting rubble and the new supports. It wavered and then it collapsed, falling on top of all those inside and cutting their enraged shrieks short.

"I saw that, Dahl," Luther said, "Couldn't have done it better myself."

The Swede smirked at Drake. "Bet you were shocked."

Drake coughed to hide a grateful smile. "Actually, I wasn't."

"Check your sixes, boys," Luther came over the comms. "But I think we just won the fucking day."

Alicia came over to where Drake and Dahl rested in the rubble, followed by Luther and Mai. Twenty spec ops soldiers held captives over by the tents and the school; a further seventy surrounded the town. Terrorist remnants were being rounded up with minimal resistance. Drake threw down his weapon and wiped the dirt from his hands.

"Tempest is fucked," he said. "At least here."

Alicia threw herself down into the dirt beside him. "Can somebody please call Hayden? I can't relax knowing they're still fighting."

Mai held up a satphone. "Already on it, Taz."

"Thank you," Alicia mouthed and closed her eyes for a moment, letting the waning sun wash the stress from her features and the horrors from her mind. A few seconds later, she opened them as Mai began to speak.

"You took them out? All of them? Gleeson and those assholes that attacked Lauren? Oh, that's great. We closed them down over here too. And Secretary Crowe is safe." Her short repeated comments were for the benefit of the people around her.

Drake found a grin stretching across his face. One more win, and without casualties. One more victory to the good guys; the ones that made the world a safer place.

"I think it's time for a vacation," he breathed, even the rubble beneath his back now feeling like a feather mattress as all the worries fell away.

"I think it's time for a drink," Luther said amiably. "And then a trip back to DC. We've been a long time absent, boys and girls, and we're far from home."

It was only then that Drake sat up in shock, catching the eyes of the SPEAR team. "Damn and bollocks, he's right! We're free. We're exonerated. Coburn will unearth all the evidence and clear us."

Alicia patted his cheek. "Yes, dear. Thanks for finally catching up."

It felt good. It felt intensely real. It felt like there really wasn't a terrible, powerful, deadly, unknown shadow rearing high above them.

Something that would change everything once and for all.

CHAPTER FORTY FOUR

Karin Blake stepped into darkness, surrounded by darkness, having just walked through an entire room full of darkness. The only way forward was to follow the small man carrying the pinprick of light.

She was alone. She didn't fear for her safety; the man that had threatened her over the phone clearly wanted something from her. Dino and Wu were back at the bar, worrying. Let them worry. She was already wondering if she really needed them.

But now the darkness ended to be replaced by a starry night. They were high up, standing on a balcony that overlooked the center of Moscow. Below, myriad sparkling lights lit up the great city. Pedestrians roamed the sidewalks and vehicles clogged the streets.

A man sat in a chair, overlooking the city, staring through the gaps in the balcony. "It is good that you are here." Thick Russian accent, but a young voice. What she could see of the figure told her he was strong too, and lithe.

"I came a long way."

"And I thank you for that. But you are also curious. You want to know who I am and what I have planned. You want to know how I discovered your greatest secret. And, in truth, you want to know if you can stop me."

Karin used her soldier's training to seek out lurkers, guards maybe. She sensed none. "I guess you could call me curious."

"I brought you here for a one-time offer. Don't worry about your safety now. You do figure in my plans a little way down the line but . . ." He paused. "No single battle plan ever stays the same."

Karin paced to the balcony and put her hands on the railing, staring at all the many aspects of life bustling below. The noise, the smells, the sights existed because so many people were content not to notice the hellish visions that passed them by in the shadows.

"Who are you?"

"I will tell you," the Russian said. "After you respond to my offer."

"Spit it out."

"Eh?"

"Please ask away. What is your offer?"

"I have a legacy. Until a year ago I could not accept it or, rather, I could not pursue it. I was forced to reclaim, rebuild and own an empire. I did that, not without sacrifice, you understand? Do you know me now?"

Karin glanced over to the shadows. "No." But there was something nagging at her. Something from the past.

"I fought tooth and nail to reclaim all that was my legacy. Loved ones died. Faithful friends were killed. I washed my hands in the blood of my enemies, fought my way back up the ladder, back to the top. Took that highest rung with my raw bones and red-hot blood."

It was a realization too terrible for Karin. The past was dead. Her brother, her mother and father were dead. The mental anguish of it all struck her once more like an axe sawing across every last nerve.

"Do you see me now?"

"I don't believe what thought just occurred to me. It can't be true. It's all wrong. You are not him."

"No, but I repossessed my legacy," the man said. "And now I will claim my revenge."

"You're trying to trick me."

"I think you know who I am. So, we'll leave it there. I have a plan to wipe out the SPEAR team. I have a plan to take and publicly destroy the President. Do you want to be part of it?"

So there it was. Karin could barely believe her agenda, her new ideals, had led to this position where a terrible madman was offering her a place in his plan to wipe out her old friends, not to mention President Coburn.

It was do or die time. Dino and Wu had been correct—her resolve had wavered as soon as she set eyes on Drake and the others back in Egypt. She recalled what they stood for, what they fought for. The world wouldn't be as safe as it was if it weren't for them.

"You have weakened?" The man was incredibly perceptive.

"I don't know what I want," she said truthfully. "But what would happen if I tried to throw you off this balcony?"

"You are welcome to try, Miss Blake. If you think we're alone."

The mention of her surname jolted her, brought everything into solid reality. She gripped the rail so hard it hurt. "I lost my brother and my parents to this," she said. "I will fight for them, as they fought for me, and as Drake and SPEAR would always fight for them."

"Then that is your answer. As I said you are free to leave. We will see each other a little further down the line."

Karin backed away, still not entirely sure who this man was, still scared of the shadows that surrounded him. "I still don't see you," she said.

He turned, and then, finally, there was no doubt. Karin stifled a scream as the face of her nightmares confronted her.

"I am Luka," he said.

CHAPTER FORTY FIVE

Somehow, the team could not rejoice, nor even relax. They were back in Washington DC, reunited, alive, nursing their wounds, but a kind of sinuous tension wove among them, a thread of threat and uncertainty. It was all down to reports and half-sentences, dark mutterings and exaggerated truths. Karin still hadn't called in, but reports told of her traveling to Russia.

From where the new darkness emanated.

They should be celebrating in their usual manner, but this time it was different. They were all sitting or standing inside a darkly illuminated warehouse, a safe area designated and guarded by the President's Secret Service staff until final announcements were made regarding their innocence.

Even Secretary Crowe was among them, determined to support the team and thank them for saving her life.

"How is Lauren?" Drake asked Smyth.

The soldier smiled. "I was with her earlier today at the hospital. Another week maybe, and she'll be okay to leave."

"Fantastic. Maybe you two can sort yourselves out then, eh?"

"I think we already have." Smyth looked younger when he smiled, Drake decided. Long may it last.

Mai stood beside Luther, both leaning across a barrel, drinks in hand and surveying the room. "It won't be long now," Mai said. "And then we'll be free."

"What's the first thing you're gonna do?" Luther asked.

"Oh, I don't know. Call Grace, probably. Grace is my foster daughter. Sort of." She sighed. "It's complicated."

"Always is," Luther said. "And after that?"

"A shower. A sleep. A good meal."

"Cool, do you want some company?"

Mai narrowed her eyes and returned the warrior's gaze with a cool glare of her own. "I'll allow you to pay for my meal, yeah."

"Well, that's a start. I assume you're allowing me to share it with you?"

"Steady on, Luther. That's a big presumption."

But even then, with her heart lifted, Mai couldn't help but stare up into the rafters where the shadows coiled. It wasn't anything physical, or obvious, just something out there in the world oppressing their contentment.

Most of the team stayed together, perhaps feeling a deeper solace in company. Drake sat with Alicia and Dahl, quietly reassured. Hayden and Kinimaka chatted a meter or so to their right, and the big Hawaiian asked her if she'd like to try again. Hayden's smile of joy was more than enough of a response.

At one point they managed to get hold of Yorgi, though the line was crackling and the young thief sounded incredibly distant.

"I am okay," he yelled intermittently, as if through thick ice. "I am being . . . I think . . . strange . . . but nothing I can rely on. It is . . . cold . . . the north."

All was good. Drake yelled out a promise to join him if they needed him but Yorgi's reply was lost to the severed connection and the snow and ice. He hated to think of their friend struggling on alone.

Luther and Molokai both sat on the hard floor, shot glasses arrayed around them like small offerings, all of them empty. Kenzie slid them over a fresh bottle with her boot. In the same movement she caught Dahl's eye.

She beckoned him over to a corner.

"I am leaving," she said. "Right now, I've done my time with this group. Earned my pardon. If you don't want me, Torsten, I don't want to be here."

Dahl felt something tug at his heart. "I can't say I'm not torn, Kenzie, but I haven't changed my mind."

"The ball and chain comes first?"

"Family," he amended. "Family comes first."

"Tell me this . . . if you didn't have children what would you do?"

The look on his face said it all but, for Kenzie, that was even worse. She didn't strike him, didn't swear at him, but he knew right then and there that their friendship was firmly over.

"I hope you get back to your family," she said.

He tried to shake the feeling of anxiety that had nothing to do with Kenzie. "Thanks. I will."

"Goodbye, then." Kenzie raised her voice to address the entire warehouse and stalked toward the door.

"Goodbye, Kenzie," Dahl whispered, closing one door and wondering if he would live to regret it.

Heartfelt farewells came from the entire team; strange for some, not so for others. Kenzie had made herself one of them with her fearless fighting, her loyalty and her determination. She would always be one of them.

Drake hated to see her go. The thought, *what's next?* rattled around his head like a crazy demon. During the hunt for Tempest he'd imagined the team taking a break, taking a vacation or revisiting loved ones, finding some form of life in the world that might help them through the coming battles.

Crowe took the call soon after that. They had all been fully pardoned.

Team SPEAR left the building.

THE END

For more information on the future of the Matt Drake world and other David Leadbeater novels please read on:

I hope you enjoyed Drake 18, *Weapons of the Gods,* and are already looking forward to the next installment! If you haven't guessed what's coming by now, I won't spoil it, but rest assured it's going to be different, action-packed, and dangerous. Not since Drake 7 has the team seen such upheaval. Drake 19 will release October 2018. The book's revealing title will be released on my Facebook page in February.

I am now writing Alicia 4, which will be available in early April 2018, and then Amazon will re-publish *The Relic Hunters* in June 2018. This will happen just two months before *Relic Hunters 2* releases, hopefully in August. For those that have already purchased *Relic Hunters 1,* the new, upgraded edition should simply appear as a free Kindle download.

If you enjoyed this or any of my other books please leave a review.

Other Books by David Leadbeater:

The Matt Drake Series
A constantly evolving, action-packed romp based in the escapist action-adventure genre:

The Bones of Odin (Matt Drake #1)
The Blood King Conspiracy (Matt Drake #2)
The Gates of Hell (Matt Drake 3)
The Tomb of the Gods (Matt Drake #4)
Brothers in Arms (Matt Drake #5)
The Swords of Babylon (Matt Drake #6)
Blood Vengeance (Matt Drake #7)
Last Man Standing (Matt Drake #8)
The Plagues of Pandora (Matt Drake #9)
The Lost Kingdom (Matt Drake #10)
The Ghost Ships of Arizona (Matt Drake #11)
The Last Bazaar (Matt Drake #12)
The Edge of Armageddon (Matt Drake #13)
The Treasures of Saint Germain (Matt Drake #14)
Inca Kings (Matt Drake #15)
The Four Corners of the Earth (Matt Drake #16)
The Seven Seals of Egypt (Matt Drake #17)

The Alicia Myles Series
Aztec Gold (Alicia Myles #1)
Crusader's Gold (Alicia Myles #2)
Caribbean Gold (Alicia Myles #3)

The Torsten Dahl Thriller Series
Stand Your Ground (Dahl Thriller #1)

The Relic Hunters Series
The Relic Hunters (Relic Hunters #1)

The Disavowed Series:
The Razor's Edge (Disavowed #1)
In Harm's Way (Disavowed #2)
Threat Level: Red (Disavowed #3)

The Chosen Few Series
Chosen (The Chosen Trilogy #1)
Guardians (The Chosen Tribology #2)

Short Stories
Walking with Ghosts (A short story)
A Whispering of Ghosts (A short story)

All genuine comments are very welcome at:

davidleadbeater2011@hotmail.co.uk

Twitter—@dleadbeater2011

Visit David's website for the latest news and information:
davidleadbeater.com